JOSEPH

JOSEPH

The Journey Home

TATE PUBLISHING
AND ENTERPRISES, LLC

Joseph

Published by Tate Publishing & Enterprises, LLC
127 E. Trade Center Terrace | Mustang, Oklahoma 73064 USA
1.888.361.9473 | www.tatepublishing.com

Tate Publishing is committed to excellence in the publishing industry. The company reflects the philosophy established by the founders, based on Psalm 68:11,
"The Lord gave the word and great was the company of those who published it."

Cover design by Gian Philipp Rufin
Interior design by Gram Telen

Published in the United States of America

ISBN: 978-1-62463-484-0
1. Fiction / Christian / General
2. Fiction / Family Saga
15.11.04

"I have watched Janice Parker live a focused and steadfast life, reaching her goals and expectations. This book reveals a life of trials and grace, evident of the Lords favor. Reading this book will increase your hope and trust in a God so that no matter what the circumstances are, he is always intervening and can restore all that is lost."

—Dottie Archuleta, His Voice Ministries

In the Pit

The dark prison cell smelled of decay. Joseph lay back on an old bed soiled from years of use. Wires from the springs in the mattress stuck into his back like pins. He had been locked up in this tiny brick cell for almost eight years. The cell was eight-by-eight with a toilet in one corner and a five-foot-long bunk bed in the other. Joseph slept on the bottom bunk.

He stretched his legs in an attempt to relieve some of the stiffness. He pulled the thin, moth-eaten blanket up around his chin to try to get warm and rested his head on the smelly pillow. He imagined sitting by the fireplace in his parents' house to escape the freezing cold air.

A guard strolled by silently with confidence, peering in on occasion before passing on down the hallway. Joseph reached down on the floor next to his bed and grabbed the journal his sister had given him. He began writing a story his father had told him about his grandfather, who had traveled on foot from Persia to Italy. Writing gave Joseph a brief diversion from his life in captivity. After an hour he put the journal down on the table. He picked up the gold pocket watch his father gave him as a graduation present and checked the time.

It was five p.m. The year was 1914. Thoughts of his family flooded his mind. It had been so long since he last saw them. Joseph thought of the time he came home from fishing with his best friend, Martino. His mother would have dinner on the table. Her pot roast melted in his mouth. He remembered the long walks he used to take with his older sister Rebecca. He smiled as he remembered the excited look on his brother Benjamin's face when he came home from school. Ben was only two then, but they were inseparable.

When he was fourteen, Joseph took a trip with his father to Toscana, an ancient city nestled in the mountains in Italy. The hills were covered with grapevines and olive groves. Sunflowers bloomed on the hillsides. They strolled through a museum filled with beautiful paintings. He would never forget that trip. He'd always been close to his father. Knowing he would never see him again filled him with despair.

Joseph wondered how God could have let him end up in a place like this. He prayed to God for his freedom. Suddenly the cell door flew open. He rolled over and saw a stocky guard. Standing next to him was a skinny, sickly pale young man with red hair.

The guard pushed him into the cell.

"Here ya go, boy. Your home for the next ten years. Get used to it!"

The guard slammed the door shut with a cold, heartless clank that echoed through Joseph's mind for several seconds.

The young man glanced around, dazed and nervous. He shrugged and took a few steps forward. He set a small brown sack containing his belongings on the floor. Joseph sat up on his bed and studied the young man. *Who is this poor boy,* he thought, *and what's he done to be brought here?* He rolled off the bottom bunk and put his feet on the cold concrete floor.

"I'm Joseph," he said.

The man looked at him for a moment. He stood still, staring wide-eyed at Joseph, his hands trembling. Finally he said, "My name's Gilbert, but everyone calls me Gil."

"Good to meet you, Gil. I hope you don't mind, but I sleep on the bottom."

"Yeah, that's fine," Gil said, still somewhat bewildered. He threw his bag onto the top bunk.

"Where are you from?" Joseph asked.

Gil opened his mouth to respond when a loud bell sounded. "What's the bell for?"

"Dinner. Let's go."

The same stocky guard opened the cell door. Joseph quickly stepped into line. Gil followed. Down the line was a sea of men dressed in black and white prison uniforms. They looked identical, down to the white socks and black shoes and anger and hatred on their faces.

"Face forward!" the guard yelled.

Joseph glanced out the corner of his eyes and saw Gil spin around. He had a terrified look on his face and avoided making eye contact with the guard.

The guards led the men down what seemed like an endless corridor until they finally reached the dining hall. Hundreds of men sat at long rows of tables. Joseph handed Gil a tray, then he picked one up for himself. A large blond-haired inmate shoved Gil. Gil turned around. The man shot him a hateful look and walked away. Joseph put his hand on Gil's thin back to calm his nerves. Gil was small in size and ordinary in appearance with a round face, bushy red eyebrows, and damaged teeth. Gils' pale face had reddened and Joseph felt him shiver as they stood on the cold concrete floor.

They shuffled through the line. The prisoner serving them placed a piece of meat the size of a fist onto their plates along with a handful of potatoes, some wilted lettuce and a chunk of stale bread. Joseph looked around the room for a place to sit. He spotted two empty chairs on the far right. "Over there," he said.

Joseph moved among the men to get to the other side of the room. Gil followed close behind him. Joseph set his tray on the table and was about to sit down when someone shoved him from behind. His head hit the floor. He sat up and reached for the leg of the chair to help him stand, but a big fat black-haired man flattened him again.

"Sorry, didn't see ya there, Jew boy."

It was Joseph's nemesis Max.

Max stared down at him and sneered.

"One day I'm gonna teach you a lesson you'll never forget. You'll wish you was never born, you stupid Jew."

Gil watched in terror as Joseph lay there. Joseph tried to remain calm. He stayed still and glared at Max; his eyes were hard. Max grabbed the chair and walked away snickering.

Joseph got up off the floor, grabbed his tray, and moved to another table with Gil right behind him. Disoriented from the fall, Joseph sat down and rubbed the back of his head.

"You okay?" Gil asked.

"Fine."

"Who was that?"

"No one."

Gil looked back and saw Max staring at Joseph from across the room. His hatred for Joseph was apparent.

"I take it he's not a friend," Gil said.

"It's no one important," Joseph insisted. He took a bite of his bread. He cringed from the stale bitter taste in his mouth. "So you never answered my question. Where are you from?"

"North Carolina." "How long have you lived in New York.

"Mostly all my life," Gil said. "I moved from Minnesota with my ma. She passed away a couple of years ago. Never knew my pa."

"So how did you end up in New York?"

"I wanted to sow my oats and venture into new territory. I ran a little low on cash, and I got in some trouble with the law. So here I am." Gil took a few bites and pushed his tray aside. "My stomach's all ready sick. This slop will make it a whole lot worse."

"You'll get used to it." Joseph glanced at the plate in front of Gil.

"Where ya from with that accent and all?" Gil said.

"Italy. I'm Jewish. My family moved to Italy when I was two."

"Long ways from home aren't ya?"

Joseph paused. "Yes, it's a very long ways from home."

"How'd ya learn to speak English so well?"

"When my father lived in Persia, missionaries from America taught him English. He taught all of his children. My English was minimal; but after eight years in prison, I speak it fluently."

"So what's the story with Goliath?"

Joseph slightly smiled. "Actually, I don't know; guess he never really took to me."

"What's he in for?"

"I'm told he beat a man to death."

"Why is it I find that easy to believe?" Gil said.

Joseph was almost done eating. Using his hand, he gently wiped the crumbs of bread from his mouth before taking one more drink of water. He lightly set the glass down and then took one more bite of potatoes. "So, what ya in for, Joseph?"

Joseph paused while his mind searched for something to say. He hesitated for a moment, and then grabbed his tray and headed for the doorway. Joseph could hear Gil's tray scrape across the table.

"Joseph, hang on. I'm comin' with ya."

They piled their trays on top of a high stack of dirty trays on a scarred, food-stained wooden table. Two guards escorted them outside to the yard.

The dust-filled yard was about half a mile wide. It was surrounded by a barbed-wire fence fourteen feet high. The fence loomed like a tower. The guards walked the yard heavily armed with guns and iron poles.

Although it was a far cry from his life in Italy, the fresh air and view of the cloudy gray sky offered a reprieve from the horrific stink and confinement of life inside the prison walls.

Gil and Joseph stood about ten feet from the gate. They watched as an inmate run several yards to catch a football. Men on both sides of the yard cheered him on.

After half an hour, a large inmate started yelling at another inmate who was smaller than him. The larger inmate pulled out a knife from under his shirt and stabbed the other guy in the chest. He fell to the ground, blood pouring out of his chest. Another inmate reached down and grabbed thin wire out of his sock and drove it into the larger inmate's neck. He fell to the ground screaming, his blood spilling everywhere.

Alarms went off. Guards tried to break up the fighting. Gil and Joseph stared in horror, unsure what to do. Joseph wanted to run but there was nowhere to go. More inmates joined in the fray. Many lay on the ground bleeding profusely from stab wounds in the chest, legs, or stomach. Soon other guards arrived. They stumbled and clashed with the inmates.

Joseph looked at the gate. Max was only a few feet away. He punched a skinny bald man in the face. The man fell flat on his back. Max walked away.

Joseph turned to Gil. "Try and run to the gate to get out of the yard. I'll be right behind you."

Gil tried to maneuver his way around several fighting inmates. One of them banged into him from behind and knocked him to the ground. Gil swung his fist and kicked him from the ground. Once he found his feet again, he got up and kept running.

Joseph wasn't far behind. He ran toward the gate, but slipped and fell on a twelve-inch iron pole. He looked up and saw a large man stumbling toward him with ripped clothing drenched in blood. The man collapsed on top of Joseph. Unsure what to do,

Joseph lay there. He tried to crawl out from under the man when he saw Max running up to them.

"Frank, Frank!" Max cried. "What'd ya do to my brother?"

Joseph could feel the rage in Max stab him like a knife. Joseph clenched his teeth in terror as Max approached him. Just when Joseph thought Max was going to kill him, a guard grabbed Max and threw him to the ground before handcuffing him.

"I'm gonna kill you! Just wait! I'll get you for killin' my brother! You'll pay for this; you low-down, good for nothin' scum!" Max yelled as the guard dragged him away.

Joseph finally managed to roll Max's brother off of him.

Joseph quickly got up and bolted to the gate where Gil was waiting.

"You all right?" Gil asked.

Joseph nodded. "I'm all right."

He was exhausted and covered with blood. Max's threat played over and over again in his mind like a phonograph. Joseph had managed to get away this time, but he knew he could get killed any day now since Max was waiting for him.

Later that night, Gil was rummaging through some old photos while Joseph lay on the bottom bunk and stared at the ceiling, completely lost in thought. Visions of Max infiltrated his mind. Max had been thrown into solitary confinement for only two weeks. One thing was certain: Max wouldn't stop until he made good on his threat to kill him. Joseph prayed silently to God to save him.

"You okay?" Gil asked. The violent outbreak had shaken him up.

"I'm fine," Joseph said.

His voice shaking, Gil asked, "That happen often?"

"No."

"I thought we were goners".

Joseph didn't say anything. He thought it'd be a miracle if he were still alive in a month.

"You never answered my question. How'd you end up in prison?" Gil asked.

"It's a long story."

"I got all night."

Joseph paused for a few seconds, his heart pounding at the thought of Max's threat. Perhaps changing the subject would bring him some relief, if only for a moment. He sighed. "Where do I begin?" Joseph replied.

"My family lived in Italy most of our lives. We are Jewish and originally from Persia. We owned a farm in a small town called Umbria. We grew mainly corn, wheat, and grapes. My oldest brothers did most of the farming. The land flourished, as did everything we produced. It always yielded a good crop. My father said that God had favor on our family and that is why we were so blessed financially. We had horses, chickens, and a donkey on the farm. My mother loved animals. We were taught to appreciate everything we had. My father, Jacob Solomon, was successful, strong, determined, and faithful. Though he was only five foot five, he was the strongest man I've ever known. He was also the wisest. Faith was important to him. It came before everything. My father was passionate when he spoke of the Lord. We were very close. You might say I was his favorite child. That's probably why my brothers despised me.

"I have five brothers and a sister: Judah, Samuel, Luke, Matthew, and my sister Rebecca are from my father's first marriage to his wife Carolyn. She passed away many years ago. My brother Benjamin and I are from my father's second marriage to Rachel, whom he truly loved. My mother was a beautiful and gentle woman. She lived life to the fullest. It took several years for her to become pregnant with me, but she never lost hope. She told me I was the completion of a promise from the Lord. My brother Judah was the oldest. He had a quiet inner strength. My brothers looked up to him. He and my father didn't get along. Actually, none of my brothers got along with my father. Samuel was the second oldest, and the reserved one in the family. I spent some time with him every so often, but I remained distant from the others. They were jealous of my relationship with my father. They hated me. Luke was the strongest of all my brothers. He was arrogant and used to getting his own way. He had the hardest time with my father, perhaps because he had the quickest temper. I think he and my father are a lot alike. He had a stubborn streak so thick you could cut through it. My brothers Matthew was the handsome one in the family. He loved only two things: girls and parties but he could build almost anything. My sister Rebecca was the last child born to Carolyn. She was beautiful. We were very close. I was fifteen years old when my mother was pregnant with my brother Benjamin. It seems like a lifetime ago. I can still hear my mother calling my name..." Joseph trailed off.

The Home I Knew

"Joseph, time for dinner!" yelled his mother, Rachel. "Come in now, and don't forget to tie up the dog."

"Yes, Mother."

It was May of 1904. Winter had been cold and spring chilly; the summer months would be a welcome change. A light rain had begun falling earlier. Now it came down with greater intensity.

"Come on, boy, let's go. I don't want you outside in the rain. Don't make me chase you."

Joseph chased the dog around the chicken coop; they squawked loudly as he passed. The dog was young, but he was tall and strong enough to out run Joseph. Running past the goat named Billy; he darted around the barn then finally jumped on top of the dog, grabbing him tightly by the stomach. He lifted the dog, took him into the barn, and tied him up.

Joseph ran toward the house through the rain. His older brother, Matthew, designed the house, but Jacob and the four boys built it by hand. They had painted it white with a light blue door. Rachel loved the color blue. The drapes she'd made and hung in the windows matched the color of the door.

The tall, broadleaf trees that surrounded the home were bare during the winter months but were now beginning to show new leaf buds. Yellow daisies laced the sidewalk leading to the front porch. Rachel loved to garden.

Joseph dashed up onto the wrap-around porch. Upon entering the home, he heard the sound of laughter and horses hooves. He squinted; from a distance, he saw his older brothers approaching, recklessly riding their horses. He entered the house through the side door. He walked on the dark shiny hardwood floors through a large kitchen with beige cabinets, a small sink, a wood burning stove, and an old, small ice box. He strolled into the dining room and sat at the table next to his sister Rebecca.

Jacob sat tall with gray hair, broad shoulders, and sun-darkened skin. "Where are your brothers?" he asked.

"They're coming, Father. I saw them up the road."

Several minutes later, one by one, his brothers stomped into the house, laughing and roughhousing. Joseph reflected on each of them as they filed in. Judah was the oldest, standing almost six feet tall with sandy brown hair and light brown skin complementing his solidly built body. Joseph knew his father regretted that Judah only completed school to the eleventh grade before he went to work full time on the family farm. Jacob tried to get Judah to remain in school, but Judah was stubborn. He refused. Joseph shifted his glance to his second oldest brother, Samuel. His father had high hopes for Samuel. Though his appearance was not striking, he was highly intelligent. He finished school with high honors. But even though he was gifted with understanding and knowledge, too often he chose what his father thought was the wrong path. He dropped out of college after only one year. His father placed him in charge of accounting for the farm.

Joseph overheard his father telling his mother that he thought his gray hair was a result of the rebellious behavior of Luke, his third son. Luke's controlling personality and overconfidence held him captive. He was handsome, with pale skin and black thick hair. Though he was average in size, he was the strongest of all the boys. His father feared Luke's arrogance and hasty temper could someday cause great hardship on him and the family.

Matthew slunk into his seat as Joseph pondered upon him. Matthew had blue eyes and sandy brown hair. His features often confused people because he didn't look Jewish. His father had ambitious hopes for him to become an architect; however, his handsome appearance and easy going manner attracted women of all ages. Immaturely, he slid into a life of self-gratification.

Joseph struck a handsome appearance; dark brown wavy hair, small brown eyes, a small chin, and sun-darkened skin. His father told him his nature was kind and gentle, just as his mother's. His father also told him he talked too much and needed to learn self-control. Joseph didn't understand what that meant, but felt some day he would learn. Although Jacob loved all his children, Joseph knew his father was most proud of him.

Jacob sat stiffly in his chair; his eyes narrowed, and in a stern voice asked, "Where have you all been, it's after seven o'clock?"

"Sorry, Father, we lost track of the time," Judah said. He held his head down, he didn't look at his father.

Jacob opened both his hands. Rachel gently placed her hand in his. The rest of the family grabbed hands and bowed their heads.

"Let's pray. Our Heavenly Father, we thank you for this bountiful meal you have placed in front of us. Let it bring health to our family and nourishment to our souls. Amen." And everyone said together, "Amen."

"Did you boys finish plowing the land?"

"Not all of it," Samuel said.

"Why not?" Jacob asked.

"We went into town and lost track of the time. We'll finish it first thing in the morning."

"Excuses," Jacob complained. "Next time I tell you to do something; I want you to do it. Understand?"

"Yes, sir," Samuel said.

"Yes, sir," Judah said.

Luke and Matthew nodded.

Her eyes wide, smiling broadly, Rebecca said, "Father, we have new neighbors."

"I know; I drove by the property. I met the new owner, Jonathan, and his son, William. They invited our family to a get together on Sunday to celebrate their new home."

"I'll bake a cake to take over," Rachel said.

Matthew grinned, "I hope there'll be women there."

Jacob set his fork down and looked over at Matthew, annoyed. "There is more to life than women, Matthew. You cannot make a living out of chasing girls; you need to put your focus on something of value."

Matthew nodded.

Luke glanced at his Father. "I don't trust them. I think they are scouting out our land."

"Why are you always so suspicious, Luke?" Jacob asked. "You don't trust anyone."

"You know how people are, Father; always looking out for themselves."

Rebecca flung her wayward bangs away from head. She took the last sip of milk from her glass and wiped her face with the handkerchief. "Can I be excused?"

Rachel tilted her head. "You've hardly touched your food. Are you okay?"

"Yes, I'm just not hungry."

"Me too?" Joseph asked.

"All right."

Jacob turned to Judah and said, "Tomorrow, I want you and your brothers to do what I asked, understand?"

"Yes, sir," Judah responded.

The next day, Saturday morning, was a warm day. Rachel got up early to work in the gardens while the older boys set out on foot to finish plowing the fields. Joseph ambled into the kitchen wearing an old pair of faded brown pants, a brown t-shirt, and a pair of scuffed up shoes. He poured himself a glass of cold milk and sat at the kitchen table eating a banana muffin his mother had made.

Rachel strolled into the house with an apron full of fresh corn. Her long, thick, wavy black hair was wrapped in a yellow scarf; her bangs covered her forehead. She wore an old blue dress. She was covered in dirt and looked as though she had been working for hours.

"Mother, where are my brothers?" Joseph asked.

"They went to take four cows across town to the neighbors, and then finish plowing the fields as your father asked."

Just then Jacob entered the kitchen. "Joseph, did you finish your studies as I told you?"

"Yes, Father."

"Good, now go and assist your brothers."

"Yes, Father."

Joseph walked along the road for over half an hour. To the right of him was a stream that had overflowed some because of the rain, but the water ran clear. Tall armies of evergreens stood on the hillside. The sky was deep blue and the steady gentle wind blew his hair from his face. The road smelled of fresh pine from the large trees.

Their home sat on thirty acres of land adjacent to the Tiber River that flowed into the Tyrrhenian Sea. The valleys were laced with green grass that covered the land for miles.

Joseph had learned to love and appreciate life on the farm, but he wanted to do something great with his life. His parents had been good to him, but his ultimate dream was to travel to America. He dared to hope that he could someday attend an American school, but he knew it was impossible. Jacob expected his entire family to run the farm.

After walking twenty more minutes, he overheard laughter coming from the lake. He stumbled down the hill to get a glimpse. He noticed his brothers' clothes lying on a rock under a huge pine tree. As he walked farther down the hill, the laughter grew louder. He looked down and saw his brothers swimming with four girls. The girls appeared to be dressed in very little, as were his brothers. He shook his head in frustration and turned back to head home.

Jacob was tending the animals in the barn. He strode out past the chicken coop and the horses tied up in a fenced yard. He moved over to the well to get a drink of water. He peered up and saw that Joseph was alone. As Joseph got closer to the house, Jacob called out to him. "Joseph, why aren't you with your brothers plowing the land like I told you?"

Joseph gave no response.

"Where are your brothers?"

Joseph hesitated and said, "I don't know." Jacob clenched his teeth. "I can tell when you are lying; tell me the truth."

Joseph finally confessed. "They were swimming in the lake."

"Go on in the house." He sounded angry.

"Yes, sir."

Joseph ran into the house and into the kitchen. After lunch, he ran to a friend's house.

Four hours later, the boys finally made their way home. They approached the house a half hour before dinner. By this time, Jacob was beyond irritated. They sauntered into the home and there was Jacob, sitting in an old rocking chair in the front room.

He rose to his feet, his face flushed, jaw clenched, and eyebrows narrowed. "Where have you been? I thought I told you to finish your work."

"We did, Father," Judah said.

"Then why did your brother see you at the lake?"

The boys froze, unable to answer.

"Father, it was such a hot day. We simply went down to the lake to cool off," Samuel said.

"Never you mind. I don't need to hear any more of your excuses. I'm sick of the lies."

His frustration grew stronger with every word spoken.

"We took the cattle to the neighbors as you asked," Luke said.

"What about the land?" yelled Jacob. "Did you finish plowing the land?"

Luke looked at Matthew and then glanced back over at his father. "We will finish the land this evening when it gets cooler."
"Do I have to plow the land myself? Why can't you be trusted to do such a small task? Leave me now before I grow angrier."

"Yes, sir," Luke said.

He climbed the stairs and Judah, Samuel, and Matthew followed. Jacob stormed out of the house and stood on the porch.

Three hours Joseph arrived home. "Joseph, you're late," Rachel said.

"Dinner is on the table and everyone is seated.

"Sorry, I lost track of the time."

When Joseph sat down, Judah stared at him bitterly, as did the rest of the boys. He sat down in his usual spot next to his sister. The family held hands and Jacob thanked the Lord for the food.

Joseph turned to his father to ask a question. "My friend has invited me to go fishing with him and his father tomorrow. May I go?"

"I don't see why not," Jacob said.

Joseph smiled and piled a big spoonful of mashed potatoes on his plate.

Ten minutes had passed and not a word had been spoken. They ate in silence for almost twenty minutes. Joseph eyes darted around the table. He could feel the animosity coming from his brothers, especially Luke. Luke's eyebrows narrowed and he clenched his jaw as he stared directly into his eyes. Joseph quickly turned his head. He wondered what he'd done to cause the obvious resentment. Then he remembered that he had told their father of his brothers' afternoon adventure.

Finally, to break the silence, Rachel asked Rebecca, "Will you help me bake a cake to take to the neighbors for their party tomorrow?"

"Yes, of course."

"Father, may I be excused?" Luke asked.

"Yes."

"Me too," Matthew said.

"Everyone's excused."

After dinner, Jacob would often migrate outside to the back porch and sit on an old wooden upholstered swing built by Matthew. He would sit and watch the sunset or meditate on world events. That was also where he did most of his praying and studying of the Word of God.

He sat glaring at the bright moon, deep in thought. Rachel joined him on the porch. She handed Jacob a cup of steaming hot tea, and then moved her long, silky black hair away from her face.

"Thank you, my dear."

"You're welcome."

She slowly sat down on the wooden chair next to his and took a deep breath. She rubbed her stomach several times, wishing she were further along than just six months. It was a difficult pregnancy; she had frequent nausea, swollen feet, and a sore back.

They sat for several minutes gazing at the stars. Jacob was preoccupied. With her deep brown eyes and naturally long eye lashes, she looked directly into Jacob's eyes and asked, "What is it? You seem a bit distant."

"I have a business to run and not one of my sons has shown me he is capable of running it, except Joseph."

"You have a deep affection for Joseph."

He took a sip of his steaming hot tea and set the cup down on the table next to the swing. "This is not about my relationship with Joseph. This is about lack of responsibility and rebellion. I'm sick and tired of their excuses. I love all my boys, but the elder ones have given me nothing but trouble. The boys will earn my respect when they have proven themselves."

She then leaned up against him and placed her head on his shoulder.

"I will have to train Joseph to someday take over the business."

"You know the boys will be angry."

"I don't care. They are irresponsible. I will no longer tolerate their lack of responsibility."

Rachel wrapped her arms around Jacob. "God will give you wisdom in all of your decisions."

He smiled and took another sip of tea. They sat outside and enjoyed the warm evening for several hours.

The Heart Break

It was Sunday, a little past two p.m., and Jacob and his family had just arrived home from attending their place of worship. Joseph raced upstairs to change his clothes and came back down again wearing his worn overalls and same scuffed up brown leather boots. He kissed his mother on the cheek. He reached into the side closet next to the kitchen, grabbing his fishing pole and a bucket for the worms. His friend Martino and Martino's father were waiting out front in their new horse and carriage. He hurried outside and jumped into the carriage and left for the fishing trip.

Meanwhile, Rachel wrapped a cake up and grabbed a brown wool shawl in case it got chilly at night. She stepped outside, moving slowly because of her swollen belly, and joined Jacob, Rebecca, and the four older boys who were preparing to go to the party. It was a three-mile ride to Jonathan's property. The boys had remained warily silent most of the way, but Rebecca was thrilled. She was boisterous and full of energy. She held her head out the wagon, smiling while the sun beamed down on her naturally smooth skin. The warm wind blew her beautiful, lush brown hair away from her face.

She glanced up and saw geese flying above her head. She inhaled the fresh pine scent from the trees. Her heart quickened with joy. *I wonder if I'll meet a nice boy,* she thought. *I'm finally eighteen and father has given me permission to date.*

Once they arrived, Jonathan graciously greeted them.

Mountains surrounding the home were towering and jagged along with tall evergreen trees and a crystal clear stream. Below was a little town nestled peacefully in the green valley. A tall, handsome, muscular man with brown wavy hair approached them. Rebecca couldn't help noticing the woman that gazed at him as he walked by. Jonathan introduced his son, William, to the family.

William glanced at Rebecca and smiled. She shyly smiled back. She watched his eyes gaze at her slender body. She wore a long, blue, and narrow silhouette skirt with a train and ruffled white blouse that complemented her figure.

"Come in, come in; let me introduce you to my wife," Jonathan said.

Jacob and the family followed Jonathan to the back of the house. Most of the neighbors had been invited, and the gathering swelled to over fifty people. A live band that included two violin players, a banjo, a singer, and a flute played folk music. Many people danced on a wooden patio next to the band. Jonathan and his family had prepared a feast: chicken, beef, lamb, potatoes, bread, and assortment of pies. Judah, Samuel, Luke, and Matthew ambled over to the table and helped themselves to the food while Jacob and Rachel sat at a table and talked with Jonathan and his wife.

Rebecca strolled over to a table on the left side of the food and poured herself a glass of punch. She turned around and watched the people dancing. She noticed William staring at her from the corner of her eye. She could tell he was studying her, though she pretended not to notice. Though she was beautiful, she was still self-conscious.

William quickly approached her with self-assurance and poise.

"Hello."

"Hello," she said, quietly.

"I'm glad you and your family were able to make it," William said.

"It's nice of you to invite us."

"You're very beautiful."

She smiled.

"Do you believe in love at first sight?"

Embarrassed, she turned her head and looked out into the crowd of people. Not knowing what to say, she simply smiled.

"Would you like some more punch?" he asked.

"Yes, please."

He grabbed her glass and refilled it; some of the punch spilled out of the top. He grabbed a white linen napkin and wiped the glass and then handed it to her.

"Thank you."

"Would you like to dance?"

"Maybe a little later."

"Well, let's at least have something to eat."

She looked up at him and nodded.

William handed Rebecca a white plate and motioned for her to go first. He then filled his plate. They sat down next to some of William's friends: a blond, handsome man; another man with black and gray hair, dressed in nice brown slacks; and woman with strands of gray hair and a slightly wrinkled face. Rebecca thought it odd that William's friends were older, but they seemed friendly.

Rebecca glanced up and noticed that Luke and Matthew were standing on the right side of the yard. They appeared to be preoccupied with meeting women. She knew that Luke was choosy when it came to women; he was arrogant and insisted on the best. He knew he was good looking, with his athlete body and black, wavy hair. She watched as Luke pulled a silver flask from his jacket and then added the contents to his and Matthew's punch. She shook her head as she watched Luke take a giant swig. He set the glass down and he and Matthew then approached two women, who appeared to be in their early thirties. Luke was only twenty-one and Matthew nineteen. Luke whispered in the ear of the red-haired woman (she had a fiery look about her), while Matthew approached the blond.

She peered right. Judah and Samuel were sitting at the table with a group of men, many of them farmers. They seemed to be enjoying the food and conversation.

Across the yard Jacob and Rachel were sitting with Jonathan and his wife, talking and laughing. Minutes later, they all got up and walked to the front of the house.

Once they finished eating, Rebecca and William went for a short walk to the edge of a hillside. The watched the cows grazing in the valley. The bright orange sun gleamed brightly in her eyes as it began to set. Rebecca felt his eyes upon her. He reached out his hand and touched her back. She flinched. He quickly removed his hand. Nervous, she turned around and took two steps.

"Would you like to go inside?" William said.

She nodded.

They went into the house from the back door. William led Rebecca to the couch and excused himself and went upstairs. He came downstairs carrying a silver flask filled. She wondered what it was for. He stepped over to the table, poured them both a glass of punch.

"Here you are."

"Thank you."

"A toast to new beginnings."

She smiled and tapped her glass against his. They sat for several minutes, Rebecca didn't speak a word. Once the glass was empty, William amiably refilled it. Once the glass was empty again, he grabbed Rebecca by the hand and led her outside to the wooden patio to dance.

They danced for several minutes. Rebecca felt a sense of warmth and happiness she had never felt before. Everything felt funny. She found herself a bit lightheaded; but she was so immersed in the mood, she didn't care. William whirled her around several times. As she spun around, she burst into laughter. William tried to keep her in step but she became quite uncontrollable.

Several minutes later, she stopped to catch her breath. She became dizzy and began to waver back and forth as though she would fall. William's hand supported her as she struggled to stay on her feet. He then grabbed her and held her tightly.

Confused, everything appeared to be spiraling out of control. At that moment she wondered if he'd slipped alcohol in her drink. He led her back into the house. He continued to console her by holding her close to him. He picked up his glass, took one last drink, grabbed Rebecca with both arms, and led her upstairs. She stumbled as she climbed the stairs.

Once they reached William's bedroom, he laid Rebecca on his bed. He kissed her on her forehead, then her cheeks, and then her lips. Rebecca was unsure of her surroundings and struggled to get away. Bewildered, she whispered, "I need to go home."

"It's okay, just relax," he said quietly. He then began to kiss her forcefully. He vehemently grabbed both of her arms, continuing to kiss her. As William continued holding her down on the bed, Rebecca persistently struggled to free herself. She began to plead with him, "Please stop, I'm begging you. Stop." William's strong arms ripped her dress from the bottom. She let out a scream, but no one was able to hear her because of the loud music. Fifteen minutes passed and Rebecca lay on William's bed, sobbing uncontrollably.

From a distance she could hear her father calling her name. She wanted to scream, but felt dirty and ashamed. Overwhelmed with grief, she lay on the bed and wept. William kissed her on the forehead. She cringed. "I'll be back," he whispered.

He left the room. Her body was shivering; she felt sick to her stomach. She lay there helpless, trying to understand what had happened. She began to blame herself. *I trusted him,* she thought. *How could he do such a thing to me?*

Minutes later, William re-entered the room. She buried her face in the pillow. She hated him and couldn't bear the thought of him touching her. He sat on the bed as though nothing had happened. He ran his fingers through her hair. Her body tightened. He told her he had asked Jacob if he could bring her home.

She lifted herself off the bed and went by the window, holding her torn dress the entire time; she slowly slid onto the floor. "I… want to go home."

He sauntered over to her. "I'll take you home soon. Don't worry. I want to take care of you, always."

Rebecca couldn't believe what she was hearing. How could he do such a horrible thing and act as though nothing were wrong? It was almost as though he thought what he did was normal.

She picked herself off the floor. William tried to hold her but she pushed him away.

"I'll take you home."

He led her out the front door towards a brown barn at the side of the house. Everyone else was in the backyard. William hitched up the horse and wagon and drove her home.

When they arrived home, she stormed into the house and dashed up the stairs into her bedroom. She didn't want anyone to see her. She lay on her floor sobbing. *I feel numb,* she thought. *I can't believe this happened to me.* She wanted desperately to bathe herself, to wash away his smell; but she couldn't move. She had no strength. She covered her mouth tightly with her hands, trying to prevent her family from overhearing her sobs.

That morning, the sun shone bright and the wind blew slightly. Joseph was sitting on the table studying a history lesson. Rachel walked into the kitchen, carrying clean clothes she had washed and hung the previous day. She sat the clothes down on the floor next to the pantry. Joseph watched as the curtains blew from the cool breeze. Rachel shut the window to prevent more cool air from entering. She had woke early to bake, so the house smelled of cinnamon bread, while Jacob sat on the porch drinking a cup of coffee and reading the paper.

It was a little past eleven a.m. and Joseph thought it odd that Rebecca hadn't come down yet. She was usually the first one up. He wondered if perhaps Rebecca was ill. He watched as Rachel picked the clothes basket up and set the clothes down on the table.

"Can I get you a glass of milk?" she asked.

"Yes, please," Joseph said.

After drinking the milk, Joseph said, Mother, I'll take some breakfast to Rebecca.

Rachel placed two slices on a plate and prepared a cup of steaming hot herbal tea. Joseph climbed the stairs and knocked on Rebecca's door. "Rebecca. Rebecca."

There was no response.

"Rebecca, are you there? I brought you some breakfast."

Still no response.

Joseph gradually opened the door and found Rebecca lying on the floor. Quiet sobs shook her slight frame as tears streamed down her cheeks. Her hair looked as though it hadn't been combed in weeks, and she was still wearing the clothes she had on from the previous night. Joseph became frightened when she saw Rebecca in such distress. She set the plate and cup of tea down on the bed, ran, and knelt beside her. "Rebecca, what is it? What happened?"

Rebecca gasped for breath and tried to regain her composure, but was unsuccessful. She began to cry harder.

"Rebecca, please," Joseph implored her. "Tell me what happened."

By this time, the crying became uncontrollable. Joseph was unsure what to do. Again he asked, "What has you so upset?"

"He—he…he hurt me!"

"What?" Rachel asked. "What do you mean?"

Again she attempted to regain her composure when suddenly she blurted out, "He forced himself on me."

"Who?"

"William…William Mesilla, last night at the party." Rebecca laid her head on Josephs lap. "I…don't know how it happened," she cried.

"Everything will be okay, you'll see, it's going to be all right," Joseph said. Joseph wanted to kill William.

Rebecca continued to weep while Joseph held her close, patting her back and rocking her back and forth.

Joseph ran downstairs to tell Jacob what had happened. Jacob was furious. He grabbed his coat, called his sons together, and headed to Jonathan's house to demand justice. Several minutes later, they arrived at Jonathan's and confronted him immediately. Jacob banged on Jonathan's door forcefully, his sons by his side.

"Jonathan, open up!"

He banged on the door again; this time using greater force.

Jonathan opened the door.

Joseph who was right next to his father watched as Jacob's chin tightened and his eyes beamed from the anger that burned within. He told Jonathan what William had done to his daughter.

"I demand justice for this disgraceful act."

Jonathan's jaw dropped. He shook his head in disbelief.

"Jacob, I'm sure there is an explanation for this. My son would not dishonor your daughter."

Jonathan waved his hand and yelled out to one of his hired men. "Bring my son to me at once." He looked at Jacob and with his outstretched hand pointing inside his home as he said, "Please, come in."

"No!" Jacob screamed.

Minutes later, William appeared.

"What is it, Father?" he said as he whipped the hay from his brown dusty pants.

Jonathan frowned.

"Did you violate Jacob's daughter, William?"

William nervously glanced at Jacob and his sons. "I never meant to harm her…I…I swear." William began to perspire. "I care for Rebecca. I could never hurt her. We…we just got caught up in the moment…that's all."

His eyes began to waver back and forth. Joseph could tell he was scared.

"I could kill you for what you have done! You have robbed my daughter of her innocence."

Jonathan looked distraught over the situation.

My son has disgraced my entire household. You are well respected and to lose your favor would be a great tragedy."

William nervously glanced at Jacob and blurted, "I would like to marry your daughter, sir."

Jacob yelled. "My daughter is devastated. Marriage to you would be incomprehensible. I won't have it!"

William held his head down in shame.

"I am sorry for what my son has done," Jonathan said. "Is there anything I can do to make it right?"

"There is no justice for the disgrace he has put on my only daughter. He has robbed her of her innocence. Only the Lord can redeem her virtue. We are a peaceful family, Jonathan, but I will say this; you must keep your son away from my daughter. If I see him near my property, I will shoot him."

"I promise my son will be punished for what he has done. If there is any way I can make it up to you, I will do it."

"Just keep your son away from my daughter and my house!" Jacob yelled.

As they turned to leave, Joseph saw the anger in Luke's eyes. This time, he felt it was justified. They immediately left Jonathan's property.

IIIIIIIIIIIIIIIIIIIIIIIIIIIIIIIIIIIIIIIIIIIIIIIIIIIIIIIIIIIIIIIIIIIIIIIIIIIIIIIIIIIIIIIIIIIIIIIIIIII

That night the four older boys gathered in Matthew and Luke's bedroom to discuss their sister's ordeal. Joseph stood by the door and listened. He heard Luke say, "He treated our sister as though she were a common whore and there was no punishment. That's not good enough!"

"I agree," Judah said. "But there is nothing we can do."

"I say we burn down their house down!"

"Don't go off the deep end, Luke," Samuel said. "Someday your temper will destroy us all."

"Well what would you suggest, brother?"

"I don't know!" Samuel yelled.

"I have an idea," Matthew said. "My friend tells me that William goes to Bellafoni Restaurant every Thursday night. We can wait for him there. We will teach him a lesson he'll never forget."

"And what if Father finds out?" Samuel said.

"We will deal with Father later!" Luke yelled. "William must be punished for defiling our sister."

Just then Joseph knocked. "Who is it," Judah asked.

Joseph opened the door. "Can I go with you?" He hated William.

Judah studied his brother's faces. "Yes, but stay out of the way. The next night, Joseph stood silently as he watched Matthew peek into Bellafoni and see William sitting next to two older, sleazy women. He stepped out to the right corner of the restaurant and waited with his brothers for William.

Finally, William staggered outside, both women hanging on each arm. He reached over and kissed one of them on the cheek, and then turned and fell drunkenly backwards. Once he regained his footage, they continued to walk.

Matthew grabbed him from behind and pulled him toward the back of the restaurant. Both women stared in terror. Luke punched William in the face. He fell to the ground and Matthew picked him up. The women screamed and ran away.

Joseph was terrified. He watched Matthew and Judah continue to hold William while Luke punched him in the stomach several times. He stood helpless. Eventually, William fell to the ground, blood streaming from his mouth. He began to cough as he gasped for air. Luke began to kick him.

"That's enough! You'll kill him," Samuel said.

"I'll say when it's enough!" Luke yelled, kicking him again.

Samuel grabbed Luke and threw him to the ground. "I said that's enough! Let's go."

They ran and jumped on their horses, Joseph was right behind him. he watched Luke glanced back at William as he lay on the dirt ground, blood dripping from his mouth and gasping for air. With no remorse, he turned his head as he and his brothers rode home.

The next day when Jacob learned of the fight, he immediately called the boys downstairs. Jacob had grown accustomed to being angry with the boys, but this time he was enraged. He was a peaceful man and believed in a peaceful home. Fighting was not the solution to justice.

They the living room and saw their father, his fiery eyes burning and his face tight with tension.

Joseph crept down the stairs and peeked into the living room.

"I received a call from Jonathan today. William was beaten badly last night outside a restaurant and had to be hospitalized. Did you do it?…Did you beat William?"

The boys remained silent; Luke held his head down. "I don't know what to do with you boys! I am ashamed of all of you."

"What were we to do, Father? Allow our sister to be treated like a common prostitute?" yelled Luke.

"And what now, Luke? Has beating young William taken the reproach away from your sister?"

Luke shifted his glance away from his father.

"How long will you continue to disappoint me?"

"But, Father..."

"Be quiet, Judah. You are worst of all. I depend on you as the oldest and that is why you disappoint me the most. I need all of you out of my sight while I figure out what to say to Jonathan."

One by one, the boys left the room.

Jacob buried his face in the palms of his hands. Rachel entered the kitchen and saw Jacob in distress. Having overheard his conversation with his boys, she asked, "What are you going to do?"

"I must apologize to Jonathan and hope the family name. This is disgraceful. I cannot understand the stupidity of these boys."

"Jacob, they were merely defending their sister's honor."

"That is no excuse. Since when do we, children of the Most High Lord, seek revenge in such a violent way? I have taught them better than this. There is no excuse."

Joseph quietly moved back up the stairs.

New Life

Fall was the most beautiful season in Italy and Joseph and Rebecca were taking advantage of this time of year at the lake. The leaves on the trees had begun to turn every deep beautiful autumn color: green, yellow, red, and orange. Joseph slumped over and picked up a rock and threw it into the crystal clear lake and watched as it skipped over the water. Rebecca gazed up at the dazzling light out of the deep blue, cloudless sky.

Three months passed and Jacob and Jonathan's families had remained distant from one another. William had moved to France to live with an uncle.

Though Rebecca didn't speak of it, Joseph knew that, at times, thoughts of William disturbed her. He could see it in her eyes; they didn't sparkle the way they used to. The joy that had once filled her spirit had grown dim.

She looked at her reflection in the water as she reached down to feel the cold water from the lake. She dipped some water up in her hand and took a sip, and then wiped her lips with the hem of her green dress. She stood and walked to a grassy spot near a stand of pine trees. She lay back on the cool, moist grass and smelled the fresh pine as she gazed up at the bright blue sky.

Joseph sat down beside her. He glanced at Rebecca, his face was sad and his voice was soft.

"Rebecca, why do you suppose my brothers hate me–especially Luke?"

Rebecca frowned. She looked at Joseph. "They don't hate you, Joseph. They're jealous of you. Father's affections for you are obvious." Joseph's voice deepened and he became angry. "I can't help that. I've never done anything to them. Sometimes I think they wish I were never born."

"Joseph, deep down inside, I'm sure they love you. I think its Father they're angry at, but they take it out on you." She reached over and gently touched his arm. "I'm sure someday our brothers will grow to appreciate you as I do. It will take time."

Joseph lay down on his back. He glared up at the bright blue sky. He squinted from the bright sun in his eyes. "I had a dream several days ago."

"About what?" Rebecca asked.

"I was standing in the center of a stage in a large building, like a stadium. Surrounding me were crowds of people, many of them thin and destitute and dressed in filthy rags. They began to approach me. It was as if they were seeking refuge. I began handing them bundles of grain. Then my brothers came and held out their hands to me. What do you think it means?"

"Perhaps you will do great things and be very important, Joseph." She laughed. "I wouldn't mention the dream to our brothers. I'm afraid their dislike for you would only intensify."

"I have a personal dream. Promise not to tell Father?"

"Promise."

Joseph's face lit up. "I want to attend one of the universities in America. I want to learn of business and economics and finance."

"That could be difficult."

"I don't want to be a farmer. I want to help people and do great things." She smiled. "You will."

Joseph sighed. "You know how Father feels about me taking over the business. He'll never let me go."

"Never say never."

She turned toward him, half sitting, her head propped on her hand. "Perhaps Father will change his mind; you know how he feels about you. He always insisted that you excel in school."

"Yes, but that's so I can take over the business."

They lay silent for a while. Then Rebecca lifted herself from the grass. She stood in front of Joseph.

"Let's go, Joseph, before we're late for dinner."

She grabbed Joseph by the hand and helped him up. They hurried home and arrived right at seven. Rebecca and Joseph flew into the house through the front door. Jacob was already sitting at the dinner table. They joined him. Rachel placed a large bowl filled with homemade rolls at the table and then sat down next to Jacob. Minutes later Judah, Samuel, Luke, and Matthew joined them.

After dinner, Luke and Matthew fed the animals while Samuel and Judah plowed the fields. Jacob sat outside on the porch reading the word of God. Joseph sat at the table finishing his history lesson while Rebecca helped Rachel with the dishes.

Rachel reached up to put a glass in the cabinet and doubled over, grabbing her stomach and moaning. The glass shattered in the sink. She grabbed for a chair.

Joseph stiffened slightly at the sound before he jumped up and ran to her. "Mother, are you okay?"

She closed her eyes, leaned on the chair, and took two deep breaths. The time had come for her to give birth to her second child.

Rebecca laid her hand on Rachel's arm. "Sit down, please."

Rachel slowly sat down on the chair, still holding her stomach. She began to breathe heavily, trying to fight the pain.

"Are you all right?" Rebecca asked.

"I'm fine. Get my coat please."

Rebecca ran to the closet and grabbed a long wool coat and wrapped it around her.

"Joseph," she whispered, "Get your father."

Joseph dashed outside onto the porch. Jacob was sitting on a chair on the back porch, reading while drinking a cup of tea.

"Father, come quick!"

"What is it, Joseph?"

"I think it's time."

Jacob leaned down in his chair.

"What?"

"Mother! She's having the baby."

Jacob stumbled to his feet.

"I'll go get the horse and carriage. You tell your brothers."

He ran to the field and called out to Samuel and Judah, "Mother is in labor, come quick."

As they dropped their plows and ran toward the house, Joseph rushed into the barn to tell Matthew and Luke. They finished tying up the horses and then ran toward the house just as Jacob walked out with Rachel. His hand supported her back as she picked her way down the stairs. "You boys stay here, except for Judah. Go and get Rachel's sister, Lillian, and tell her to meet us at the hospital."

"But, Father, we wish to come," Matthew said.

Jacob helped Rachel in on the passenger side of the carriage. "All right, you boys hitch up your horses and meet us at the hospital."

Joseph and Rebecca jumped in the back.

Once they arrived, Rachel clung to Jacob, slumped over and cried out in pain. Once her feet landed on the door of the hospital, she knelt down as her energy depleted. "I can't walk anymore. The pain grows stronger every minute, like a bomb exploding in me. I feel like I'm dying," she cried.

A nurse ran to them and immediately called for a wheel chair. The nurse and Jacob lifted her into the chair and took her to a hospital room.

Just then. Lillian arrived with Judah by horse and buggy. Jacob had called her because it was she who had helped to deliver Joseph. Joseph's birth took place in the home. The labor was too difficult and there were complications so Rachel vowed to never give birth at home again.

Jacob paced slowly back and forth in the narrow hallway of the old hospital. The siblings all sat silent in the waiting room. Joseph could see the anxiety in his father's eyes. The fear seemed to deepen as he heard Rachel cry out in pain over and over again.

Three hours later, they heard the sound of a baby crying. Joseph watched his father's face, it was filled with joy.

Minutes later, Lillian ran down the hallway towards them.

"There are complications. The doctors don't know what's wrong.

Joseph watched Jacob's face turn pale. Jacob placed his hand on his heart as though it was causing him pain. Rebecca who was right beside him held him.

After many painful minutes of waiting that seemed like hours, the doctor finally walked in. "The baby is fine."

"And Rachel?" Jacob asked.

"We're not exactly sure what happened. She started to hemorrhage and now she's in a coma."

Tears rolled down Jacob's face as he heard the news.

"May I see her?" Jacob asked.

"Yes, she's in room 5B."

Jacob sat at Rachel's bedside for several hours. Joseph and his brothers and sister stayed close. Rebecca brought food, but Jacob was too distraught to eat. Matthew walked in the room with a glass full of water, some of it spilling on the floor.

"Here you are, Father."

"Thank you, son."

"She's going to be okay," Matthew said.

Jacob reached up and grabbed Matthews's hand and nodded.

That was the first time Joseph had ever seen any sincere sympathy come from his brother.

"Father, shall we bring in the baby?" Rebecca asked.

Jacob shook his head.

The family watched for Rachel to show a glimpse of action. Joseph had never seen his father so distraught. He knew his father couldn't bear to live in an empty house without his mother's radiating presence, or lie alone in the bed that they'd shared for so many years, or sit at the table without her. His father truly loved his mother.

Jacob shared with Joseph how he had met Rachel many years ago.

The year was 1864. Jacob sat on a bench in a small one-room schoolhouse. The paint on the outside was cracked and tarnished, and the room smelled of mildew. Twenty-four students attended the school. The room was painted white; there were five benches, a small wooden desk up front where the teacher sat, and an old chalk board. Jacob was seventeen years old.

One day, a young girl walked in. She had long hair, deep brown eyes, high cheekbones, and fair skin. She wore a bright yellow dress. Her name was Rachel. She was only fourteen years old, but she was by far the most beautiful girl he had ever seen. He fell in love with her the first moment he saw her. Jacob knew he had met the girl of his dreams and that he would someday marry her. One week later, the two began courting. He would walk her home after school. Her parents were strict, so he would say goodbye outside of her father's property.

Carolyn, Judah, Samuel, Luke, Matthew, and Rebecca's mother attended the school as well. Carolyn stood five feet five inches tall with long brown hair and was ordinary in appearance. Jacob often noticed Carolyn staring at him, but he had no interest in her.

One evening, a little past six p.m., Jacob had finished his chores. He walked out of the barn and there stood Carolyn. She had followed him home. She pulled from her bag a bottle of wine she had found in her father's shed. Jacob had never had alcohol before; but, out of curiosity, he decided to try it. The two laughed and drank for over one hour. Carolyn made advances toward him and they were intimate.

He learned several months later that she was pregnant. The two were forced to marry. She died five years after Matthew was born. Within three months, Jacob married Rachel, the woman he truly loved.

Five hours had passed in the dreary hospital room. Joseph and his brothers stayed by Jacob's side the entire time. Jacob was resting his head on the desk next to Rachel's bed when Rachel slowly opened her eyes.

"Father, Father," Rebecca cried, shaking his shoulder and grabbing his arm.

Jacob looked up, overwhelmed with joy. He took her hand and began to cry. She stared up at him, unable to speak. Joseph ran to get the doctor.

Five minutes later the doctor walked into the room. He reached over and felt Rachel's pulse.

"It was close, but she's going to be okay."

Jacob breathed a sign of relief. He kissed his wife on the cheek. She smiled slightly and in a soft voice asked, "Where's the baby?"

Just then a nurse walked in with a fragile, pink baby boy; his thick sandy brown hair tumbling over his forehead.

"He weighs 6.4 pounds," the nurse said.

Jacob stood up and the nurse handed him the baby. He laughed. The family was overflowing with joy. He knelt down beside Rachel's bed. She smiled, gently rubbing her fingers across the baby's head.

"Let's see, what shall we call you?" Jacob asked.

He paused. "Your name shall be Benjamin. Benjamin Jotham Solomon.

A Dream Comes True

The time was eight a.m. The family was used to rising early; the day usually began at six. Jacob, Judah, Samuel, and Luke spent the day picking bushels of corn. They planned to go into town later to sell them to the local merchant. The store owner was close friends of the family and purchased all of his produce from Jacob's farm.

Matthew, with the help of his brothers, finished building a red barn large enough to hold twenty-five cows. He walked out of the barn, his torn black pants and old white shirt covered in white paint; he had just finished painting the front door.

Rachel sat on the front porch knitting a black scarf for Jacob while Joseph vigorously chased the two-year-old, Benjamin, through the yard. Joseph picked him up and swung him around several times. Benjamin laughed as he flew around and around in a circle. Joseph's playful dog, Champ, leaped on his back while he held Ben. He gently placed Ben down and wrestled with his dog to keep him from licking his face. Joseph laughed as he grappled on the grass, trying to control his feisty dog.

"All right, Champ, I give up," Joseph said.

He lifted himself off the ground, picked up Ben, and dashed up on the porch. He set Ben down next to his mother. "Mother, where is Rebecca?"

"She went for a walk with Dan." Joseph smiled.

Rebecca had met Dan several months earlier. His parents owned a lumber mill right outside of Tuscany. His gentleness and kindness helped her to forget the terrible experience. They were deeply in love. They planned to be married by the end of the year.

"Your lunch is on the table. I packed an extra sandwich in case you decided to go fishing afterwards."

"Thank you, Mother."

Joseph ran into the kitchen and grabbed his lunch. He rushed out the side door and ran to school. The school was two miles away from his home, and class started promptly at eight thirty.

He headed into the fields, swishing through the wild grass and towering Douglas firs with long strides and carrying stacks of books. He entered the building and moved down a narrow hallway into the far right classroom. The walls were white, the floors wooden, and twenty four desks were arranged in neat rows. Twenty-two students filled the room. The old school, which carried 150 students, had been added to and now held 250 students.

On the back of the wall were two brown bookshelves. In the front of the room were the teacher's desk and a chalk board. An Italian flag with three vertical bands of equal width in green, white, and red, hung from the wall on the right side of the classroom.

Joseph loved school; he devoted himself to his studies. Math was his favorite subject. He had been blessed with great intelligence and an inner drive to be the best at everything he did. He would be graduating in two weeks and it was important to Joseph to finish at the top of his class.

Final examinations were approaching. Joseph studied at every opportunity he had. The school teacher, Mr. Tanelli, who stood tall with black, wavy hair, invited a guest to speak to the students today.

Everyone, please settle down," Mr. Tanelli said. "Mr. Earl Rodgers is here from the United States of America. He is in Italy on business; however, he is an old friend of mine and has graciously agreed to speak to us today. Mr. Rodgers is a retired professor from New York University. He is here to talk on the subject of engineering, as well as other job opportunities in America."

A quiver of excitement passed through Joseph.

The elderly professor had striking white hair and a beard. He spoke with an indistinguishable accent and was dressed quite well in a dark suit with a white waistcoat and dotted necktie. He carried a fashionable top hat. *He must be wealthy,* Joseph thought. He stood with such poise and his mannerisms were quite refined. He had a look of wisdom and intelligence. *I wonder if everyone in New York is rich.*

Joseph found his hour-long lecture informative and engaging. Mr. Rodgers discussed engineering and marketing and showed the class photos of the University. Joseph was engrossed in the lecture; like a sponge, he absorbed every word spoken. Once Mr. Rodgers concluded, the class applauded.

"I have a very important announcement to make," Mr. Tanelli said. "As you know, you will be given a final examination on Monday."

The students all let out a sigh.

"Hold on, hold on, let me finish. Mr. Rodgers has graciously arranged to offer the two students with the highest scores a free trip to visit New York University and the City College of New York."

Joseph was sitting so far on the edge of his seat that any minute he could drop to the floor.

"Once the tests have been graded, I will announce the two winners. Mr. Rodgers will cover the cost of travel and the room. You have all weekend to prepare; I suggest you get started."

Joseph's heart began to beat rapidly; he could barely hold back his excitement. The opportunity that had just presented itself to him was the chance of a lifetime and he planned to do everything he could to win.

He studied from dawn till dusk all weekend, taking breaks only to eat and do his chores. He told only Rebecca about the opportunity to go to America. She was hopeful, but told him, she knew if he won the trip it would be hard to convince their father to let him go.

When Monday came, Joseph rushed to school; his hair was barely combed, and his face was pale. He had studied and worked the whole weekend with little sleep. The thought of winning the trip consumed him.

The teacher passed out the exam and asked the students to keep the paper face down until all of the exams were handed out. Joseph had never been this nervous in his life. He held his hands down flat on the table to keep them from shaking. He took two deep breaths to calm himself.

When every student had an exam, they were allowed to begin. It took almost two hours. Although Joseph felt he did well, anxious thoughts overwhelmed him. The results were to be shared the next day.

When Joseph got home, he finished his chores and went to bed early. Too stressed to eat, he lay awake all night in anxiety.

The next day in class, Joseph sat upright, gripping his seat. His stomach felt nauseated as he waited to hear the results of the exam. He prayed silently to the Lord for divine favor.

Mr. Tanelli stepped into the classroom. Joseph took deep breaths to calm his nerves.

"I have the names of two students who, I must say, are very deserving of this trip," Mr. Tanelli said.

He glanced around the room. Was it Joseph's imagination, or did his eyes linger on him?

"While the majority of you did well, these two students received the highest scores in the class."

Joseph clenched his teeth.

"The first student is...Peter Antonio."

The young boy smiled and the other students, including Joseph, applauded.

"The second student is Joseph Solomon."

Again, the class applauded.

Joseph could barely breathe. He wanted to jump out of his seat, but managed to maintain his composure.

"Thank you," he said.

"You're welcome, Joseph, you deserve it," Mr. Tanelli said.

After class Mr. Tanelli told Joseph to tell his parents at once because Mr. Rodgers was planning to leave right after graduation. Joseph promised that he would.

He ran home to tell his family. This was the most exciting day of his life. He wasn't sure how his father would take the news, but he was going to do everything in his power to convince him to let him to go.

He dashed into the yard and up the steps, swinging the door open so hard it slammed into the wall. He trampled on the freshly mopped, damp floor yelling, "Father, Father."

Jacob's voice came from the living room. "What is it, Joseph?"

"You'll never believe it," he said, gasping for air. Joseph stood next to his father who was sitting down on the couch.

"Joseph, slow down, slow down."

His face was flushed from the long run home, his shirt soaked from perspiration. He took a deep breath. "I won a prize; I have been chosen to go to visit an American college."

Jacob smiled. "Well, that's quite an honor, but how, Joseph?"

"Mr. Rodgers, a friend of Mr. Tanelli. He is from the United States. He spoke to our class a few days back and offered free trips to two students who received the highest final exam scores in the class. I won! He has agreed to pay all costs. The school is in New York City. May I go, Father, please?"

"That's very far away, Joseph."

"Father, I must go, please."

"Joseph, what will become of this?

"It would only be for the experience," Joseph explained.

"When will you return home?"

"In one month."

Jacob paused for several moments. "You are only fifteen Joseph. I cannot allow you to travel alone. Your brothers will go with you."

Relieved and elated, Joseph hugged his father, and then ran upstairs to tell Rebecca.

Two days later, Jacob entered the house after a long walk. Judah, Samuel, Luke, and Matthew were sitting at the table eating breakfast. Rachel placed two pancakes on a plate for Jacob and set them down next to Samuel. Jacob walked over to the hallway closet near the kitchen, opened the door, and pulled out a brown package and a little black box. He went to the foot of the stairs and called for Joseph. "Joseph, come down here. Come quickly."

He then strolled into the kitchen.

Joseph ran down the stairs and into the kitchen.

"I've bought you something," Jacob said, smiling. He handed Joseph the neatly wrapped package.

Curious, Joseph studied it, "What is it, Father?"

Jacob laughed. "Well, open it."

Joseph ripped open the package and threw the wrappings on the floor. His brothers waited to see what their father had gotten his favorite son.

He pulled out a brown suit and held it up.

"I can't believe it. It's a suit, a brand new suit."

"You'll need something nice to wear when you go to America."

"Thank you, Father."

Judah set his fork down and glanced over at Samuel with an angry expression.

"Wait, there's something else."

He handed Joseph a little black box. Joseph opened the box and pulled out a beautiful gold pocket watch. Joseph stared at the gift in awe; he had never owned a watch.

"This has been in our family for years, Joseph. I want you to have it."

Joseph hugged his father, murmuring, "Thank you."

Jacob nodded. "You're welcome. You can pass it on to your son."

"I will," he said, looking at the watch in his hand and smiling.

Luke got up from the table, grabbed his plate, slammed it down forcefully on the kitchen counter, and stormed outside. Gradually, the other three boys joined him.

Luke unhitched his horse and said, "Everything is Joseph. It's as though we don't exist. I grow to hate our little brother more and more everyday. I wish he would go to America and disappear forever."

Matthew laughed as he unhitched his horse, "Perhaps he will. Father said we are to accompany Joseph to America. Once we get there, we will throw our little brother in the ocean."

Samuel threw down his saddle. "Enough of that talk! Our dislike for our little brother isn't going to change the way Father feels about him."

"He's right," Judah said. "Let's go down to the lake and try to forget Joseph exists."

They rode down to the lake where they spent the rest of the day.

Journey to America

Joseph ran down the stairs and stumbled; dropping the bag he'd just finishing packing.

"Joseph, calm down. You'll be leaving soon enough," Jacob said.

"Sorry, Father. I'm very excited."

He picked himself up and grabbed the bag.

"Have you packed everything you need?"

"Yes."

"Judah, Samuel, Matthew, Luke, hurry, it's time to go," Jacob shouted.

The boys loaded their luggage onto the carriage.

Rachel hugged Joseph tightly, smiling while tears ran down her cheeks. "I will miss you," she said hoarsely.

"I will miss you too, Mama."

She held him for another moment, and then kissed him goodbye. She smiled brightly as she said, "Hurry home."

Rachel hugged each boy goodbye.

Joseph picked Benjamin up and hugged him.

"Be good, little Ben, and I will bring you something back from America."

Benjamin smiled and nodded.

Rebecca, flushed with excitement, approached Joseph.

"I have something for you."

She handed him a journal.

"I want you to keep a record of everything you do and see, okay?"

He riffled through the blank pages of the little black book. He smiled. "I will." He hugged her. "Thank you."

Joseph and his brothers, along with their father, rode to the city of Grosseto. The city lay on the shore and stretched across the hillsides, covered with lush bushes, shrubs, and flowers. Joseph squinted from the sun and took off his jacket once they arrived. His excitement intensified as he stared at the boats anchored on the water. The boys had to take a boat to France to catch a larger ship to America.

Jacob turned to Joseph one last time. Tears came to his eyes. "You make me proud, Joseph. The Lord has special plans for you. You were chosen to do something great. You are a fruitful vine near a spring whose branches climb over a wall. Someday you will understand what those words mean, Joseph."

He hugged Joseph one last time. He then turned and hugged Judah. "Judah, you are the oldest; I am depending on you to look after the others—especially Joseph."

"I will, Father."

He hugged Samuel, Luke, and then Matthew. "Try to stay out of trouble."

They each responded with, "Yes, Father."

"I will see you all in one month."

As the boys boarded the ship, Joseph turned one last time to wave goodbye to his father.

The boat sailed across the Liguran Sea and arrived in the city of Cannes, France. The city sparkled, lying on the shore surrounded by rich mountains and the beautiful Mediterranean gold coast, with stretches of rocky beaches. Joseph watched the families stroll by while admiring the brilliant view.

With a motionless stare, he froze once he saw the ship. The giant vessel, painted white, held a maximum of three hundred passengers. There were funnels side by side located on the far left with lifeboats carried low in a hull and five decks.

They boarded the ship; two hours later, the ship set sail.

The next day, Joseph stood on the deck. It was an endless stretch of water. The sun was shining bright, but his face was cool from the sea breeze. His wool blue jacket rustled in the wind. He stared at the sea for hours. *I can never get bored,* he thought to himself. He smiled as he watched a dolphin fly above the deep blue, peaceful waters.

Finally he would see America. He wondered what would be in store for him once he arrived.

Several days passed. Joseph had seen very little of his brothers. They spent most of their time drinking and partying with women aboard the ship. Joseph enjoyed walking along the far right side of the deck where few people visited. Jacob had given him plenty of money, which was a good thing; if he had been dependent on his brothers, he would have starved.

Peter, the other young man who won the trip, told Joseph that Mr. Rodgers had been seasick and was spending a great deal of his time in his cabin. Joseph had dined with Peter and his parents on occasion, but spent most of his time alone.

One evening, Joseph strolled across deck from the raised roof. Rich people dressed in elegant attire strolled across the oriental carpet. He heard a voice from behind him.

"Got a light, kid?"

He turned around and there stood a sandy-haired man with a big belly and an odd-shaped long nose holding a cigarette. He was dressed in a black tux.

"No, sir," replied Joseph.

"Where ya from, son?" the man asked.

"Italy."

"Ah, beautiful country."

"Yes, sir."

"What's in New York?"

"I am visiting American universities. I hope someday my father will allow me to attend one. Where are you from, sir?"

"New York. The wife and I vacationed in Europe and now we're on our way home. I went to New York University; very good school. What's your name?"

"Joseph."

"Well, Joseph, I'm Taylor Parks."

Just then, a lovely woman dressed elegantly in an off-white gown walked over to the man.

"Darling, I've been looking everywhere for you. Let's hurry before we are late for dinner. I told the Joneses we would join them at eight."

"Yes, dear. Well, son, maybe I'll run into you some day in New York."

"Yes, sir, it was a pleasure to meet you." Joseph glanced at the woman. "Ma'am."

She gently nodded her head and smiled before she slipped her arm between Taylor's arm and they walked away.

The next day was Sunday—another beautiful day. They were due to arrive in New York. As Joseph strolled along the deck, he stared straight ahead, his heart throbbing with excitement. With a sudden burst of energy, he ran downstairs into the room and yelled, "We're here! We're in New York!"

His brothers jumped out of their beds.

Joseph ran back upstairs onto the deck and stared in amazement. His brothers stumbled out on deck, still buttoning their shirts. They stood next to Joseph and watched as the ship sailed past the Statue of Liberty. They looked in wonder at the enormous female figure dressed in a robe. It was even larger than it appeared in the history books Joseph had read. *People are actually walking into it,* Joseph thought. They looked ahead and there was New York City in its splendor: a tall, large city, lying on what appeared to be an island. The sun shone brilliantly over the city.

The boys held their bags and moved slowly as they disembarked from the ship. They searched for transportation to their hotel. They decided to cross the street where they saw several horses and carriages. Joseph lagged behind, caught up in his surroundings. It was quite different from Italy. The architecture was unique; the buildings stood tall and long, and there were more cars on the streets than he'd ever seen in his life.

"Joseph, stop day dreaming and come over here!" Judah yelled.

Joseph ran and caught up with his brothers.

Judah pointed with his outstretched arms to an empty carriage. "There's a driver."

The boys loaded their bags onto the carriage, climbed in, and handed the driver the address of the hotel.

Twenty minutes later, they arrived at their destination.

"Here you go. Midtown," the driver said.

Judah handed him the money for the ride and said, "Thank you."

They arrived at noon. The building was made of red bricks and was four stories. Upon entering, Matthew appeared to be examining the crafted hardwood floors. On the right were two beautiful velvet beige chairs and an attractive brown couch. It had a quiet and relaxed atmosphere. Joseph found it to be intimate and charming. He peered right where a silver haired man with an almond-shaped head and sideburns sat. He was dressed in a three-piece suit consisting of a sack coat with a matching vest and a tall hat. Joseph had never seen anything like it.

They slowly approached the illustrious looking gentleman.

"We'd like to check in," Judah said.

The man studied Judah carefully. He cleared his throat in a refined voice said, "Your name?

"Joseph Solomon."

The clerk searched his documents on the open desk. He handed the keys to Judah and said, "There is a message for Joseph."

Joseph took the note.

Hello, Joseph. I'm sorry I couldn't spend much time with you on the ship. Meet me at the university on Monday at nine a.m. sharp to begin the first tour, Mr. Rodgers.

"What is it, Joseph?" Samuel asked.

"Mr. Rodgers has asked that I meet him at the university tomorrow morning at nine."

Joseph was thrilled to have half a day to explore the large city. They climbed three flights of scratched wooden stairs. They found room number twenty-eight and entered. It had two double beds. Joseph went over to the window and looked out and saw the alley and another shorter brick building. He moved over to one of the beds and started to set his bag down, but Matthew shoved it onto the floor. "You sleep on the floor."

Joseph, annoyed, picked up his bag, and set it beside an old dresser drawer.

"I'm hungry," Luke said.

"We'll unpack our bags, and then we will get something to eat," Judah said.

After unpacking, they ate dinner at a diner across the street. One hour later, they walked out of the diner.

"Let's go, brothers. There's a whole other world here to explore," Luke said, smiling.

"Joseph, you stay in the hotel room," Judah said.

Joseph frowned. "But I want to go."

"I said no," Judah said."

"But Father said we were to stay together…"

"Joseph, shut up and do as you're told!" Luke said.

Joseph watched as they walked on ahead into the crowded busy streets of downtown New York. It was apparent his older brothers had deserted him. Irritated, he shook his head. He looked around at the city and decided to explore it on his own.

There was too much to see; he refused to spend it locked up in a smelly hotel room. At first glance, the city was overwhelming. He tried to remember every street name so he could find his way back.

Joseph strolled north along the busy streets. People were everywhere, as far as the eye could see, dressed in so many forms of fashion. Some wore elegant and sophisticated attire, while others appeared to be quite poor. The sound of cars filled the streets, many odd looking and shaped in different sizes. He examined a car parked on a street corner. A small emblem read *Ford.* He'd never heard of it. He stopped by a restaurant. A sign read, "Best Barbeque in Town." The smell radiated through his body. It was quite a contrast from the acrid smell of horse manure on the farm.

He peered up and stared at a gigantic building with a bell tower on the very top. It was astonishing. He wondered how they built such a tall building. He read the small print: "The Woolworth Skyscraper."

At one corner stood a young, thin boy with a green cap on his head, yelling, "Get your paper here! Get your paper."

A man reached out his hand and grabbed Joseph's shirt and said, "Hey, son, get your scarf here, only ten cents; buy now while it's hot."

Joseph politely said, "No, thank you."

"Hey, young man," said a woman who was standing on the second floor balcony of a tall faded brick building. Her blouse straps hung off her shoulders, a cigarette dangled in her right hand. "I can show ya a good time."

Embarrassed, he turned his head and continued to walk. He passed Gothic Trinity Church. He thought it was unusual in appearance with its Gothic style. It was the largest church he'd ever seen.

Joseph went east on Broadway and downhill to South Street arriving at Wall Street. Elaborate marble buildings lined the street.

He walked the busy crowed streets filled with people, mainly men. Stopping at 18th and Broadway, he stared at the spectacular building. The name inscribed on the top of the building read, "New York Stock Exchange." *What is a stock exchange?* Joseph thought to himself. *It must be important, look at the people coming in and out of the building.*

Joseph walked North of Canal Street and arrived in what was called Little Italy. The streets were crowded; there were immigrants, laborers, and peasants. He peered right at a woman who appeared to be in her early thirties with a young boy who was wearing filthy short pants and knee socks that were torn on the right side above his ankle. His face was covered with dirt. She was wearing a long wool shirt with a gray shawl wrapped around her, and her hair was nicely tucked in a bun. The pain and sorrow on her face revealed she was desperate. She unzipped a torn, small, brown bag and pulled out a penny and purchased an apple from a fruit vendor. She handed the apple to her son who looked to be about seven. He smiled and graciously bit into it. *This is a very different world from Wall Street,* he thought.

He continued to walk for two more miles; he stopped and looked left at stairs leading underground. The sign read, "New York Subway." He stepped down two flights of steps and saw what appeared to be an underground train.

The ceilings were made of ornamental moldings, and the panels were decorated with narrower moldings. The bases of the walls were brick, and above that was glass tile. The track was made of timber and rails and centered between iron poles. Tracks were leading into four different directions and curved around, entering a dark tunnel.

He approached a man behind the ticket counter. "Excuse me, sir. Where does the train go?"

"North Broadway, lower Manhattan, Brooklyn. Depends on where ya wanna go, kid."

He handed the man twenty cents and then boarded the train.

The train started slowly then entered massive speed. Joseph smiled, gripping his seat. As the train got ready to stop, a conductor yelled, "Manhattan Street near 128th Street!" Several people detrained. Joseph wondered where the train would go next. It went to Broadway, 137th, and then Broadway and 145th Street. Joseph rode back to his original spot. He couldn't remember when he'd had so much fun.

Joseph pulled out his pocket watch from his coat jacket and checked the time. It was five thirty. He returned to the hotel at seven because he wanted to make sure he was well rested for the next day. His brothers didn't come back until around two a.m., intoxicated from a night of drinking. They woke him with their loud singing and laughing.

Annoyed by their rudeness, Joseph forcefully grabbed his pillow from under his head and covered his face with it. He clenched his teeth to try and hold in the frustration as he lay on the cold hardwood floor.

The next day, while his brothers slept, Joseph rose early to meet Mr. Rodgers at New York University. Peter spent the day before with his mother and father, but he and Joseph agreed to walk to the University together. He pulled the directions that Mr. Rodgers had given him out of his pocket and knocked on Peter's hotel room. He was staying in a room down the hall.

"Hi, Joseph."

"Hi, Peter. Are you ready?"

"Almost, I need fifteen more minutes."

"I'll wait for you in the lobby," Joseph said.

"Okay."

It took them a little longer to get to the University than they thought. They rode the trolley to Market Street, then walked left on Mills, and then took a right on to Broadway. There stood New York University—a massive group of brick buildings covering at least two blocks. Joseph was astonished. The photos Mr. Rodgers had shown him did not do the campus justice. They entered the university; Joseph's feet were ringing on the marble floors. The ceilings were high. To the far right were white walls with inscriptions on them. They were too small and too far away to make out the words. Hundreds of students strolled in the hallways, most carrying books. Joseph felt important just being among them.

"Joseph! Peter! Over here."

The two looked behind them and there, standing next to a counter, was Mr. Rodgers.

"You're ten minutes late."

"Sorry, Mr. Rodgers," Peter said. "It was my fault."

"It's okay. Let's go, there is much to see. New York University is a private university. The school was founded in 1831 and is the largest institution of higher education in the state," said Mr. Rodgers.

They moved through the history, mathematics and engineering, and medical buildings. They talked to the chestnut-brown haired history professor who looked to be in his early forties about the history of New York City. Joseph was captivated; he thought it was remarkable. His desire to attend the school burned deeper and deeper within his soul. The knowledge acquired here far exceeded anything he felt he could learn on the farm.

Once the tour was completed, the boys walked back to the hotel. Peter had planned to join his parents for dinner.

"See you tomorrow, Joseph."

"See you, Peter."

Joseph looked across the street into the diner and noticed his brothers having dinner. He strolled into the restaurant and headed toward the table. As he sat, Matthew pulled the chair from underneath him. He fell flat to the floor. Matthew laughed hysterically. The others remained silent, while he lay on the floor embarrassed and bruised. He climbed to his feet, took hold of the chair back, and sat down. Attempting to start a conversation he said, "The university is amazing. There are so many buildings."

Judah and Samuel continued eating, neither looking at Joseph.

"We plan to spend the next two days at the university. Next week, we will see City College of New York."

"The women are more beautiful here than in Italy; don't you think, big brother?" Matthew said, glancing at one of the waitresses.

Luke nodded.

It was obvious to Joseph that his brothers were ignoring him. Joseph had grown accustomed to his brothers' rudeness and distance toward him.

He ordered a turkey sandwich and a glass of milk and ate silently for twenty minutes. Once he was finished, he left the restaurant and went back to the hotel room.

Reaching into his black bag, he pulled out his little black journal and sat at the desk and wrote for almost thirty minutes. Once he finished, he brushed his teeth, changed clothes, and went to bed.

A Divine Encounter

Joseph carefully and quietly rose off the hardwood floor early as his brothers lay in the bed, snoring. He'd been in New York for two weeks now and hadn't gotten a decent night's sleep once. Sleeping was uncomfortable in the summer heat. He'd heard an intense rain shower drench the city; but now, at six a.m., the last of the rain was falling. As he finished getting dressed, the weather cleared and the sun broke through. He finished buttoning his shirt and tying his shoelaces; he grabbed his hat, and crept out of the room.

It was only seven a.m. and it was already hot and humid. Joseph decided to walk alongside the shore today. The road narrowed as he turned left. He stood motionless for several minutes staring out into the big open water; the brilliance of the sun shining upon the waves. He watched the boats drift aimlessly over the quiet water. There was peace and serenity about the scene.

A sign read, "South Street Seaport." Tall ships were moored there. People stood on a wooden dock and some entered a boat while others were talking and laughing. Children were jumping and playing and couples were embracing, strolling side-by-side, and holding hands.

Near the dock was a restaurant, a short, stout man selling hats at a little shop, several horse and carriages lined up along the road, and a couple of cars parked on the street.

He glanced up and saw the Brooklyn Bridge. Joseph had read an article on the bridge; it had been built in 1887.

Joseph walked for one more mile until he came upon a dock with a sign that read "Parks Shipping Company." He entered through a black, rusty iron gate. From afar, he saw several men aboard a massive, silver steel ship. He heard the noise of drilling; it looked as if they were repairing the ship. Directly ahead was what appeared to be an office. The grounds were bare. The sound of the drilling got louder; when he got closer, he covered his ears.

Three men strolled out of the office wearing suits, one was short and stocky and held a cigar in his mouth. The man smoking the cigar seemed familiar, but the sun shone so brightly in Joseph's eyes that it was difficult to know for sure. Two of men walked away, but The man with the cigar hesitated, then he approached Joseph. As the man got closer, Joseph recognized him—it was Mr. Parks, the man he had met on the ship from Italy.

"Can I help you, boy," he said.

"I was just looking around," Joseph said, nervously. He was, after all, trespassing.

"Do I know you, kid?

"Yes, we met on the ship almost two weeks ago. My name is Joseph."

He studied Joseph. "Ah yeah, I remember. Italy, right?"

"Yes, sir."

"So, how ya like our great city?"

"It's quite beautiful. Better than I imagined."

"Good, good. So what brings you to my neck of the woods?"

"I was walking along the docks and happened to notice the sign. I decided to get a closer look."

"Well, allow me to give you a tour."

Excited, Joseph followed Mr. Parks through the grounds.

Mr. Parks owned two ships that delivered cargo throughout the United States, fifty foreign ports, and the United Deep Waterway System of Russia. He carried all types of cargo, including timber, timber products, and paper.

They boarded the power-driven ship. It was employed exclusively in commercial transportation of commodities. The ship drew twenty tons, was five hundred feet long, and was seventy-five feet across the beam. The ship had three funnels and was nearly two stories and had five times the cargo capacity for only three times the cost of a smaller ship.

Mr. Parks told Joseph he wanted to venture out and someday open a Chevrolet dealership in the state of New York. He was, to Joseph's surprise, one of the wealthiest men in the state.

They stepped into the kitchen. "Ya hungry?"

"Yes," Joseph said.

Mr. Parks looked over at a tall, bronze-toned man with thick black hair and said, "Hey, Sal, prepare a meal for us, will ya?"

"Yes, sir."

They ate salmon, baby red potatoes, a green salad, and French bread. Mr. Parks spoke of his road to success.

"The folks were poor. We lived in a small town in Iowa."

Joseph took a bite of his salmon and listened attentively.

"I managed to save enough money doin' odd jobs. I worked in a grocery store stockin' groceries, and I was a bell boy. You name it; I did it. It paid for my education. Once I graduated, I landed a job as a salesman in a clothing store. I became one of the most successful salesmen they'd had. Two years later I was appointed director; then five years later, president."

Joseph smiled as he listened to the energetic and confident man. *He seems aggressive yet gentle: tough yet kind,* Joseph thought. Joseph lifted his glass and took a drink of water as he listened.

Mr. Parks straightened his tie and leaned back in his chair and continued to talk incessantly.

"I saved a lot of money and got this brilliant idea. Why not invest in a shipping company? That's where the money is. A friend of mine had a company in North Carolina. I invested some money; and, tell you what, kid; it paid off. I saved a ton of money and eventually purchased my own boat. You're sittin' on it."

Joseph could tell that Mr. Parks was highly intelligent and probably successful at everything he did. Joseph hardly knew the man, yet he felt a bond forming between the two of them.

"Ambition and vision is the way to success," Mr. Parks said.

Joseph smiled and nodded.

"So, what do ya want to do with your life?"

"I'm not sure."

"Well, Joe…You don't mind if I call you Joe, do ya?"

"No, sir."

"Joe, you seem like a bright young man. Ya ever need a job, look me up. Here, let me give you one of my cards. I'll write my personal telephone number on it."

Taking the card, Joseph said, "Thank you. I'm very grateful you would take the time to show me around. And thank you for lunch."

"You're welcome, Joe."

As Joseph turned to leave, Mr. Parks patted him on the back and said, "Son, I believe you're gonna do great things."

"Thank you, sir," Joseph said.

Sweat was dripping from Joseph's nose and his cotton shirt was soaked. He wiped his forehead with his sleeve and headed west.

He started looking for the closest opportunity to escape the heat. Turning left, he came upon Madison Street and peered at a large red brick building. The sign read, "National Academy Museum." He entered the building and slowly walked down the hallway. On the wall hung a plaque explaining the history: "The National Academy Museum and School of Fine Arts is one of the oldest artist-run organizations in the United States. Founded in 1825, they have always fostered the promotion of the Fine

Arts in America, and house a sizeable collection of American Arts, over eight thousand works!"

Joseph strolled along the aisles, viewing the elegant artwork. It was just as fascinating as the university's; the history was remarkable. One painting read, "Twilight in the Wilderness" (1858). He smiled as he thought his father would probably have to sell his entire farm to purchase one of these small pieces of art.

A half an hour later, he'd only touched the surface. He took the time to examine each piece of art and study its history. Being so engrossed in the artwork, when he moved around a corner, he bumped into a young woman. She fell to the hard marble floor and dropped her small white handbag and two books.

With a dazed expression on her face, she reached to her right side and picked up her purse.

He was instantly apologetic and concerned. "I'm so sorry; are you okay?" he said as he reached out his hand and helped her up.

She shrugged, "It's okay; I wasn't paying attention to what I was doing."

She straightened her shirt and smoothed her long black hair. He picked up her books and handed them to her. "I'm really sorry."

"No really, it's okay. I should have been paying better attention."

Joseph stood there awkwardly.

"My name is Sasha." She reached out her hand to shake his.

"I'm Joseph."

"Hello, Joseph."

Joseph's eyes widened as he stared at the slender girl with radiant brown eyes and a smooth white complexion. She was wearing a pink skirt with a beautiful embellished white blouse with insertions of lace down the side. She was the most beautiful girl he'd ever seen.

"You aren't from around here, are you? I can tell from your accent."

"No," he said.

"Where are you from?"

"Italy."

"That's quite a long ways away."

"Yes, I am here visiting universities."

"Oh, what school are you planning to attend?"

"I'm not sure."

"I am planning on attending college too; I'm just not sure which one. I'd love to study art."

"Do you come here often?" he asked.

"Oh yes, I love this museum; it feels like a second home."

"How long have you lived in New York?"

"All of my life."

Joseph's hands had begun to perspire. He wiped them on his pant legs. His heart was beating fast and he found himself immersed in the conversation. He felt warmth and affection for her. Something he had never felt for any girl before. She was polite and pleasant to talk to. She appeared refined, yet simple.

"Would you like to look at more of the art with me?" she asked.

"Yes."

He and Sasha strolled down the aisles viewing paintings and sculptures. She mentioned she had studied art at her private school and was well-versed on the museum's collection. He listened intently while staring into her deep brown eyes.

Joseph wanted to spend more time with her. *I'll invite her to dinner,* he thought.

He took a deep breath and finally got the courage to ask. "Would you like to have something to eat?"

"I would love to, but I'm meeting my parents for dinner tonight. Maybe another time."

Trying to hide his disappointment, he said, "I'll look forward to it."

"Oh wait, there's one more thing I would like to show you before I go," she said. "It's on the top floor."

Joseph followed her to the top floor of the museum. There was an exquisite, brilliant diamond. It was, by far, the most beautiful piece of art at the museum. The inscription read, "The Star of Africa: The largest stone cut from the Cullinan and the British Crown Jewels. It weighs 530.20 carats and has seventy-four facets and is still the largest cut diamond in the world."

"It's only here for one month; it's then being shipped back to Africa." She spoke softly but he could feel her inner strength. He was impressed with her knowledge; she was not only beautiful, but also intelligent.

"Well, I really need to go," she said. She gently tapped his arm and smiled. It was nice meeting you and talking with you, Joseph. You are very kind. I do hope I run into you again." He wondered if he would ever see her again.

"I enjoyed meeting you," he said. Joseph didn't want to see her go. *Should I ask her out now? What if she says no?*

She slowly began to move away. "Goodbye, Joseph."

He watched as she walked away. She glanced back at him one last time and smiled.

Will I ever see her again, he thought to himself. He signed and checked his pocket watch. It was four thirty. When he left the museum, his thoughts were filled with Sasha.

When Joseph returned to the hotel, his brothers weren't there. He took the journal and pen out of the desk and wrote of the day's activities. He also wrote a brief letter to his family back home.

Hello, Father, Mother, and Rebecca. This city is so amazing—unlike anything I could have ever imagined. Today I had a tour of a shipping company from a man I met on the ship. It was fascinating. Later I toured a museum. I met a new friend. I wish so desperately you were here. This experience has been unforgettable. It has only been two weeks; yet, it feels like we arrived just yesterday. I will try and write at least two more times. Tell little Ben I bought him a surprise. I miss you and love you and will see you soon. Love, Joseph.

He didn't want to mention to his family that the new friend he'd met was a girl. He was shy and slightly embarrassed. That night, as he lay down to sleep—his back aching from the hardness of the floor, he decided he would visit the museum every day with the hopes of seeing Sasha again. The emotions that gripped him were both frightening and exciting. He wondered if he was in love.

The Heist

The next day, Judah and Samuel decided to tour the east side of the city since they had remained midtown the majority of the trip. Luke and Matthew stayed in downtown Manhattan.

The roads were congested and it was another hot and humid day. Luke and Matthew stopped into a diner to get a cool drink. After that, they went in and out of stores to escape the scorching heat. The time was two thirty p.m. and they'd spent much of the day gapping at every young lady that crossed their path.

Luke glanced across the street and noticed an unusual building. It looked elegant, with brown cement walls and beautiful stained glass windows. The people going in and out appeared to come from money. A woman entered the store leading an odd-looking, short dog that had more hair on it than the fur shawl she was wearing.

"Let's go this way," he said as he dashed across the street, trying to get a closer look.

"Wait!" Matthew yelled. "Where are you going?"

Luke weaved his way in and out of people. Matthew, trying to keep up, bumped into a stout gentleman dressed in a suit and tie who had just crossed the street. "Excuse me," he said. The gentleman gave him a rude look and walked around him.

Once Luke reached the building, he stopped and peered in the window. It was filled with beautiful diamonds, rubies, and emeralds. He glanced up and noticed the name of the store. It stated in big letters: "Helzberg Jewelers."

He entered the jewelry store and Matthew followed. The people working behind the counters were beautifully dressed. A police officer was standing on the far right side, watching as people entered the building. Toward the back, a man was working behind a desk in an office.

Luke and Matthew strolled from case to case, eyeing the exquisite jewels. Both men found themselves overwhelmed by the beauty. Luke had dreamed of someday being a wealthy man—although the only skills he had came from working on the farm. He never finished school; he never saw the need. As he gazed at the beautiful jewelry, he imagined himself being able to purchase any piece he wanted.

"Look at this one," Matthew said. "Isn't it beautiful?"

Luke glanced in the case and saw a large diamond necklace. It was stunning. "What do you think its worth?"

"Enough to buy our own farm and animals—and women to go along with it," Matthew said, snickering.

In the next case were gorgeous diamond rings in different shapes and sizes. It was hard to believe that there were people who could afford to buy such valuable jewels. They gawked at the jewels for half an hour.

Suddenly, two men with black masks on their faces rushed into the store. The taller one pointed his gun up and pulled the trigger, sending a bullet into the ceiling. "Everyone get down on the floor now!" he barked.

People began to scream. Matthew and Luke froze, not sure what to do. The officer reached for his gun, and the shorter man shot him in the chest. He fell backwards, blood pouring from his body. A woman screamed and clutched her small child to her. Another woman fainted, hitting the floor face down. "Please, I'm begging you! Don't hurt me," an older man said, pleading for his life.

"Shut up!" the taller thief said. "I said I want everyone down on the ground; and keep your faces down."

Matthew and Luke dropped to the floor, terrified and in disbelief that this could be happening. Thoughts raced through Luke's mind. *Would they be able to get out of this alive? Were the robbers planning on killing the hostages?*

Luke glanced at the men out of the corner of his eye; the whole situation made him curious. He watched as the men broke one glass case after another and stole the valuable pieces of jewelry. They were stuffing the jewels in large black bags like it was candy.

The shorter one approached the case next to Luke. Luke immediately turned his face toward the floor. The man broke open the glass case and was reaching inside when, suddenly, he was shot in the leg by a jeweler standing behind the counter. The taller thief whirled around and shot the jeweler once in the head. Luke was sure he was dead when he hit the floor.

The wounded thief next to Luke grabbed his leg and fell to the floor. Blood was pouring out of his thigh. He was pale, sweating, and perspiring profusely. He moaned as he picked himself up off the floor. He leaned on the jewel case next to Luke, clutching his leg. But he couldn't stop the bleeding. Blood poured between his fingers.

"Let's get out of here," he said, hoarse.

The uninjured jewel thief ran over to him and wrapped one arm around him, dragging him out the front door.

"Are they gone?" Matthew asked, his cheek glued to the floor.

Luke's heart was pounding like a hammer. "Yes."

Luke glanced quickly around the room. Everyone lay on the floor too frightened to move. Police sirens sounded in the distance.

Luke knew any minute the police would be surrounding the place. He reached into the broken case above him and grabbed a handful of jewelry, stuffing them into his pocket.

Matthew stared in horror. "What are you doing?"

"Shut up," Luke said. "Let's get out of here."

"But how?" Matthew asked.

Luke looked up one more time. Police were getting out of the car. "Let's get out of here now before they come into the store."

He grabbed Matthew by the shirt and the two ran out of the jewelry store and down the street. They ran in and out of alleys. When Matthew could go no farther, he slumped into an alley and leaned up against the wall. "I'm tired, I have to rest."

He tried to catch his breath. He doubled over, breathing heavily. Terrible thoughts raided his mind. It was like being in a horrible nightmare. "Tell me you didn't steal jewels from that store."

Luke remained silent, gasping for air.

"Do you know how stupid that was? What if you got caught?"

"Come, we must hurry. We've got to get back to the hotel."

They ran for what seemed to be endless blocks. The whole time they felt as though the police were pursuing them.

They dashed into the hotel and ran upstairs. Luke, exhausted, tripped on the stairs. He picked himself up and continued to climb with Matthew right behind him.

They entered the room, trying to catch their breath. Samuel, who was resting on the other bed, looked up at them. Matthew was drenched in his own sweat.

"Did it rain?" Samuel asked.

New York often got dosed with a quick rain shower or two.

Matthew fell backwards onto the bed, breathing hard. Luke sat down beside him, breathing heavily.

"What is the matter with you?" Samuel asked.

Just then, Judah entered the room.

"You both look as though you have seen a ghost. What is it?" Judah asked.

Matthew was restless. He stood up and stumbled over to the window and nervously glanced outside. He turned and looked directly at Luke. They stared at each other in silence for several seconds. "We were in a jewelry store that was robbed by thieves," Matthew said.

"Where? Are you okay?" Samuel asked.

"We're fine," Matthew said.

Luke sat on the bed in silence.

Matthew looked at Luke with trepidation. "Show them Luke."

"Show us what?" Judah asked.

Luke sat up, still breathing heavily.

Again Judah asked, "Show us what?" This time his voice was stern.

Luke slowly took the jewels out of his pant pocket and laid the jewelry on the bed—four diamond necklaces and three diamond bracelets. Their value must have been at least twenty thousand dollars. Judah and Samuel stared in horror.

Judah grabbed Luke by his shirt and picked him from off the bed. "What have you done? Have you gone insane?"

"Wait," Luke said. "It's not what you think. We didn't do it."

Samuel, outraged, said, "What do you mean!"

"Let me explain," Luke said.

Judah threw Luke back down onto the bed.

"We went into the store to look at the jewelry, when, all of the sudden, two men rushed in with masks on their faces. They had guns and forced all of us to get down on the floor. One of the thieves shot and killed a police officer. He was then shot in the leg by the jeweler. The other thief killed the jeweler. They ran out of the store. When no one was looking, I grabbed some of the jewels. I swear to you; no one saw me. Once it was clear, we ran out of the store."

Both Judah and Samuel stared at Luke in utter shock. Matthew buried his face in his hands and shook his head, and then looked up at his brothers. "I didn't know he was planning to do it. I swear this wasn't planned."

"I cannot believe you have done this. You are foolish. What possessed you?" Samuel yelled.

"These jewels are worth thousands and thousands of dollars. Don't you see? We are rich," Luke said, with a glimmer of hope on his face.

"What if you'd gotten caught?" Judah yelled.

"Well we didn't. Just think of the things we could buy," Luke said.

"Just think of how much time we would have spent in prison had we gotten caught!" Matthew screamed.

After a moment of silence, Samuel said, "We must dispose of them at once."

"No!" Luke said. "Brothers, we're rich. No one knows we have them. The police are searching for the jewel thieves. They've probably been caught by now. Think of all we can buy."

"How will we sell them?" Matthew asked.

"We'll worry about that in Italy," Luke said.

After a long pause, Judah asked, "Where will we hide them?"

Their eyes searched the room, seeking a temporary place to hide the jewels.

"We can hide them in here," Luke said. He pointed to the drawer next to the bed.

"And let the maid come and find them?" Samuel said. "That would be stupid."

Matthew glanced to the right. "What about our suitcases?"

"No," Judah said. "If we got searched, that would be the first place they would look."

After several minutes of studying the room, Luke noticed Joseph's bag lying on the floor next to the desk. "I know the perfect place for them."

He walked over to the floor and picked up the bag and set it on the desk. "We will place the jewels here."

"And why would we chance our little brother getting into trouble for your foolishness?" Samuel said.

"Well, do you have any other ideas?" Luke argued.

"No, but Joseph should not be to blame for this."

"I agree with Luke," Matthew said. "We have no other choice. If Joseph gets caught, we will deny ever seeing them. We should hide the jewels in Joseph's bags and no one will ever know."

"It is the only thing we can do," Luke said.

A brief pause. "Do we all agree?"

Judah hesitated for several seconds. He glanced over at Samuel briefly and then said, "Agreed."

Luke placed the jewels in a side pocket of Joseph's black bag.

"I want no part of this," Samuel said. He stormed out of the room.

"We will speak of this to no one, understood?" Judah said.

Matthew and Luke both nodded.

"And what of Samuel?" Matthew asked.

"He won't speak of it," Judah said. "We must leave tomorrow."

Several hours later, Joseph arrived back at the hotel. He ran upstairs, carrying a small brown bag. When he opened the door, he saw both Luke and Matthew lying on the bed and Judah sitting at the desk. He thought it odd that his brothers were there. They were usually out until much later. Perhaps they were too overwhelmed by the heat and needed to take a break today.

"Hi," Joseph said.

Matthew and Luke remained silent.

Judah asked, "Where have you been, Joseph?"

"I visited the university and went to the museum."

"What did you do today?" Joseph asked.

Luke looked up at Joseph, grabbed his cap, and left the room.

Joseph glanced down at Matthew and asked, "Is there something wrong?"

Matthew looked at Joseph nervously and said, "No."

He got off the bed and walked out of the room.

Judah remained quiet for several minutes.

Finally, to break the silence, Joseph said, "This city is so amazing. Father would be fascinated, don't you think?" Judah nodded.

"I hope someday to return to America and—"

"I'll be back. I must get some air," Judah said.

Once Judah left the room, Joseph walked over a small bag down on the table. He had bought a necklace made of colorful gems for his sister at a small jewelry stand on the street. He pulled it out of the small bag and glanced at it one more time and smiled. *Rebecca was sure to like it,* he thought.

Joseph turned around and noticed his large black bag was sitting on the desk. He tilted his head, wondering how it got there. Grabbing the bag, he stuffed the necklace on the inside and put it back on the floor.

After dinner, Joseph decided to head straight to bed so he could get an early start in the morning. He planned to spend a great deal of time in the museum, hoping, to once again run into Sasha.

Several minutes later his brothers returned, earlier than usual. Joseph kept his eyes closed, pretending to be asleep. He wondered what was up with their suspicious behavior and what made them stay in most of the day. They each bathed and went straight to bed. A few minutes later, Joseph fell asleep.

The next morning, Joseph heard a large bag drop onto the floor. He looked up and saw Matthew picking his bag off the floor and placing it back on the bed. Joseph turned on his side slightly and saw that his brothers were packing their things. "What are you doing?"

"What does it look like?" Judah said. "We are leaving."

"But we are scheduled to stay for two more weeks." This was the trip of a lifetime and Joseph wasn't ready for it to end.

"We changed our minds," Judah, said. "Now get your things together. We're leaving."

Joseph again argued with his brother, "But I don't understand. Father said..."

"Joseph, be quiet and pack! I don't want to hear what Father said. We are in charge now, and we say we are leaving today!" Samuel shouted.

His heart began to race with anxiety. He slowly rolled himself up off the floor. There was still so much to see. He had to fight to keep the tears from falling. What could have caused this sudden turn of events? He began packing his clothes in defeat.

The ride to the docks in the carriage was a long one. Joseph was saddened by the fact that he would never see this city again, and, even worse, the thought of never seeing Sasha again brought anguish to his soul.

Once they arrived at the docks they were in luck, a ship was leaving for France in just a couple of hours. They purchased their tickets. They stood in line for at least an hour waiting to board, the sun burning down on them. Joseph noticed the police searching the bags of several passengers. He wondered what they were searching for. He tapped the tall gentleman in front of him on the shoulder. "Excuse me, sir; do you know what they're looking for?"

"A jewelry store was robbed and one of the guards and a jeweler were killed. They are searching for the jewel thieves."

Joseph briefly noticed Matthew turn and stare at Luke. Matthew looked as though any minute he would get sick.

The boys were almost on board the ship. They had just taken three more steps then heard the voice of a police officer.

"Wait one moment, boys."

As the police approached, Judah whispered, "Stay calm and just do as you're asked."

Luke and Samuel remained calm. Again Joseph stared at Matthew. He looked as though any minute his heart would leap right out of his chest. Joseph wondered why such anxiety was flooding Matthew's emotions.

"We need to check all your bags before you board the ship," a stout blond-haired officer said.

Judah wiped the sweat from his forehead. One at a time, they searched each bag and jacket. The officer spoke to Joseph. "Open your bag, son."

Samuel's face was flushed, his eyes wide. Joseph opened his bag. The police officer searched inside and found nothing. Once he finished the search, he said, "Okay, go on."

As they began to move slowly on board the ship, the same police officer said. "Wait one moment. I need to see your bag one more time."

Joseph once again calmly handed the bag to the officer. The officer reached into the side pocket and pulled out a large diamond necklace.

He glared down at Joseph and said, "Now where did this come from?"

Joseph's jaw dropped. "That's not mine."

The officer pulled several other pieces of jewelry from Joseph's bag. Joseph looked at Judah, hoping for an answer. Judah wouldn't look at him.

"I've never seen that in my life," Joseph said.

"So it just happened to end up in your bag by accident?" the officer said, glaring down at Joseph.

Luke yelled, "Joseph, what have you done? Have you disgraced us and our father?"

Joseph, staring in horror said, "You have to believe me; I've never seen those jewels in my life. I swear!"

The officer called for several other officers. Judah and Matthew stood there speechless, pretending not to know a thing.

Joseph looked at Samuel and said, "You must believe me."

The blond officer looked at the others and said, "How do we know you aren't all a part of this?"

"Sir, I swear, we knew nothing about this. We will do whatever we can to help," Luke said.

Joseph stared in disbelief. *I can't believe what I'm hearing,* he thought. *This can't be happening.* Joseph's emotions were scrambling as he tried to sort out what was being said. "I swear I'm innocent."

The officer immediately placed Joseph under arrest. Joseph was hustled into a police car. Judah stared at Joseph with a look of dread on his face and watched him being driven away. This was a terrible mistake and Joseph was sure that it would be taken care of once he had a chance to explain. He had never stolen anything in his life.

"We're going to need you boys to come down to the station so we can ask some more questions," the blond police officer said.

"Oh course, we'll do whatever we can to help," Judah said.

Joseph was taken to the station and locked up.

When the boys arrived, they were interviewed for several hours. They denied ever seeing the jewels.

Two hours later, they were then asked to wait in a small room.

"Are you sure we did the right thing?" Matthew whispered.

"It's too late to turn back now," Judah replied.

Samuel frowned and looked at Luke. "You got us into this mess, and now Joseph has to pay the cost."

"We," Luke said. "We got him in this mess; you are just as much to blame."

"Yes, but I didn't steal the jewels!" Samuel argued.

"Yes, but you did nothing when the police took Joseph!"

"Enough!" Judah shouted. "It's too late now. What's done is done."

After a moment of silence, Matthew finally asked, "What do we tell Father?"

"I don't know, but we have a long trip home to come to a decision," Judah said.

"What will happen if Joseph is sent to prison? What will happen when he gets out and Father learns the truth?" Samuel asked.

Judah turned to Samuel. "If Joseph is sent to prison, Father will probably be dead by the time he gets out. Besides, we can't worry about it now."

The Trial

They threw Joseph in a small, cold jail cell. Terrified, he lay on a smelly old cot about four feet in length. His legs bunched up. The waiting was unbearable.

"Someone help me, please," pleaded Joseph, weeping. He was startled by a loud banging on his door. The guard yelled, "Shut up!"

"I'm begging you! I'm innocent, please let me go!" he cried.

Joseph heard the guard walk away, not listening.

How? Why? I don't understand? he thought. *Could my brothers have done this? Could they hate me this much? How could my brothers do such a thing? Did they detest me this much?*

The next day was set to be the arraignment. He trembled at the thought; he could barely keep down his food: stale bread and a small slice of baloney.

A short man with glasses, who was escorted by a tall, muscular guard, approached his cell. It was the lawyer that had been appointed to him by the courts.

He met with Joseph for twenty minutes in his small cell. Joseph cried as he told him the story. The lawyer appeared sympathetic but realistic. The evidence they had against Joseph was colossal. It would take a miracle to get him off.

The lawyer left the cell and one hour later, the tall muscular guard led Joseph into the courtroom in handcuffs. Joseph moved slowly; he felt the cuffs chafing against his bony wrists. His legs were weak, and his heart was pounding. He peered right and his brothers were sitting at the back of the court room. They didn't look at him. Joseph sat at a table in front next to his lawyer.

A gray-haired judge sat stiffly at the front of the courtroom behind a tall bench, dressed in a black robe. He knocked his gavel on the table twice and said, "Will the defendant please rise."

Joseph's lawyer stood and then petitioned for Joseph to stand.

Witnesses at the jewelry store said one of the robbers shot the jeweler and the other robber shot the guard, so the prosecution had sufficient evidence to try Joseph on armed robbery and second-degree murder.

"On the count of armed robbery and murder in the second degree, how do you plea?" the judge asked.

The lawyer cleared his throat and said, "Not guilty."

The trial was set to begin in two days.

It was Wednesday, June 13, 1906; the first day of the trial. The prosecutor gave his opening remarks.

He almost whispered at first, but the power of his voice made every sound heard throughout the room. He looked deeply saddened when he spoke of the victims' families. He looked at the widows and told of their lifeless future without their husbands. The jewelry owner, Mark Myer, left behind a wife and four children ages two, three, seven, and twelve. The prosecutor was eloquent and poised, but his words were sharp and precise. With just his opening remarks, he was annihilating Joseph.

A juror with a thick mustache and bushy beard glared at Joseph with an angry expression, and then he turned his head. Sweat surfaced above Joseph's eyebrows; his heart was pounding.

The prosecutor questioned several witnesses, including the police officer who had found the jewels on Joseph. The prosecutor then called Luke to the stand.

Joseph watched Luke move slowly to the front of the room. Though he had a non-empathetic expression in his eyes, Joseph thought for sure Luke would tell the truth. *He won't allow me to suffer for a crime I didn't commit,* he thought.

"Do you swear to tell the truth, the whole truth, and nothing but the truth?" the man asked, holding a Bible.

Luke, with his right hand on the Bible and left hand rose high, said, "I do."

The prosecutor asked, "Can you tell us where Joseph was the day of Sunday, June 10, 1906?"

"No. Actually, my brothers and I didn't spend any time with Joseph," Luke said. Luke didn't stare at Joseph.

"How did Joseph appear the day after the robbery when he entered the hotel room?"

"He seemed to be in a hurry, like he'd been running."

"Was he carrying anything?"

Luke paused. "Yes, he had a brown sack with something in it." Another pause. "Like jewelry."

"I object!" Joseph's lawyer said.

Voices of people murmuring filled the courtroom.

"Order in the courtroom!" the judge said, banging his gavel on his table. "I will have order in this court!"

Joseph's jaw dropped as he listened in horror. He felt the color drain from his face. A flashback of the jewelry bag carrying the necklace he had purchased for Rebecca came to mind. He glared at the twelve men sitting to the right, who would determine his fate. Their faces were hard, stern, and unsympathetic. A man with a sagging, bulging neck gave him a stony look before he turned his head.

"What happened next?" the prosecutor asked.

"I left the room."

"When you returned to the hotel room, did you see the bag anywhere?"

"No."

"No further questions."

Joseph's attorney stood. "Did you ask Joseph what was in the small bag?"

"No."

"Then you have no idea what was in the bag? Is that correct?" the lawyer said, glancing at the jury.

"No," Luke said, quietly.

"I'm sorry, we can't hear you."

"No!"

"Have you ever known Joseph to steal anything in his life?"

"No, sir."

The lawyer looked at the judge. "I have no further questions."

The judge leaned back in his chair. He cleared his throat and turned to Luke.

"You may be excused."

Two days later, the jury had heard all the evidence and were sent away to deliberate.

Joseph was taken back to his cell, legs shaking, feeling cold and sick.

He lay in his cell, silently weeping and praying. He begged God to spare his life.

After three hours, the verdict was in. He saw his brothers sitting in the back row. They turned their faces once they saw him.

Once again, the judge Joseph asked to stand. His heart began to beat so fast that he thought he was going to have a heart attack.

The judge looked over at the foreman and said, "How do you find the defendant?"

The brown-haired man with a bushy beard stood and said, "In the count of armed robbery…we find the defendant guilty."

Joseph's heart sank.

"In the count of second degree murder, we find the defendant…guilty."

Joseph felt a sharp pain in his stomach. His breathing got heavier. He held his stomach. He was gripped with fear. Gasping for air between pains, he said in a whisper, "I swear by Almighty God, I'm innocent."

In a stern look, his eyebrows lowered, firm voice, the judge said, "You have been found guilty of the charges before you, and I sentence you to twenty-five years in the New York State Penitentiary."

The guard grabbed him and handcuffed him.

"No please! I'm innocent, I swear," he shouted, tears streaming down his face. "Brothers, tell them, tell them I'm innocent, please."

The guard's grip tightened on Joseph, shoving him through the door.

His brothers left the courtroom.

Joseph didn't see his brothers again.

The Revenge

Tears seeped down Joseph's face as he finished telling Gil the story. It was like reliving a dreadful nightmare all over again.

"I was hoping it was a horrible dream and any minute I would wake up; but when they slammed the prison doors shut, I knew it was a reality."

Joseph's story left Gil stunned. "What about your father? Wouldn't he have come lookin' for ya?"

"They probably told him I was dead. I knew my brothers hated me, but I didn't know how much."

Just then the bell rang, and they heard the loud voice of a guard saying, "Lights out!" Within seconds, everything went dark.

"I can't believe it, Joseph. I thought I had it bad. I don't know what to say."

"All I have left is my brain, my strength, and my God."

"Shut up in there. Lights out, you know what that means!" the guard, banging on the door.

"Goodnight, Joseph."

Joseph rolled over to one side. "Goodnight."

The next day, Joseph and Gil were awakened by the sound of the loud bell.

He and Gil, along with hundreds of other inmates, did their usual daily routine—gathering in the dining hall for meals, doing laundry, and shoveling dirt alongside the road.

Two weeks later, Joseph and Gil sat at a table on the far side of the dining room, eating breakfast. Max was to be released from solitary confinement that day. Joseph tried hard not to focus on it. He sat straight and tall in his chair, yet he could feel his heart knocking up against his ribs. Joseph took a bite of watery oatmeal. The food was horrific, but to keep his strength he had to endure it. He had just picked up his glass to take a drink of cloudy, dirty water, when, out of the blue, a paper airplane landed on his plate. He turned around and noticed that six men sitting at a table nearby were glaring at him, snickering. Gil sat staring at Joseph while he unfolded the paper. The penmanship was horrible; there were food stains on the sheet. It read: *Doomsday.* Joseph threw the paper to the floor right beside him and pretended not to care, but he was scared.

"What's it say?" Gil asked.

Joseph sat silent for several seconds. He took a bite of dry, brittle toast. "Nothing."

They finished breakfast and went about the daily duties. Joseph prayed the whole day to God for protection.

That evening, Joseph and Gil were standing in the yard. Joseph's eyes darted around the compound. A guard suddenly motioned for Joseph. He walked over to him; he could feel Gil close behind.

They went into the building only a few steps when the guard abruptly stopped. He looked over at a couple of men and nodded. The three men nodded back.

He turned to Joseph and Gil and said, "Stay here." Then he walked away.

They were only a few feet from the door, so they attempted to go back out, when three men ambushed them. One of the inmates grabbed Gil around the neck, making it impossible for him to yell. The other two inmates snatched Joseph and pulled him by a narrow hallway.

"I told you I was comin' after you, ya stinkin' Jew; didn't I?" Max said. "I told cha you'd pay for what cha did to my brother."

"I didn't touch your brother. I swear. You have my word. He fell on me…"

Max's fist slammed into Joseph's face. Joseph felt a tooth break and he spit it out. He felt blood spurt out of his mouth. He tried to cry out, but within a matter of seconds he could feel his mouth begin to swell.

Max punched him in the stomach and chest and then across his face several times. Joseph hung on the arms of the two inmates, helpless. Joseph then felt a sharp item penetrate the right side of his face. He felt his skin rip open. Max had cut him with a knife. Blood was streaming from his face, and his nose felt as though it were broken. The pain was excruciating. Max kicked him in the legs and stomach. Joseph felt pain strike through his bones like lightning. Two guards who heard the fighting came crashing in the hallway. Max and the other three inmates ran toward the dining room.

One guard chased Max and the other inmates while the other guard tended to Joseph.

Joseph felt week. His body was shaking and blood was dripping from his face. He felt as though his chest were collapsing, as if air were too thick to inhale. Every cough sent knives of agony through his body.

"Can you move?" the guard asked.

Joseph laid helpless, unable to form words.

"Joseph, you'll to be okay," Gil said.

Joseph could see tears welling up in Gil's eyes.

"I need some help over here!" yelled the guard.

Another guard ran over.

"Go get a gurney."

He returned with a metal stretcher with wheeled legs. They transported Joseph to the infirmary.

Joseph lay bleeding on the bed.

The doctors ran several tests. The warden came to see him. Joseph overheard the doctor explaining his condition to the warden outside the door.

"He has two broken ribs and some internal bleeding, but his face was beaten the worst. He has a broken nose and several lacerations to his skin. The knife wound severely ripped the inner lining of the right side of his face. We'll have to perform surgery, but I'm not sure we can repair it completely."

Why didn't you let them kill me God and end this life of misery? Joseph thought.

The doctors performed surgery the next day. When he awoke, his entire head was swaddled in dressings. His eyes were covered with ice packs. There was a numbness and tightness underneath his jaw and around his ears. He felt like he'd been at war. The doctors had him drugged with morphine, so the pain was at a minimum.

Three days later, the doctor entered his room. He slowly unpeeled the bandages from his face. The doctor gently pressed his right thumb up against the right side of Joseph's face. Joseph jilted his head back slightly and clenched his teeth.

The doctor removed his hand. "The bruising will go away and the swelling will recede. The scar might completely heal. It could have been worst."

Once the doctor left the room, Joseph slowly lifted himself from the table, cringing from the pain in his chest. He moved over to the mirror. A bout of fear leaped in his spirit once he saw himself. The surgery had somewhat altered his appearance. He rubbed his fingertips along his face. His nose was smaller and his cheekbones looked slightly higher. A scar lined the right side of his face from his jaw to his ear. Tears came to his eyes as he wondered if the scar would fade. The doctor had told him that in due time he would feel normal. Joseph had felt his identity drifting away for years, and now even his appearance had been altered.

He slowly moved back to his bed, laid down, and cried.

One week later, Joseph's health had all ready improved. The pain was still agonizing, but the doctor kept him medicated. His ribs were bandaged, but healing.

The warden came to see him again. He sauntered over to Joseph and stood to the right of his bed. A guard stood near the door.

"How are you feeling, Joseph?"

"Better," he said quietly.

"What happened?"

Joseph paused. He glanced at the guard, edgy, and then looked up at the warden. Joseph's mind was filled with fear. Snitches in prison didn't just get beaten—they got killed. In a quiet voice, he said, "I fell."

The warden scowled and shook his head. "Tell me what happened."

Again, Joseph said, "I slipped and fell."

"Look, Joseph, you've been a model prisoner, but I won't tolerate this kind of behavior. You either tell me what happened or suffer the consequences."

Joseph remained silent. He turned his head away from the warden and closed his eyes.

The warden turned to the guard and said, "All right, when the doctor gives the okay to release him, put him in the hole for three days."

Three days later, when the doctor released Joseph from the infirmary, the guard threw him in solitary confinement. The hole was smaller than the outhouse on his father's farm. It was dark, cold, and smelly. The only human contact he had was with the guard who brought him food.

Time passed by slowly; one day was like a month. Questions filled his mind. *What would happen once he got out of solitary confinement? Would Max finish the job?* At times, depression would seep in; he wanted to die, but he fought to maintain his sanity. He prayed day and night. He told himself that one day he would be free from this misery and reunited with his family.

The night before Joseph was to get out of solitary confinement, he had a dream. There were several men working in a big brick building. Max was sweeping the floor. The building began to shake, crumbing around him. Max was buried alive.

The next morning, Joseph pondered on the dream. He felt that soon God would vindicate him.

His first morning out, Joseph was assigned to scrubbing down the kitchen. He wiped the sweat from his forehead and then poured water from a bucket over a plate to remove the soap suds. He slid the plate back on the rusty steel rack.

The kitchen felt like an oven. He filled his hands with water and ran them through his hair to cool off. He picked up a dirty cup from the sink and scrubbed it with a torn dishrag and a bar of soap.

A thin, bald guard named Larry approached him. "Hear the news about Max?"

Joseph tilted his head.

"He was shoveling dirt along the roadside and there was a mudslide. Four prisoners were buried. Three of them got out, but Max is dead."

Joseph remained calm and straight-faced, but a spring of hope burst in his soul. He knew that God had protected him. *If only God would release me from this nightmare I live in,* he thought.

The War

When Judah, Samuel, Luke, and Matthew returned home, they told their father that thieves had shot Joseph in a jewelry store and he died at the scene. Once Jacob heard the news, he fell to the ground and wept uncontrollably in his distress. He wept for days.

Rachel, too, was heartbroken and became detached from everything and everyone around her. It was as though her heart had stopped beating. Her spirit grew fainter everyday. She neither ate nor drank for weeks. She came down with the fever and died. Jacob had not only lost his beloved son, but the only woman he had ever loved.

Judah couldn't bear to see the anguish of his father's suffering, so he moved to France and settled in Cannes. He became a successful farmer. He grew mainly wheat, corn, and rice.

He married a woman named Salama and had two sons of his own. His first child died at the age of four. Soon after, his marriage fell apart, and he and his wife later divorced. He remarried and his second wife, Michele, gave birth to a son.

Judah watched as Michele laid their son down in a small wooden crib in their bedroom.

He smiled as he stared at the small, brown wavy haired boy. He then moved into the living room and sat by the fireplace.

He sat staring at the distant sun though the window, completely lost in thought. He shook his head as the events from eight years ago played over and over in his mind. The grief and shame of what they'd done still haunted him. He'd often had nightmares concerning Joseph.

He sat silent, remembering a letter he'd received from Matthew several weeks ago. Matthew too has had nightmares concerning Joseph. Matthew said that Samuel was stricken with sorrow every time Joseph's name was mentioned, but Luke never spoke of him.

Judah's eyes filled with anguish, as he remembered the look on his father's face after learning of Joseph's death. *I wonder if God is tormenting us for what we did,* he thought. *Trying to forget Joseph is an impossible task.*

Minutes later, there was a knock on the door. Michele answered the door. She poked her head into the living room. "Judah, its Nicholas."

Judah ambled out on his front porch. "Nicholas, so good to see you." He placed both his hands on Nicholas shoulders.

"It's good to see you," Nicholas said.

"Please sit down," Judah said.

"How are you my good friend?" Judah asked.

"I'm well. My wife gave birth to a daughter several weeks ago. She is beautiful."

Judah smiled. With his right hand, he patted Nicholas on the back, "Congratulations, I'm so happy for you."

"Thank you."

Michele stepped out on the balcony carrying a tray with two glasses of iced tea and a plate of oat bread and honey. She had chipped some ice from an ice block. She set the tray down on a small wooden table.

It was a hot summer, with no breeze to bring relief. Nicholas wiped the sweat off his forehead before taking a drink. He grabbed a slice of oat bread, poured a heap of honey on top, and took a big bite. Nicholas owned a farm five miles down the road from Judah.

"I read the newspaper before leaving the house. It said that Nationalism has created violent tensions in the Austro-Hungarian Monarchy. Russia, Great Britain, and France have created an alliance. People are leaving Cannes by the dozens. War is coming for sure," Nicholas said.

"I know," Judah said, troubled. "There have been rumors of war since January. I would have never believed that Germany would declare war with France. Here it is, July 1914, and it has truly become a reality."

"Times will be hard, especially for Jews. It will be difficult to make a living. People will starve, diseases will destroy many; it's inevitable," Nicholas said. "My wife and I will be traveling north to Denmark. We want to get as far from France as possible. What will you do?"

Judah tensed. He took a drink of tea, sat back, and inhaled deeply. "I once traveled to America many years ago. Perhaps it may hold hope."

"I have a friend. He would surely sponsor you and your family."

"I would be very grateful, my friend," Judah said.

"And what about your family in Italy? Have you heard from them?"

Judah hung his head. "Only my younger brother Matthew, he keeps me abreast on my family's dealings."

Judah looked up and squinted to shield the sun in his eyes. After a brief moment of silence, "I must reunite with my father."

"When was the last time you saw him?"

"It's been eight years. After my brother passed away, I couldn't bear my father's grief, so I left."

"Well, perhaps time has healed old wounds,"

Judah nodded. "Perhaps."

"What will your family do when war breaks out?"

"I don't know. I hope to convince them to move, but my father is very stubborn. It would take a miracle."

"Let's hope God works in your favor. This war could be the destruction of us all."

They sat on the porch for two more hours talking about the coming war.

After Nicholas left, Judah sat outside for the rest of the day, pondering on the future. Judah knew there was only one thing he could do.

Jacob slowly made his way into the kitchen, carrying a newspaper. He poured himself a glass of milk, and then sat down next to Benjamin at the table. Benjamin was reading his history book on Napoleon. Like Joseph, Benjamin was kind and gentle and devoted himself to his studies. It was Jacob's desire that Benjamin would someday run the farm.

Jacob opened the newspaper and saw images of men marching off to war, and the faces of women and children in distress. He shoulders tightened from distress.

Jacob was reading a story about a family whose home was destroyed by enemy fire, when Matthew dashed into the house.

"Father, Father," he gasped.

"What is it, Matthew?"

"It's Judah; he's home."

Jacob ran outside.

Judah climbed out his car, a 1914 Kissel, along with his wife and two sons. He glanced at his father, running toward him.

Jacob grabbed Judah's face with both hands. He hugged him and kissed him on the cheek. "It's good to see you, my son," he said, hoarse.

"I've missed you, Father."

"And I you. It's been a long time, Judah. You look well."

"As do you."

Matthew was standing next to Jacob.

"Matthew, so good to see you." The two men embraced.

"I see you are as handsome as always. I can't believe some woman hasn't snatched you up."

Matthew laughed. "It's not because I haven't looked. Welcome home, Judah."

"Benjamin, you have grown so much. I almost didn't recognize you. Your hair and your complexion are darker than when you were small. You are as handsome as Matthew, and almost as tall."

Benjamin hugged his eldest brother and welcomed him home.

"This is my wife, Michele," Judah said.

She gave a round of hugs to the three men.

"These are my sons, Elijah and Micah."

Jacob hugged each of the boys, rubbing his fingers through young Micah's bushy, black hair.

Just then, Luke and Samuel strolled in from working the fields. They began to run once they saw Judah.

Covered in dirt, Luke hugged Judah.

"You look well, Luke. You've grown a beard; it suits you."

"Thank you, you've been missed," Luke said.

"I'm sorry to hear you and your wife divorced, Luke. I know what you are going through. Do you see your two daughters much?" Judah asked.

"Once a month. She moved to the city of Arezzo. I visit as often as I can."

"I'm sure things will work out, little brother."

Luke nodded.

Judah smiled when he saw Samuel.

"Samuel, it's been a long time." He placed both hands on Samuel's shoulders.

"Too long." Samuel hugged him.

"Matthew told me in letters he sent me that you have two sons."

"Yes, they are in town with their mother shopping."

"I look forward to meeting my nephews and my sister-in-law."

"Where is Rebecca?" Judah asked.

"She gave birth to her second child two weeks ago, a daughter named Hadassah. They are at their home; they live only a mile from here. I will have her and her family join us for dinner tonight," Jacob said.

"Good, good, I look forward to seeing her and my new niece."

"Please come in, come in," Jacob said.

Judah climbed the stairs and slowly strolled into the house; it had been a long trip. The place looked the same, but the atmosphere had changed. The warmth that had once filled the home seemed to have faded away.

He joined his father and brothers in the living room. They spent much of the day talking and catching up.

After dinner, Jacob and his sons sat on the front porch enjoying the cool, cloudless, summer evening while the children played. Rebecca swept out onto the porch, carrying two plates with slices of pie on them; her baby strapped to her chest with a black cloth.

"I made an apple pie," she said, smiling.

She handed the plates to Jacob and Judah.

"Thank you," Judah said as he stroked his niece's dark hair with the tips of his fingers. "Her deep brown eyes, black hair, soft skin; she is as beautiful as her mother."

Rebecca smiled. "Thank you."

She went back into the house and returned with Judah's wife. Between them, they carried four pie plates for Samuel, Matthew, Luke, and Dan, Rebecca's husband.

Judah lifted his fork and took a bite of pie. "Rebecca makes the best pie in Italy," he said before setting the plate down on his lap.

Judah began to fidget. He rubbed his chin with his right hand several times. He frowned and leaned back in his chair. Finally, taking a deep breath, he said,

"Father, this war could grow enormous."

"I know this; it is a horrible thing, war," Jacob said.

"How do we know Italy won't soon be involved? Germany, France, Austria-Hungary, Russia, Serbia, and Belgium are all ready mobilized. It's only a matter of time before Italy joins the fight," Judah said.

"I have read that Italy will remain neutral," Jacob said. "This war is between France, Germany, and Russia."

"But how can we be sure?" Samuel said. "I have heard and read that Italy's entry into the war will be determined by the course of the war. No one may be safe."

Jacob crossed his arms and sat straight in his chair. "God will keep us safe."

"But even God gives us warnings," Judah said. "Many people, especially Jews, are leaving. I suggest we do the same."

"You're making too much of this."

"I've thought long and hard about this too, Father," Samuel said, "and we can't take the chance that Italy will not enter this war."

"And where would we go?" Jacob asked.

Judah was almost afraid to say it, but felt he had to. "I would suggest we move to America."

"America!" Jacob yelled.

"Yes, Father, it is the safest place."

"No!" Jacob said, sternly. He leaped up from his chair and strode over to the side of the balcony. "I will not tread upon land that robbed me of my precious son."

"But, Father, it could be dangerous to remain here," Samuel pleaded.

"No! That is my final word. That country has brought me nothing but grief. We'll have no more talk of leaving."

Jacob walked into the house and went to his bedroom for the remainder of the night.

A week had passed, and Judah and his family temporarily moved in with Jacob. It was early evening and the family had just finished dinner. Judah and Samuel sat on the couch reading the newspaper while Luke, Benjamin, and Matthew were in the barn feeding the cows.

Though the sun had shone bright earlier that day, it had been an unusually cool night. The fire was burning in the fireplace. Jacob threw a black scarf that Rachel had made him around his neck. He listened to the laughter of his grandchildren and watched them play.

"Grandfather!" Rebecca's son, Joel yelled. "Look what I've found." He held out his closed fist.

"What is it?" Jacob asked, smiling.

Joel opened his hands and a big green grasshopper jumped out. "Oh wait, it just got away," the boy said, running to catch it.

Jacob laughed.

"Father, we need to speak to you inside." Judah was standing by the door.

"What is it?"

"Please come in."

Jacob lifted himself from his chair.

"Luke, Matthew, Benjamin; join us!" Judah shouted.

They were standing near the barn, covered with hay from feeding the animals.

Jacob followed Judah into the house and sat down on the couch in the living room. Seconds later, Luke, Matthew, and Benjamin joined them.

"Father, we were reading the paper. Listen to what it says," Judah said.

"Today, August 23, 1914, German forces now occupy Belgium and are moving quickly upon France with two armies. The fighting between French and German forces has taken place in the region of Alsace-Lorraine in Southeastern France. The French and British armies tried to halt the advancing Germans, but they found themselves under heavy fire from long-range German artillery. The Allied Powers may quickly be forced to retreat."

Judah set the newspaper down on the table, stood up, and paced back and forth across the living room floor. "Italy is safe for now—but for how long."

"What are we supposed to do? How we will survive? We can't just flee for our lives not knowing how we will manage once we get there," Jacob said.

Samuel moved next to his father. "We will sell everything and build a new farm. There are more opportunities in America."

Benjamin walked over to his father and laid his arm on his shoulder. "You always say God will provide."

Luke, who had remained silent up to this point, finally spoke. "We could be doomed here."

"I agree, Father," Matthew said.

"So do you agree, Father?" Judah asked.

Jacob stood, without words. With his head down, he paced around. He moved over to the window and watched his grandchildren playing in the yard. His family was everything to him, and their safety was crucial. Although Italy had remained neutral up to this point, he didn't want to risk placing his family in harm's way.

"All right, I fear we have no choice. We will move to America."

It took one month for each member of the family to sell most of their possessions. They packed their things and boarded a ship.

While New York was enthralling, Jacob found it large and congested—nothing like his home in Italy. He'd lost his son, his wife, and now he was losing his home. He wondered if he was doing the right thing.

The family learned from Americans aboard the ship that there were acres of cheap land available in the state of Missouri.

They traveled by train and settled in a small town named Jackson right outside of Kansas City. They purchased twenty acres of land and harvested many vegetables, including corn, tomatoes, lettuce.

While there were difficult times, the favor of the Lord still rested upon Jacob.

Out of the Pit

Joseph, now thirty years old, had been in prison for twelve years. He had earned the respect of the warden, who believed he was a man of integrity and honor. He had been assigned lenient task—working the office four hours a day, four days a week for two years. While Joseph was unsure of what the future would hold, he had gained a great deal of knowledge in finance and accounting.

With Max gone, things seemingly settled down. He had been responsible for much of the corruption behind the prison walls. The work brought Joseph some relief from the horrors of prison life.

Joseph was often asked to assist with taxes. As the warden gave him more and more responsibility, he let him bring Gil in as his assistant.

Joseph sat at a small, scuffed, wooden desk; stacks of papers were piled high. His desk was near a window, so often he would gaze outside and watch the horses with carriages drive by. It was summer time; the sky was deep blue and the sun shone bright.

Joseph riffled through some green-lined papers and set one of them on his desk. He handed some of the stacks to Gil. "Gil, will you file these documents in the brown cabinet?"

"Will do."

He began to write when Bill, the guard, strutted up to his desk, his belly bouncing.

"Warden's on his way."

"Okay."

Joseph straightened his desk and tucked in his shirt.

He finished completing a tax form then looked up at the doorway, and the warden appeared. Standing on either side of him were a young attractive woman with brunette hair and a little red-haired girl with freckles who looked to be five.

"Joseph, allow me to introduce you to my wife, Barbara. This is the young man I was telling you about."

"It's very nice to meet you, Joseph," she said.

"It's a pleasure to meet you as well."

"And this is our daughter, Samantha."

"Hello, Samantha," Joseph said.

She glanced up at him shyly then turned her head.

"She's a bit shy at first," Barbara said, slightly laughing.

"I thought my daughter was old enough to see where I work. I'm taking them for a little tour—first inside the prison, and then outside where some of the inmates are working. Why don't you join us, Joseph?"

Joseph eagerly agreed. Getting outside the prison walls was a like a welcomed oasis.

They walked through the mess hall, the small library built several years ago, and through the chapel. The cells were off limits, even to the warden's family. As they moved through the yard, Barbara tried to cool herself by removing her jacket. They then went outside of the yards where they saw several inmates putting up telephone poles.

Samantha ran several feet to catch a butterfly.

"Samantha, please don't run off," Barbara said.

Samantha, bored and annoyed, said, "But I want the bug."

"I said no, darling. Stay with Mommy."

She scowled and crossed her arms in frustration.

"I think it's wonderful—the work that's being accomplished here. Just think; soon, every home might have a telephone," Barbara said.

"Joseph's been very helpful, especially with organizing the finances. The government gives the prison quite a bit of money to assist with projects such as this one."

"You must have gone to a good school, Joseph."

"Yes, ma'am. Actually, math was one of my strongest subjects. But I've learned a great deal here."

They watched the men working a little while longer; then, without warning, they heard a loud sound. Barbara grabbed the warden's right arm. Joseph turned toward the noise. A rope that held one of the telephone poles steady was getting ready to snap. The pole was leaning, as though any minute it would fall. Several prisoners near it began to back away.

One prisoner yelled, "Move out of the way! It's getting ready to fall!"

All of the sudden, Barbara screamed, "Samantha."

The warden's daughter had wandered away and was right in the path of the leaning pole.

Joseph dashed toward the young girl just as the pole broke loose and began to fall. The warden was right behind him.

Barbara screamed again as she began to run toward the girl. "Samantha!"

Joseph pushed the little girl out of the way; but the pole slammed into him, and that was the last thing Joseph remembered.

Joseph came to in the ambulance. He lay on the cot gasping for air in excruciating pain. His head hurt. It felt like a ton of bricks had dropped on his chest. He felt worse than he had after the beating from Max.

He was diagnosed with four broken ribs, a broken wrist, and a concussion. He spent three weeks in the hospital. The incident was reported in the newspaper. Joseph was a hero.

It was Tuesday morning. Joseph was discharged from the hospital and had to go back to the prison. Coastal clouds began to thicken into a gloomy overcast over the city. It modeled Joseph's mood—depressing and grim.

As Joseph was escorted into the large, dark building by Nathan, a gray haired guard in his late fifties, he glared miserably at the brick walls. Joseph's heart sank once the doors behind him shut. He moved slowly to prevent the pain from his chest from escalating. He was only a few feet away from his cell when Bill approached.

"Wait," Bill said.

Both Joseph and Nathan turned around.

"The warden wants to see him."

Joseph wondered why the warden wanted to see him. The guard immediately turned Joseph around.

Joseph had known Bill and Nathan for years. Nathan was a friendly man. He never married. He'd worked at the prison for over twenty years.

Bill was in his early thirties, had three children, and was expecting another child. He had worked at the prison for five years. Joseph genuinely liked them both.

They moved past the infirmary, a dark cell in the back building where Joseph had worked, and into the warden's office.

Nathan opened the door, and there was a short man with glasses standing next to the warden.

"Joseph, have a seat," the warden said.

Joseph sat down on a chair right next to the warden's desk.

"How are you feeling?"

"I'm still a little sore, but much better."

"Good, glad to hear it. I guess you're wondering why I've called you here so soon after your release from the hospital."

Joseph nodded.

The warden placed his right hand on Joseph's shoulder. "Joseph, you saved my daughter's life."

"I'm glad she's okay sir."

"Well, thanks to you she is. I can never truly repay you for what you have done. But there is one thing I can do for you."

The man at the door handed the warden what appeared to be a scroll and smiled. The warden unrolled it. The warden began to read, "It has come to my attention that Joseph Solomon risked his life to save another's. As the governor of this great state, I hereby, this 14th day of July, 1918, grant Joseph Solomon, a full pardon."

Joseph's heart began to beat rapidly. In utter shock, he leaped to his feet. Questions filled his mind. *Can this really be happening? Can this be another one of my dreams?* he thought. *Has God truly granted me freedom?*

The warden smiled. "You're free, son."

Joseph would have jumped up and down, but his injuries didn't allow it. Tears came to his eyes. It was truly a miracle.

Joseph returned to his the cell to gather his things. Saying goodbye to Gil, he could no longer hold back the tears. He fell to the floor and sobbed uncontrollably.

Gil laid his hand on Joseph's shoulder. "Congratulations, Joseph. I'm happy for you."

"At last God has vindicated me."

He picked himself up off the floor and regained his self-control, struggling to say the words. "You have been like a brother to me…I will never forget you, Gil."

Tears rolled down Gil's face. He smiled and said, "I'll be out in two years. I'll look you up."

The two men hugged.

A New Beginning

Joseph smelled the fresh air and tasted the sweetness of freedom as he stepped out of the horse and carriage—even more so than when he walked out of the prison walls. He gazed up at the deep blue sky. he was filled with joy. He felt as though any minute he could burst into laughter. A scripture his father had often prayed came to mind. *Weeping may endure for a night, but joy cometh in the morning*. It was morning. His heart sang in silence as he thanked God for restoring his liberty.

There was so much to do and so much to see. The buildings seemed larger than he remembered, and some of them different in appearance. His eyes glanced to and fro as he strolled along the street peering inside each store and building he passed.

Right in front of him, he noticed a young man getting into a peculiar looking motor vehicle. It had an odd shape with a green and black fender, black leather interior, and a wooden dashboard. It was unique, as all of the other cars on the streets, each in different shapes and sizes.

Up the road stood a little gray-haired man scooping ice cream out of a canister set in ice. He dropped the scoop into the cone and handed the treat to a little boy.

Strolling up to the man, Joseph said, "I'd like a vanilla ice cream please."

The slightly bald, jolly old man scooped the ice cream and handed it to Joseph.

"There you are. That'll be five cents."

After paying the man, Joseph sat down on Main Street and watched as people strolled by.

Many people of many different races had migrated to New York. He watched as a woman stepped by with a peculiar-looking fur hat with brown, beige, and white all intertwined on her head and a fur shawl draped over her shoulder. He wondered why she was wearing such a thick hat and shawl in the middle of summer. A man dressed in black with a small, black derby hat on his head and black suit helped her into the back seat of a large, black car. The car looked expensive.

After finishing his ice cream, he continued to stroll down the busy streets. Joseph was in good shape, but now his joints ached as he moved from one street to another.

Looking for some relief, he searched for a restaurant to rest his body and quench his thirst. He turned the corner and came upon a familiar street—Burlington Avenue. There was the diner he had remembered eating in years earlier. He peeked inside. The furniture looked newer and was in different colors, but the diner's owner looked the same; now gray-haired and stout, yet full of laughter and still managing to keep his customers amused.

He looked across the street and froze, overwhelmed with both nostalgia and sadness. There stood the hotel he and his brothers once stayed in. The building was dilapidated with the faded red bricks. Joseph stared at the building for several minutes before deciding to cross the street. He slowly made his way to the other side then stopped, staring at the hotel for some time. A sign on the door read: *Condemned*. Still, he decided to enter.

Carefully opening the door, he stepped into the musty, old hotel. A spider crawled its way up a cobweb right next to the door. The lobby looked older. The walls were cracked and the wood oak floors scuffed and filthy from years of use. To the left were a couch and two faded beige chairs. The fireplace was a few feet away; a rat made its way across the floor, entering into it. To the right was the same old desk where the clerk once checked in hotel guests.

Joseph slowly climbed two flights of stairs, arriving on the third floor. He paused. A feeling of grief struck through his bones. He approached the room he and his brothers had stayed in. Unable to face the heartache that stood behind the door—any minute he would become sick, he turned around, ran down the stairs, and darted outside, stopping into a nearby alley and leaning up against the wall. He wiped the tears from his face. He vowed never to return to this part of the city again.

He walked four miles toward midtown and found an old hotel. It was cheap, but clean. After unpacking, he ate dinner two streets up the road at a small restaurant. It was the best hamburger he'd ever tasted in his life. The French fries melted in his mouth.

With his stomach full, he went back to the hotel, took a bath, and lay down on the bed. His feet were still aching and head was pounding. It had been a mentally and physically stressful day. Exhausted, he fell fast asleep.

The next day he ate at the same restaurant. This time, he had scrambled eggs, steak, and fresh biscuits.

He peered right and saw a fat man with an unbuttoned shirt, thinning brown hair, and an unshaven face. His belly moved when he laughed. Joseph studied the face of the waitress after she listened to the man. She frowned and grabbed his menu before walking away. She slipped behind a bar and poured a cup of coffee. Turning back to the man, she set the coffee down.

The waitress had a polite smile; a smile he'd seen so many times—his mother's. His heart began to ache as he saw visions of her laughter in this stranger.

He bit into his biscuit and reflected on the cinnamon bread his mother used to make that would melt in his mouth. He wondered how his parents were. He missed his mother's sweet caring nature and his father's strength. His heart ached when he thought of his family, especially Rachel and Benjamin. Ben would be almost fifteen years old. Joseph would have given anything to have watched him grow and develop into a young man.

Anger burned within him when he thought of his older brothers. He never wanted to lay eyes on them again as long as he lived. But he couldn't allow his hatred to keep him from reuniting with the rest of his family.

Joseph thought long and hard of what to do next. He had been given a new suit and enough money to get by for a couple of months. However, he knew if he was going to survive, he must find work. His plan was to earn enough money to buy a ticket and sail back to Italy. At least, that was what he wanted to do. He had, of course, heard about the war and wasn't sure if his family was still there, even though he had read Italy remained neutral.

He decided to write a letter in hopes that it would reach them. He pulled out his journal from his pant pocket. The edges were ragged and the pages were beginning to fall apart; he'd filled it to the last page. A large, blond waitress sailed by. "Miss, you wouldn't happen to have an extra sheet of paper would you?"

"Hang on," she said.

She stepped behind the counter, ducked, and came back waving an order pad. "Here you go. Will that do?"

"Yes, thank you."

"Can I get you anything else?"

"Just more coffee."

She grabbed his cup and returned with it filled.

"Thank you."

"You're welcome," she said as she walked away.

He wasn't sure where to start. He kept the letter brief.

Hello Father and Mother,

I'm not sure what my elder brothers told you, but I am alive and well and living in New York. I'm sure you are wondering why I've decided to write you after so many years. My life's circumstances caused me to be falsely imprisoned. I've been in the State Penitentiary in the state of New York now for twelve years. I hope to find employment soon so that I can earn enough money to take the next ship back to Italy. I will explain everything to you when I see you. Tell Rebecca and Benjamin that I love them and I will see them soon. Here is the address of the hotel I'm staying in: 33 Nelson Way, New York, NY. Write back soon. I love you, Joseph.

He didn't say what his brothers had done for fear that it would destroy their father. He folded the letter and stuffed it in his pocket. He finished his coffee, asked the waitress where the nearest post office was, and then left the diner. He stopped by a nearby store and purchased an envelope. Two miles south, he came upon a post office. He entered the small brick building and purchased a stamp. After sealing the letter, he hesitated for a brief moment and then dropped the letter in the box. He wasn't sure if it would ever reach his family, but he had to try. He felt deep in his heart that God would, in time, reconcile him with his family. Now he had to try to find work.

Where do I start? he wondered.

There was a man distributing newspapers on the corner.

"I'd like one please," Joseph said.

Handing him the paper, he said, "That'll be two cents."

After paying him, he leaned against a building. Glancing at the cover, it read: *The New York Times.* He searched for any help-wanted ads.

The choices were few: store keeper, grocery clerk, and receptionist. It wasn't much, but it was a start. He set off on foot to find the locations the ads stated were requesting help, stopping along the way at every help-wanted sign. Everywhere he turned was a no.

After hours of walking in the sweltering sun, his shirt dripping with sweat, still, nothing had turned up. His head ached and he felt dehydrated and weak. He stopped into a diner and drank a soda before continuing his search. At one point, a rain shower drenched the city for several minutes. It was a welcoming and refreshing break from the heat.

Four long hours had passed and it was seven thirty. The receptionist job required typing skills. The storekeeper and grocery-clerk positions had just gotten filled earlier that day.

Later that night, Joseph ate dinner at an Italian restaurant two blocks up the street from his hotel. He took his last bite of ravioli, drank his milk, and then went back to his room.

He sat at the edge of the bed. With his shoulders slumped and elbows on knees, he exhaled loudly and realized how exhausted he was. He stretched his arms above his head to remove the stiffness.

He tried hard not to get discouraged. It had only been a few days and New York was a big city. It would be a greater challenge than he had imagined, but he was determined to find a job.

A Familiar Face

One month slipped by quickly, and Joseph had still not found a job. Money was running low.

He was up before the sun and dressed quickly; putting on the same faded black pants, blue shirts, and scuffed shoes he'd worn for a week. He brushed his teeth and then left the hotel. He rubbed his eyes, feeling the stiffness in his body. He'd remembered seeing a library when he first arrived in New York.

Moving past 42nd street, he came upon the brilliant structure—The New York Public Library. The building was almost two city blocks in length.

He climbed the stairs and went into the massive concrete building and stared in awe. A pair of marble lions stood proudly before the majestic Beaux-Arts Building.

He stepped inside. The building had a unique stone vault above a white marble interior with an elaborately decorated ceiling. A great gallery extended along the north-south axis of the building on the first floor. He peered right and saw a stunning stairway.

Joseph mounted up the stairs, stopping at the second floor. Hundreds of books on every subject filled the shelves. Strolling down the aisles, stopping at the history section, he grabbed the thickest book he could find. He leaned up against the wall and leafed through several of the pages.

He put the book back and then walked farther down the hallway, entering into another room. Looking right, there were stacks of newspapers on a shelf. Flipping through a few, he noticed they were dated as far back as ten years. He grabbed a stack and sat down at a small table toward the back of the library. When working in the warden's office, he saw a newspaper only occasionally, so now he was hungry to find out what he had missed.

Joseph studied the newspapers, learning of every major event that had occurred over the past twelve years. He educated himself about the past presidents, economics, business, and any other subject he came across. Joseph knew that knowledge would be one of his greatest assets.

As he continued to read, a familiar face in a photo caught his attention. The man was standing next to the governor of the state of New York and other distinguished looking men. He studied the photo. His hair was gray, skin wrinkled, and he was larger in size, but Joseph recognized the odd-shaped nose.

The lines at the bottom read: "Governor Al Smith, Councilman George McGovern, Councilman Rodger Montana, and businessman Taylor Parks attend a special dinner for Governor Woodrow Wilson at the Mt. Vernon Hotel."

Yes, Taylor Parks, the man I met at the shipping yards over twelve years ago. Joseph glanced down at the date: January 7, 1917. *That was a little over one year ago.*

Farther down it read: "Taylor Parks is a successful businessman. He owns one of the largest shipping companies in the United States."

Joseph remembered the words that Mr. Parks had spoken to him; *"Son, you ever need a job, look me up."* He kept the card Mr. Parks had given him with the telephone number stashed away in the back of his journal. It was a long shot, Mr. Parks probably wouldn't remember him, but it was worth a try.

He returned to his room at half past six. Grabbing the journal he kept in a small brown bag next to his bed, he pulled out the business card. It was too late to call, but he would make a visit first thing in the morning.

Exhausted, he fell backwards onto the bed. He was sick to his stomach and his feet were throbbing. He managed to lift himself up to pull his shoes off. His feet were blistered. After soaking them in hot water, he went straight to bed.

The next morning, he dialed the number, using the hotel phone, but the number had been disconnected. He decided to visit the shipping company where he had first met Mr. Parks. His mood lifted with this slim hope. While he planned to fervently search for Mr. Parks, he knew he needed to be realistic. He would accept any job offer that crossed his path.

Joseph sauntered along the docks for two hours, finally arriving at Parks Shipping Company.

It had grown from a small office to a three-story building.

He stepped into the large building with white walls and wooden floors. There were doors to the far side of the building, which looked like offices. There was an older woman with gray hair, wearing a brim hat and glasses, sitting stiffly behind an old wooden desk.

"Can I help you?" she asked.

"Yes, I'm looking for Mr. Taylor Parks."

Her chin high, she said, "Do you have an appointment?"

"I'm an old friend," Joseph said.

"Well, Mr. Park's office was moved to downtown Manhattan several weeks ago."

She picked up a pen and paper from her desk and wrote some notes. "Here's the address."

"Thank you."

Joseph took a bus since the office was almost ten miles from the docks. Reading the card, it read: 350 Eighth Street.

This must be it, he thought.

He stepped out of the bus and stared at the five-story brick building in east Manhattan. Standing by the door was a large black-haired man with a bushy, sandy-brown beard in brown pants. Joseph approached the man cautiously. The man glared down at Joseph.

"Whatcha looking at boy?"

"Uh, well…"

"Well, what is it, boy? Speak up!" the man said. harsh.

"I'm looking for Mr. Parks, Taylor Parks. Do you know him?"

The man sized Joseph up.

"What do you want with Parks?"

"We met several years ago. I was hoping I could see him. Can you tell me where I might find him?"

The man gaped at Joseph for a couple more seconds. "You got an appointment?"

"No, sir, but…"

"Get lost."

"Sir, please,"

"I said get lost!"

Joseph pretended to walk away, but instead slipped around the corner of the office. Peeking around to the side of the building, he spotted a side door. He shot a quick glimpse around the corner to see if the man was still there. The man pulled out a cigarette and soon two other men joined him. Desperate to see Mr. Parks, he snuck inside.

Two men stood talking next to an office toward the back. One peered over at Joseph then turned his head. Straight ahead were wooden stairs. Hearing the noise of men talking, he shot a glance behind him. The man was entering the office. Joseph ran up the stairs so he wouldn't be noticed.

A young woman, wearing eye glasses and her hair styled in a bob, was sitting at a desk talking on the telephone. "Yes, sir. I'll see that Mr. Parks receives it."

She hung up the phone and asked, "May I help you?"

Joseph cleared his throat, "I'd like to see Mr. Parks."

"Well, do you have an appointment?"

"No, I'm an old acquaintance."

"I see."

"I was hoping he might have a few minutes to talk to me."

"Well, Mr. Parks is a very busy man and you'll need an appointment."

It had been a long journey and Joseph had battled discouragement for weeks. He was willing to do anything. "I understand, but I've come along way; if I could just have ten minutes."

"I'm sorry, sir."

Just then, three men walked out of the inner office. A gentleman in a black suit stood at the entrance. Joseph recognized the man.

"I'll see that the merchandise is delivered first thing Monday morning."

"You never let me down, Parks; looking forward to a long working relationship."

"Good day, gentlemen. Grace, hold my calls."

Joseph stood to his feet and before he could speak up, the woman said, "Uh, sir…Mr. Parks…"

"What is it, Grace?"

She strode over to Mr. Parks. "There's a young man here to see you."

"Does he have an appointment?"

"No, sir, but he says he is an old acquaintance."

Mr. Parks peered at Joseph, not recognizing him, and then turned his head.

Joseph stood with his heart beating rapidly. Desperate, he thought, *I've got to see him.* Not sure what to do, he stood still.

"Well, what's he want?"

"I'm not sure, sir; but apparently he's been trying to locate you for days. He's come a long way, sir."

"All right, send him in—but only for a minute."

"Yes, Mr. Parks."

She walked back to her desk, her chin high. "Mr. Parks will see you now."

"Thank you."

Joseph moved slowly to the office door, his hands trembling.

"Well, don't just stand there. Come in, boy."

He cleared his throat. "Hello, sir. My name is Joseph."

Mr. Parks sat in his chair and gazed up at Joseph. He opened a desk and pulled out a cigarette.

"Cigarette?" he asked.

"No, thank you," Joseph said.

"What can I do for ya."

"Well, sir, you probably don't remember me. We met many years ago. The first time was on a ship from Italy to America, and then again at your shipping company. We had lunch together."

Mr. Parks lit his cigarette with a match and took a giant puff. Smoked filled the room. "Tell me more."

"You gave me a tour of your shipping company. You also offered me a job and gave me this."

Joseph handed Mr. Parks the business card. Mr. Parks studied the card carefully. "That's certainly mine, and that's my old phone number on the back. Have a seat."

"Thank you."

Joseph took the chair directly across from Mr. Parks.

"So, Joseph is it?"

"Yes, sir."

"How can I help you?"

"Well, sir, I recently relocated here to New York. I was wondering if the job offer you made would still be a possibility."

Mr. Parks took another puff of his cigarette. "Well, that was quite a while ago."

"I realize that, sir, but I'm an excellent worker—great with finances; and I could really use the work."

"Tell me about your previous experience."

"I did some financial consulting for a large organization," Joseph said, cautiously.

He prayed that Mr. Parks wouldn't ask for references. He thought to himself, *It wouldn't look too good to have the warden write a letter of recommendation.*

"I also worked on a farm for many years. I'm a good worker and very strong. I'm willing to do anything."

He continued to study Joseph. "I'll tell you what. You seem like a man of integrity. And seeing that you have a card with my writin' on it, I'm gonna give you the benefit of the doubt. I have a position open as an assistant to my manager at my shipping company."

A bout of joy leaped in Joseph's spirit.

"Do ya need the address?"

"No, sir. I can't tell you how much this means."

"Well, Joe, you don't mind if I call ya Joe, do ya?"

Joseph nodded.

"I like you—and there are very few people I like, but I have a good feelin' about you."

"Thank you, sir; you won't be sorry."

Mr. Parks and Joseph shook hands.

He opened his door and patted Joseph on the back. "Goodbye, Joe."

"Thank you again," Joseph said.

"Grace, call Nelson Peterson and tell him he's got a new assistant startin' tomorrow."

"Yes, sir."

Joseph was elated. At last, a job. He ran down the street. Any minute he was going to explode. Everything looked different, brighter, and more colorful. He had forgotten to ask what it paid, but he didn't care.

He stopped into a clothing store to pick up a few items: a blue tie, black socks, and a new pair of shoes. He had worn holes in the only pair he had.

That night, as Joseph prepared for bed, he thanked the Lord and vowed to work diligently every day. He looked in the mirror. He had matured. His appearance had changed, especially after the surgery from the beating from Max in prison. He was still handsome though. He'd grown more than five inches since he first came to America. His naturally curly hair had lightened some, and he had grown a small brown mustache. He had broad shoulders, a muscular body, and sun-darkened skin.

He still hadn't heard from his family. Hope for reconciliation grew dimmer and dimmer every day.

Joseph was not only physically a different person from the boy from Italy, but mentally as well. His identity had changed. He had been given a fresh start, and it was a new day. He needed a new name. *From this day forward, I will no longer be Joseph Abraham Solomon. My new name will be Joe Abrams.*

Joseph Prospers

Joseph rolled over on his left side and picked up his pocket watch off a small black table next to his bed. He glanced at the watch for the tenth time; it was five a.m. Five minutes had passed from the last time he checked. He had barely slept that night. He lay awake with questions racing through his mind. *What will I be doing? Will they like me? I wonder if I'll meet friends.* He'd been alone and felt isolated since leaving the prison. A companion would be a welcomed bonus.

Twenty-five minutes later, at five thirty a.m., he rolled out of bed, put on the suit given to him before being released from prison, and put on his new shoes. He darted down the hallway to get to the bathroom. After brushing his teeth and shaving, he went back into his room and over to the mirror. He combed his hair, patted down his mustache, and knelt down beside the bed to pray.

"God, thank you for this job. Give me strength and wisdom; and grant me favor in this job, so that I might please you."

He stood in front of the mirror one last time and straightened his tie. He dropped his watch in his pants and then stepped out of his room.

It took him a little over an hour traveling on the trolley to get to Parks Company. Joseph was to report to work at eight o'clock, but he arrived at seven. He didn't want to chance being late. To pass the time, he walked around the grounds to familiarize himself with the layout. At eight, he entered the office.

The same older woman he saw the previous day was sitting stiffly behind her desk. "Can I help you?" she asked.

"I was told to come here for my first day of work. Mr. Parks referred me."

"You're the young man I saw yesterday aren't you?"

"Yes."

She glanced down at a piece of paper lying on the desk. "You must be Joseph."

"Yes, but I go by Joe."

"I see," she said, reserved. "Mr. Peterson is expecting you. Follow me."

She stood. Her orange dress was ruffled and she was wearing a helmet-shaped hat and white stockings. She walked him down a long hallway to the very last office on the left. She knocked on the door.

"Who is it?" a coarse voiced man asked.

"Mr. Peterson, Joseph—I mean, Joe is here."

"Just do as you're told!" the man behind the door said.

Joseph heard the sound of the phone being slammed down. "Send him in."

"You may go in now."

Joseph nodded and said, "Thank you."

He opened the door and went into the office. A large man with black hair, a black beard, chubby face, and tan skin gave him an angry look. His face looked as though he'd been in several fights. He had two thick scars—one across his forehead, and one down the left cheek that went from his eye to his mouth. He looked and smelled as though he hadn't bathed in weeks. For a moment, the sight of this man brought back memories of Max.

The room smelled of cigar smoke. Staring down on the desk, Joseph noticed an ashtray filled with cigar butts. Stacks of paper covered the desk. The office hadn't been cleaned in a very long time; thick dust lay on the desk. The wooden floors were filthy with dirt scattered throughout, and several cockroaches were crawling on the walls.

"Well, don't just stand there; sit down!" he barked.

Joseph immediately sat down. His empty stomach became nauseated.

"Sir, I'd like to thank you for this opportunity..."

"Shut up and listen! I'm not used to someone decidin' who I hire. You musta done a real job on the old man, gettin' him to hire ya. While you're here, boy, you'll do exactly as you're told or your days are numbered. Got it?"

Joseph nodded.

He had a strange, cutting tone, spoke clearly, yet he was threatening and abrasive.

"I can't hear you, boy!"

"Yes, sir."

"Follow me."

Peterson stormed out of his office and down the hallway with Joseph not far behind. He stopped at a closet near his secretary's desk, grabbed a broom, and slammed the door shut. He led Joseph outside and aboard the deck of the ship. It was the same ship Joseph had toured with Taylor over twelve years ago, but now freshly painted.

He turned to Joseph, threw the broom at him, and said, "Now get to work. You'll start with this entire deck, and when you're done with that you can do the grounds."

"Yes, sir," Joseph said.

Joseph knew that Mr. Peterson would be difficult to work for, but none the less, he was grateful for the job. He thought in time, perhaps Mr. Peterson would get to know him and like him, although he wasn't holding his breath.

Joseph was assigned several tedious tasks. He worked in the yards and in the office, sweeping and mopping floors. Cleaning the bathroom was the worst with its foul smell and filthy stalls. He didn't make much, but it was an income. He had been taught to do everything as unto the Lord, so he put one hundred percent into his duties.

Six months passed. Joseph had moved into a small two-room apartment in a poor area of Manhattan. The surrounding buildings suffered from obsolescence and were in poor condition. The apartment had a stove, a rusty old sink, an old couch, a small bed, and a bathroom with a sink and small, stained tub. It wasn't much; but it was a place to lay his head.

It didn't take long before Joseph earned the respect of the other employees at the shipping company. He had a humble approach to his work.

One day, Mr. Daniel Makaski, the senior manager, showed up unannounced. Mr. Makaski was a gentle, genuine man in his fifties. He stepped aboard the ship while Joseph was busy cleaning the deck. The weather had grown cold as the fall months were coming to an end. Joseph turned up the collar of his coat. The icy weather reddened his face; his hands were red and raw. He leaned on the railing and shivered in the cold wind he continued scrubbing the deck.

Joseph watched from the corner of his eye as a paled-faced man he had never seen before walked by with Mr. Peterson. Peterson snarled at Joseph as they passed.

Mr. Makaski, with his stretched right arm, pointed to Joseph. "Come here."

Joseph moved slowly toward them, guarded.

"You are responsible for cleaning this whole deck?"

"Yes, sir."

"I've been here many times, but I have never seen it this clean. What's your name?"

"Joe Abrams."

"Well, Joe, keep up the good work."

He patted Joseph on the back several times.

"Thank you," Joseph said.

He smiled as he walked away. It was nice to hear that he appreciated his work. The encouraging words brought peace of mind. The only feedback he received from Peterson was negative and harsh.

Later that day, while Joseph was in the office mopping the floor, he looked into the spare office near the center of the building. Mr. Makaski and Mr. Peterson were having a meeting. He mopped for several more minutes before he looked up again. This time, Mr. Makaski motioned for Joseph to come into the room. Joseph glanced around to make sure Mr. Makaski was talking to him.

Slowly making his way to the door of the office, he tensely stood waiting. Mr. Makaski and Mr. Peterson had spent most of the morning in meetings. Mr. Makaski laid out several written documents on a long brown desk. "It's a new advertising campaign to increase sales. What do you think? I could use someone else's opinion."

Joseph, taken back, stared at Mr. Makaski. Not sure why someone of his caliber would want his opinion, he approached the table cautiously. He took a breath to calm his nerves and then studied the ideas presented before him carefully. It listed several marketing strategies for domestic and foreign buyers. Taylor planned to increase cargo distribution to more than fifty more companies. He'd put Mr. Makaski in charge.

Joseph had paid attention to every detail of the business and made several notes on creative ideas he had to improve sales.

"Well, what do you think, Joe?"

"Well, sir, they're great ideas. Can I make another suggestion?"

Mr. Peterson smirked. Mr. Makaski Joseph asked to explain.

"Well, as you know, a low cost product always attracts consumers. If the company wants to establish a relationship with more consumers and at the same time increase sales, then why not deliver additional, higher-margin products, with the low-cost product? Give the customer exactly what he wants, but increase the types of cargo. We deliver timber, why not add metal?"

Joseph continued to share his ideas for a little over fifteen minutes. While in prison, he had read books on a wide variety of subjects, especially business.

Mr. Makaski stared at Joseph in silence. "You know something, Joe, I think you're onto something," said Mr. Makaski enthusiastically. "That's brilliant. Why didn't I think of it?"

Peterson glared at Joseph in repugnance.

"We might just be underestimating your abilities here, Joe. We'll give these ideas of yours a try and see what happens." He smiled.

Joseph was excited and nervous. A part of him could not help wondering what would happen if the ideas didn't work.

On a cold January morning, three months later, Joseph was hard at work sweeping the deck as usually. He had on two shirts, a scarf wrapped twice around his neck, and a heavy brown coat. Tiny pieces of ice stuck to his hair. He rubbed his hands up against his pants to warm them. Mr. Makaski stopped by early that morning to meet with Peterson. He was sitting in the spare office finishing up a telephone conversation. He yelled out to his secretary. "Joan, get Peterson in here. And get Joe Abrams too."
"Yes, Mr. Makaski."

Joseph entered into the office, and one minute later Peterson appeared. Peterson looked at him with abhorrence. Joseph stood next to the door with his arms crossed. He nervously checked his watch and glanced at the dimly lit sky through the window before he concentrated on Mr. Makaski. From the corner of his eye, he could see Mr. Peterson continuing to glare at him. He couldn't afford to lose his job—it was all he had.

Mr. Makaski smiled warmly at Joseph. "Have a seat, Joe," Mr. Makaski said. "Can I offer you a cigarette?"

"No, sir." Joseph tried to relax, but his heart was pounding.

Mr. Makaski pulled a cigarette out from his coat pocket and lit it by striking a match on his shoe. "I put those ideas you had for increasing production to domestic and foreign ports into place."

Joseph watched with a feeling of anxiety and prayed a silent prayer. Mr. Makaski blew one large puff into the air and set the butt in an ashtray on his desk.

"They worked. I've seen an increase in production."

Joseph breathed a sigh of relief.

"I have a new project I'm working on, and I'd like you to be in charge."

Peterson looked at Joseph, gnashing his teeth, his eyes narrowed. Joseph, pretending to ignore his enraged expression, stood stunned. "I don't know what to say, Mr. Makaski."

"First of all, call me Daniel; and second, say yes."

Joseph smiled. "Yes."

"Good, good, we'll start on this tomorrow."

Joseph walked out of the office smiling in utter shock, unable to grasp what had just happened.

"Looks like ya got lucky," Peterson said. "Don't think this means anything. Once a low scum .janitor, always a low scum janitor. It's in your breeding." Peterson said.

Joseph, too excited to be intimidated, walked away.

To celebrate, he went downtown to have dinner at an Italian restaurant. He stepped off the carriage onto the slippery sidewalk and moved slowly though the crowd past vendors selling minces pie and people haggling with peddlers. He went into a restaurant, Antonio's. He ate spaghetti and meatballs.

He smiled to himself. *In less than one year, I've received a promotion.*

A Reunion

Joseph stood in his small kitchen, measured the grounds for his coffee, and poured the water into a kettle. He had moved to the upper west side of Manhattan in a residential area in a two-story building that had been renovated. His apartment had four rooms: living room, kitchen, bathroom, and bedroom. The living room had a brown couch, beige chair, and one small brown table; Joseph wasn't much on decorating. It had a single bed. It was small, yet cozy.

He smiled, shaking his head. Only one year and three months at Parks Shipping Company and he'd been appointed general manager. Daniel Makaski had retired early, so Joseph took over his responsibilities.

It was summer of 1920, and business was booming. Things were going well and he loved his job. He strived to be the best at everything he did. He bit into a slice of slightly burnt toast, placed it back on the plate, and finished getting ready for work.

He shot a glance at his watch—half past eight. He was dressed in a three-button wool sports jacket, a vest, and brown designer pants that were cuffed at the bottom. His pocket watch was slipped on a chain to his vest. He straightened his beige cotton tie one last time. Then, he grabbed his car keys and ran down the stairs. The car was parked on the street.

He climbed into the front seat of his new, red Chevy Deluxe Amesbury Special Roadster with wire wheels and leather interior.

After arriving at work a little past nine, he opened the door and stepped over to his secretary, Mrs. Madison's, desk.

He pointed to the file cabinets next to her desk. "Mrs. Madison, grab the notes filed under Baltimore from the brown file and bring them into my office, please."

Wearing a perfectly ironed, plus-size green dress, she looked through her reading glasses at him. "Yes, sir."

Joseph's office was bright from the sun shining through the window. He pulled out his black leather chair and sat behind the nicely polished mahogany brown desk. The office had wooden floors, white walls, and a brown bookshelf.

Joseph sat back in his chair, stretched out his back, clasped his hands behind his head, and stared out into the bay. He watched small boats drifting out into the still, large body of water.

I love my job, he thought to himself.

A knock on the door. "Mr. Abrams?"

"Come in, Mrs. Madison."

She walked into the room smiling, carrying a sheaf of papers in one hand and a glass of water in the other. "Here you are, Mr. Abrams."

"Thank you, and thank you for the water."

"You're welcome." She returned to her desk, closing the door behind her softly.

He flipped through the pages, studying the contents of the third page. It was a seamlessly constructed architectural layout of a docking area in Baltimore, Maryland.

Another knock on his door.

"Come in."

Peterson stepped into the room carrying a thick stack of papers. Nelson Peterson had been made assistant manager to

Joseph three months earlier. Although the downward move was humbling, Joseph was a sincere and kind man; he treated Peterson well.

Joseph stared at the big stack in Peterson's hands. There must have been at least fifty pages.

"Taylor left these over the weekend. Went out of town for a few days; said he wanted you to get through them by the end of the week."

He unloaded the pile onto Joseph's desk.

Joseph shook his head. "It's going to be a long week."

Peterson nodded. "You need anything?"

"No, thanks."

He stepped out of the office. Joseph casually fanned through the papers. Most of the pages were mimeographs of notes. He'd had a meeting the previous Friday with Taylor. Taylor had purchased another cargo ship and was working to establish another shipping company in Baltimore. Joseph was assigned to assist in the founding of the new company. He'd been learning the business from the ground up. The experience and knowledge gained were priceless.

The telephone rang. He lifted the pile of papers from the bottom and moved them to the side of his desk as he answered the phone.

Joseph could feel the ache in his back from sitting in one position to long. He'd been on the phone for almost three hours talking to potential buyers. He shrugged to relieve the stiffness.

"You go with us and we'll deliver better, faster, and more efficient services. Trust me, I won't let you down."

With his phone glued to one shoulder, he reached in his drawer and pulled out an envelope. "Where do you want the shipment sent? That's 1132 Oak Boulevard; got it."

Just then, there was a knock on his door.

Ignoring it, he said, "Good, you won't be sorry. I can get you a delivery as early as next week."

He rubbed his right eyes several times and moved his neck to the right and then to the left.

Once again, a knock. "Mr. Abrams," his secretary said.

Placing his right hand over the speaker part of the phone, he said, "Just a minute…Call me once the shipment arrives. Thank you and a pleasure doing business with you. Goodbye. What is it Mrs. Madison?"

She poked her head through the door. "I'm sorry to bother you, sir; but there's someone here to see you."

"Does he have an appointment?"

"No, sir."

"I'm very busy, Mrs. Madison."

"I know, sir, but he says it's urgent."

After a brief moment of silence and a sigh, he said, "All right, send him in."

The man entered the office. Joseph gradually looked up, eyes wide. "Gil!" Joseph jumped out of his chair. "I don't believe it. Is it really you?"

Gil snickered. "It's me."

Joseph hugged him. Placing both hands on his shoulders, he asked, "How did you find me?"

"I saw your picture in the paper. I didn't recognize the name Joe Abrams, but I'd know that face anywhere."

"When did you get out?"

"A month ago. I was released early on parole."

"I'm so glad to see you, Gil. Sit down. I want to hear everything."

Gil sat on the chair right across from Joseph.

Joseph studied his good friend for several seconds. His shoulders had broadened, his rusty red hair had lengthened, and there were deep faint lines around his eyes. He seemed less innocent, though stronger and more confident. It was obvious the years in prison had been hard on Gil.

"I just can't believe you're here. How are you?"

"I'm okay." He shook his head several times. "Life was hard when you left. You were my only friend. I never thought I could be so lonely."

"I missed you too, Gil. Not a day went by when I didn't think about you. Did you get my letters?"

"They were the only things that kept me going. I looked forward to them. I counted the days when I'd be released. I prayed to that God of yours and it musta done some good. The warden released me eight months early." Gil sat silent for a moment. "He died two weeks after."

Joseph's eyebrows lowered, his mood dampened. "How?"

"Heart attack."

"I'm sorry to hear that…He was good to me."

"Yeah, he was a good man," Gil said.

Joseph took a drink of water. "Can I get you some water, coffee, tea?"

"No, I'm okay."

"So, what have you been doing with yourself since you got out?"

"Well, I'm looking for a job." Joseph smiled.

"Well, that's one area where I can help. Consider yourself hired."

"Just like that?" Gil said, surprised.

"Just like that."

Leaning back on his chair, Gil asked, "How'd you ever manage to land a job like this, right out of prison?"

"Hard work and a lot of prayer."

He laughed.

Glancing at the pile of papers on his desk, Joseph hesitated at first, then said, "Let's get out of here, spend the day in the city."

"Sounds good to me," Gil said.

Joseph grabbed his suit jacket and wrapped his arm around Gil. "Mrs. Madison, I'll be out for the rest of the day; take any messages."

"Yes, sir."

They spent the remainder of the day in the city reminiscing about old times, both good and bad.

It was Wednesday afternoon, and Joseph had been in earnest discussion with Taylor and another board member, Al, all day regarding the plans for the new company in Baltimore. Gil had worked as a file clerk for the last three months, and on occasion, assisted with ship repairs. Joseph planned to use Gil's skills on the new construction project.

He followed Taylor out of his office; the meeting was over a little past noon. After shaking hands with the men, he slipped into the bathroom. It was a hot day and the building was humid. He wet some toilet paper under the faucet with cool water and smoothed it across his face as an attempt to cool off.

Stepping out of the bathroom, his shirt damp, he approached Gil, who was kneeling at one of the cabinets by Mrs. Madison's desk organizing files. "You hungry?" Joseph asked.

Gil peered up at him and said, "I'm starved."

"Let's get something to eat. How's Mel's sound?"

"Okay by me."

"I'll be out for about an hour, Mrs. Madison."

"Yes, sir."

The diner was bright, lively, and adventurous. An aroma of thick, juicy hamburgers and crisp, mouthwatering fries filled the room. A busboy placed two glasses of water on the table. Gil gulped the entire glass down within seconds.

"I don't know if I really ever got the chance to thank you for this job."

"It's not much, but you're welcome. You've been a good friend. I don't think I would have made it through prison if it hadn't been for you. I plan to use more of your talents with the Baltimore project. Your repair skills will come in handy."

Gil nodded.

"So how are things going with you and Georgia?" Joseph asked.

"Never better. Walked into Bloomingdales, met her, dated her for one month, and all ready it feels like I've known her for years."

Joseph smiled.

"What can I get you?" the thin and pretty blond waitress asked.

"I'll have a burger, fries, and vanilla shake," Joseph said.

"I'll have the same," Gil said.

Gil watched the waitress walk away. "She's very pretty."

Joseph took a quick glimpse and nodded. Joseph could tell Gil was hinting at something. Pretending not to notice, he gazed at the people in the restaurant.

"Have ya dated since ya been out?"

Joseph took a sip of water and set the glass down and said, "No."

"Why not? You're a successful businessman now. Isn't it time you thought about settlin' down?"

"I've been so immersed in my work; I haven't had time to think about it."

Just then the waitress reappeared at the table. "Here you go—two vanilla milkshakes. Your burgers will be up in a minute."

"Thank you," Joseph said.

After swallowing a large gulp of the shake, Gil wiped his mouth with his hand then dried it on his pants. A brief pause. "Have you ever been in love?"

Joseph smiled. "There was a girl once."

"What's her name?"

"Sasha. I met her when I first came to America. We met at a museum." He tilted his head back and sighed. "She was the most beautiful girl I'd ever seen. I remember the conversation I had with her, almost word for word."

Warmth and affection flooded his face when he spoke of her.

"I can still see her face and those beautiful brown eyes. She had a kind spirit. She reminded me of my mother, caring and gentle."

"What happened?" Gil asked.

His eyes narrowed and his chin dropped. "My brothers happened. Prison happened."

Anger, frustration, and disappointment filled his spirit. Glancing out on the street, he said, "Even though I'd only known her for a short time, I never forgot her."

"Why don't you try looking her up?"

"It's been over fourteen years. I'm sure she's married."

"You won't know until you try."

"It was hard enough knowing I'll never see her again. I think seeing her happily married would be even more painful. For now, my focus is on my work."

The waitress stepped up to the table, carrying their food. "Two burgers and fries."

"Thank you," Joseph said.

"Can I bring you anything else?"

"No, this is fine, thank you,"

She set the tab down on the table.

Taking a giant bite of his burger, Gil said, "There's more than just one girl, ya know."

"I know," Joseph said, right before biting into a fry. "How about we change the subject?"

Gil laughed and took another bite of his burger.

After lunch they hurried back to the office.

Joseph sat at his desk. He made several phone calls and attended a late afternoon meeting.

On the drive home, thoughts inundated his mind of the girl he'd met so many years ago. He wondered what she looked like. *Did she have children? Did she ever attend college like she'd planned?* He wondered if he would ever see her again.

The Chases

Sasha lay in bed, half asleep in her large and elegant bedroom in her parents' thirty-room mansion. She lifted herself from her bed, placing her feet flat on the floor. She went into her bathroom and placed a towel where she could reach it. She ran the bath and dipped her leg in it to check the temperature, and slowly stepped in. She reached for the soap and lathered up.

She soaked for ten more minutes before getting out and toweling off. She went to the closet, pulled out her white nurse outfit, and slipped into it. She brushed her bangs out of her face; her silky black hair was pulled back in a bun today. Her hair complemented her thick lashes and flawless skin. Her slender figure fit nicely in her white nurse outfit. She dabbed a little makeup on her face—pale powder and cream rouge, and headed downstairs.

She walked into the kitchen, pulled out a jar of milk from the refrigerator, and poured it into a glass. She then strolled into the dining room where her father was sitting, reading the newspaper.

"Madam, may I bring you some breakfast?" the thin, gray-haired butler said.

"No, thank you, George," Sasha said.

Two maids, a butler, a gardener, and a driver were among those employed by the Chase family.

She entered the large, elegant dining room. A glass case filled with beautiful crystal dining ware stood in one corner while a glass table with a crystal vase filled with white tulips sat in another.

"Hello, Daddy," Sasha said.

"Morning, dear."

He took a drink of his coffee and continued reading the newspaper.

Sasha's father, Robert, had graduated Harvard Law, finished top of his class, and worked in a well-known law firm for ten years. At the age of forty-four, he decided to run for the United States Senate. After an aggressive campaign, he was elected a senator.

Sasha gulped down the milk. Drops spilled over onto the expensive Persian carpet that lay on the rich, polished ebony floor.

Robert straightened his reading glasses. "You might try slowing down once in a while, Sasha."

"No time. I don't want to be late."

She wiped the milk off her upper lip and rubbed her hand on her dress to dry it.

She kissed her father on the cheek. "Tell Mother I'm working a double shift at the hospital today, so I'll miss dinner."

"Don't work too hard."

"I won't."

She rushed to the closet by the front door and pulled out a light sweater, then grabbed the keys to her yellow Ford model automobile and drove to Valley Memorial Hospital.

She started making her rounds and checking on her patients.

Two hours later, she approached the last room next to the nurses' station. She stepped into the room. "How are you feeling, Mr. Watkins?"

Mr. Watkins, a seventy-four-year-old, white haired and white-bearded man, struggled to say the words. "I'm in a bit of pain, but okay."

Sasha placed two fingers on his wrist and took his pulse. "I'll give you more pain medicine in an hour."

He nodded.

"Would you like more blankets on your bed? Perhaps that might make you a bit more comfortable."

"Yes," he said hoarsely.

She slipped out of his room, and re-entered two minutes later carrying a white cotton blanket. She gently laid the blanket on top of the sheets.

"There, hopefully that's better. I'll check on you in an hour."

He nodded and closed his eyes.

Sasha tiptoed out of his room and sat down to do paperwork at the nursing station. A red haired, heavyset nurse approached. "So did you tell the folks you found a house you want to move into?"

"No, not yet. I'm sure they'll be fine with it; it's just Mother's always envisioned me living with my husband, not alone—even though I'm thirty-one," she said, rolling her eyes.

"Well, the sooner the better," responded the nurse.

"I'm planning to tell them this weekend." Glancing down at her watch, she added, "Betty, mind if I go to the cafeteria to get something to eat?"

"No, go right ahead."

"I'll be back in thirty minutes."

"Take your time."

She entered the clean cafeteria half past three. She'd been working now for seven hours and wasn't due to get off till ten. She grabbed a tray and strolled down the line.

Glancing up at the cook, she said, "I'll have a turkey sandwich, some potato salad, and a glass of milk."

After purchasing her food, her eyes canvassed the room for a nice, quiet spot. She sat down at one of the far round tables. She took a bite of potato salad and wiped her mouth with a napkin.

Glancing around the room, she saw a tall, athletic, blond-haired young man sitting down next to an attractive blond woman a few tables away. When he glanced in her direction, she turned her head. He reminded her of her late husband, Winton.

Sasha had dreamed of owning her own art gallery, but her parents—especially Mother, managed to convince her that it was foolish, so she decided to go to college instead. She wanted to become a nurse and travel to other countries to help the poor.

One day, while attending one of her mothers' charity events, she met a handsome, blond, blue-eyed man named Winton Grant III. Winton was intelligent and determined. His family was among the wealthiest families in New York. They owned two banks.

Winton and Sasha began dating, and Sasha fell in love. After they'd been seeing each other for six months, Winton proposed, and they were married one year later.

Sasha wanted a small wedding with family and a few personal friends, but her mother insisted on a large ceremony—inviting three hundred people.

Sasha moved into Winton's home in Connecticut. Her dreams of attending college faded away; she became immersed in charity work and entertaining Winton's business associates and their wives.

Time passed, and it was suddenly a week before Christmas. The couple had been married for two years. Winton went skiing with a friend in Aspen. There was an avalanche. The two men tried to out ski the slide, but only Winton's friend survived.

Sasha was devastated. She sold her house and moved back in with her parents, vowing never to marry again.

A year after Winton's death, she decided it was time she pursued her dream of becoming a nurse. She enrolled in New York Medical College and Hospital for Women and graduated at the age of twenty-seven, accepting a job in the emergency department at Valley Memorial Hospital.

She lifted her fork and took another bite of potato salad and washed it down with her milk. She heard her name being called from a distance.

"Sasha, that you, my dear?"

She turned around and saw a short man smiling at her. "My goodness, Mr. Parks, I haven't seen you in quite some time."

He walked over to her table, bent down, and hugged her. "Call me Taylor. You make me sound like an old man. Your father never told me you worked in the hospital. Now what's a pretty little thing like you doin' in a place like this?"

"Oh, I've worked as a nurse here for a few years. Please sit down."

Taylor sat across from Sasha.

"I almost didn't recognize you. You've grown into quite a young lady," Taylor said.

"Thank you."

"So how is your father, that son-of-a-gun? I haven't seen him since the Governor's Ball."

"Oh, he's quite well. He and Mother are planning to celebrate their 35th wedding anniversary. It's going to be a grand event; you really should come."

"I wouldn't miss it. The wife and I got the invitation just yesterday."

Taylor glanced at a scrawny, freckle-faced cafeteria assistant who was walking past, carrying a stack of trays. "Say, kid, bring a cup of coffee would cha."

"Yes, sir."

"So Mr...I mean Taylor. If you don't mind my asking, what brings you to the hospital?"

"Visiting an old classmate."

"I'm sorry to hear that. I hope he'll be okay."

"He'll be fine. Doc says he'll be good as new in a couple weeks."

"That's good to hear. Well, I really should get back; I have patients to see," Sasha said.

She stood and grabbed her tray.

"Here, let me get that," Taylor said, removing the tray from her hand. "You go see your patients."

"Thank you. It was good seeing you again," she said.

"You too, my dear, and I'll see you at your parents' bash."

She smiled. "I'll see you then."

After a long night, she arrived at her parents' home on the upper side of Manhattan, a little past eleven p.m. She slowly crept up the stairs.

Exhausted, she flung her clothes off, threw them on a chair next to her bed, put on a pink nightgown, and went to bed. Within minutes, she was fast asleep.

The next morning, Sasha could vaguely hear her name being called. "Sasha, are you up? Breakfast is ready."

She opened her eyes in a daze, hoping she was having a bad dream. She covered her head with her pillow.

Once again, she heard her name being called. Heaving the blanket off her body, she let out a loud sigh. "I'll be down in a minute."

Fumbling out of bed, she walked over to the mirror. She patted her wayward hair down and went into the bathroom. After a bath, she put a little make up on her face—light blush and ruby-red lipstick, and threw on a green blouse and a plaid skirt. She strolled down the stairs into the dining room and sat next to her father.

"Hello, Daddy."

"Hello, Dear."

"Hello, Mother."

Sasha's mother was sitting in the dining room, dressed in a kimono-style embroidered silk dress, her black hair medium-length and styled in waves, said, "Well, it's about time you got up. What took you so long, Sasha? It's almost eleven thirty."

"So nice to see you too, Mother," Sasha said sarcastically.

Sasha poured herself a cold glass of orange juice.

"You almost missed breakfast," Ellen said.

"That's okay, I'm not very hungry. I worked the long shift last night so I ate late.

With a silver, shiny coffee pot in one hand and a sideboard on the other, the maid said, "Coffee, sir?"

"Yes, thank you."

She poured hot, steaming coffee into his cup and set the sideboard with a plate of melons, strawberries, grapes, and danish in front of him. He took a bite of his danish, then took his glasses from his breast pocket and set them on his nose. He picked up the business section of the newspaper that had been left at his place.

Ellen, Sasha's mother cut a piece of melon and placed it in her mouth, and then gently wiped her lips with a napkin. Placing the napkin back on her lap, she looked up and said, "Robert, Senator Basin phoned. He said to call him back today." His face buried in the paper, he mumbled, "Will do."

"Maggie, tell Andrew I'll be ready to leave by one o'clock," Ellen said.

"Yes, ma'am."

Oh, Daddy, you'll never guess who I ran into at the hospital."

"Who's that, dear?"

"Taylor Parks."

"Well, I'll be. I haven't seen him in a while. How's the old man doing?"

"Quite well. He's planning to attend your mother's wedding anniversary."

"Good thing, it'll be nice to see him."

Sasha took a large swig of orange juice, watching her mother's glare from the corner of her eyes.

"Sasha, I really do wish you would wear one of your more suitable dresses."

Sasha frowned and rolled her eyes. "What's wrong with this one, Mother?"

"Darling, how do you ever expect to meet a husband dressed like that? It's been a long time since Winton's death, God rest his soul. Don't you think it's time you moved forward?"

She crossed her arms and sat back in her chair. "I have moved forward; and if I ever decide to marry again, my husband will have to love me for who I am on the inside—not for the dress I'm wearing. I need to go," she said, standing abruptly.

"Where are you going?" Ellen asked.

"I'm meeting Alena to play tennis."

"Well, what time will you be home?"

"For goodness sake, Mother. I'm thirty-one years old. I don't know. I'll call you if I'm late. Bye, Daddy."

"Bye, dear."

"Mother."

Stopping by the closet near the door, she grabbed a white large bag and a tennis racquet and dashed out of the house.

She drove to the tennis court, arriving a half hour later at a distinctive private club with an upscale golf course, indoor and outdoor seating for guests, and four tennis courts.

After changing into a long white skirt and shirt, she hurried out to the courts where she'd planned to meet her best friend, Alena.

"Hi, Sasha," Alena said.

"You have no idea how glad I am to see you," Sasha said.

"Problems on the home front again? When are you going to tell the folks you're moving out?"

"Just as soon as I put a down payment on my place—which is later on today. I can't wait. My mother is driving me to drink!"

Alena peeked over Sasha's shoulder.

"If you don't watch out, she'll have you married off to Wellford."

Sasha turned around and there stood a tall, thin, awkward, and large-nosed man playing tennis on the court next to theirs.

"Don't even think about it," she said.

The two erupted into laughter.

"Let's play," Sasha said.

The Party

Joseph stood tall in front of twelve board members in a large conference room, but his hands were trembling as he strolled on the Skyline Maple hardwood floor. He distributed the reports to twelve board members, including Taylor Parks, sitting around a large, shiny mahogany table. He'd spent hours preparing the night before.

The sun was shining bright into the room. Joseph grabbed a handkerchief from his pant pocket and dabbed it on his forehead. Photos of past and present board members hung on the deep green wall in front of him. The photos made him even more nervous.

It was a Friday, August 4, 1921, and Joseph had become a highly respected businessman. Profits had doubled under his leadership as general manager.

He straightened his brown cotton tie, cleared his throat, and said, "Good morning gentlemen."

With the exception of Taylor, the men—many gray-haired with wrinkled skin, sat watching him in silence. Taylor nodded and smiled.

In a stern and confident voice, Joseph said, "I'm going to provide you with an analysis of the advertising campaign I created. If you open the documents I've placed before you, you'll see a detailed layout of the plan."

A gentleman to his far right, James, pulled out a pair of reading glasses from inside his suit jacket to read the document, while the others focused intensely on the plan.

"I have completed a thorough and accurate assessment of our current financial portfolio; and I feel that, with this new advertising campaign, we will see a significant gain in foreign ports within the next six months. We decide the best way to get the consumers attention and how to communicate the unique aspects of our business to them."

Joseph spoke for over twenty minutes.

"In conclusion, gentlemen, this is precisely what we have to do in order to achieve our goals: get the public's attention, and sell them on our company. I believe this detailed report showing the strategic steps I have talked about can make it happen."

Once the presentation was complete, half the board applauded while the others either nodded or sat smiling.

"Well done, Joe, well done. Very pleased with your work," Taylor said.

"Yes, Joe, very pleased," said Al, the board member sitting to Joseph's right.

Grinning, Joseph said, "Thank you."

One by one, the gentlemen left the room.

Taylor clapped him on the shoulder. "Oh, by the way, I'm going to a party tonight. Friends of mine, Senator Chase and his wife, are celebrating their 35th wedding anniversary. The wife was supposed to accompany me, but she's a bit under the weather. Why don't you come, Joe? The governor will probably be there along with other important men you should meet. It'll do ya some good to get out. Ya know what they say: too much work and not enough play."

Joseph chuckled. "I'd love to go. Where's the party?"

"I'll give my house address to your assistant. We'll go together; meet me at seven p.m. sharp."

Except for an occasional dinner with Gil, Joseph hadn't socialized much in the past few years. A burst of excitement flowed through his body. *A party at a senator's house...the governor...beautiful women are sure to be there. Could life get any better?* he thought.

He finished up his last minute paperwork, grabbed his suit jacket and car keys, and drove straight to Saks Fifth Avenue to get a new suit.

After being fitted for a stylish black suit and shiny black shoes, he drove home.

He'd received a healthy salary increase, so he moved into a newly built, lavish apartment in the upper west side. A marble fireplace sat in his living room.

There were a handful of good restaurants in the neighborhood, along with a bookstore and a few shops. The culture was rich with Italian, Black, and Asian people. Joseph spent most of his evenings walking and studying the people. Children played and people sold items on street corners. The smell of salmon sautéing and fresh crab often circulated down the street from his home; he dined out twice a week. He loved the weekends the most—they were bustling, diverse, and filled with restaurants, crowded streets, and young college students.

Joseph put on a white tailored shirt and slowly buttoned it up. He straightened out the collars before tucking the shirt in his pants. He tried to appear at ease, but it was difficult. *In just a few hours I'll be surrounded by eminently successful people. I wonder what the home is like.* He smiled. *I bet it's spectacular.*

Sasha sat in her bedroom at her vanity applying cream rouge on her cheeks. Relieved to finally be in her own place, she smiled as she glanced around the small room. It was simply decorated with a single bed, a dresser, and a painting of wild horses hanging over her bed.

She'd only been in the house for a week, but already, it felt like home.

It's not much, but it's mine, she thought.

The house was in midtown Manhattan. The move didn't come without a price; she promised to join her parents for dinner at least once a week.

Sasha shook her head and laughed as she thought to herself, *Mother's probably invited every eligible bachelor in the city to the party.*

She softly penciled in thin arches to her eyebrows before applying a brilliantly red lipstick to her lips. She combed her shiny, black hair away from her face, and then pinned two gold Spanish-style hair combs on the sides of her hair. She hung a long strand of pearls around her neck. She glanced at herself one more time in the mirror.

Picking up her cat, she said, "Don't wait up, Jasp."

Setting him down next to the bed, she clutched the gift she'd bought for her parents in one hand, grabbed her car keys in her other, and hurried off to the party.

Sasha arrived little past six p.m. The party was set to begin at seven. She entered, taking in the sight of the large ice centerpiece in the middle of the hallway. The banister on the staircase was laced with white and red roses. A red rug channeled from the top of the stairs to the bottom and into the dining room. When she opened the door, Ellen walked into the entrance. She was dressed in a pink robe and pink slippers.

"Sasha snarling you look wonderful." She kissed her.

"Thank you."

Just then, two men walked in carrying a large ice centerpiece shaped in the form of four roses. They set it down in the entrance.

"No, no, how many times do I have to tell you? The center piece goes into the dining room, not the entrance," Ellen said, frantically.

The men turned around and moved the centerpiece.

"Everything needs to be perfect."

How can I help, Mother?"

"See that everything is perfect the patio, darling. I'm going to see that the caterer has put the last finishing touches on the food."

Sasha darted back under a vaulted ceiling, which was the entrance leading to the reception hall. The room had over twenty small well-made wooden tables and chairs with crystal vases and white tulips as centerpieces. There was an expensive carpet with autumn colors—orange, red, and green, lying on the shiny mahogany floor.

She opened the sliding glass door and stepped out on the patio. To the right, there was a beautiful rose garden with ten chairs perfectly spaced out for the orchestra. Fifteen small wooden tables, with four wooden chairs surrounding each, were placed on the close-cut grass. The mansion was on a hill with a perfect view of downtown Manhattan.

She went back inside. From the reception room, there was a long passageway with stained-glass windows on both sides, leading further to a gallery. The living room was secluded on the other side of the reception hall.

Robert strolled down the stairs, wearing a dashing new tuxedo, hair perfectly parted near the center and slicked back with gel.

"Darling, you look lovely," he said.

"Thank you, Daddy."

Just then Ellen walked back in. Ellen's two yorkies ran down the stairs; but before they could go any farther, she bent down and grabbed them. The butler, George, was not far away.

"George, see that Molly and Mabel are locked up for the night. I don't want them getting in the way."

"Yes, madam."

George climbed the stairs, holding one dog in each hand, to put the pets in their room for the night.

"Mother everything looks wonderful. The patio is simply stunning."

"Thank you, daring."

"Try not to worry," Robert said, as he straightened his tie.

"That's my job. Oh my, I seem to have lost track of the time." She hastened up the stairs to finish getting dressed.

Thirty minutes later, the guest started to arrive. Ellen, dressed in a beautiful, deep blue dress with a gold band around her head, and deep blue high-heeled shoes, approached Sasha. The ten carat diamond around her neck sparkled like the stars.

Have you seen your father?"

"No; when I do, I'll tell him you're looking for him."

Just then, an older woman with black hair highlighted with streaks of gray, wearing an elegant gold-fringed flapper dress and a long strand of beads dangling around her neck walked up to Ellen.

"Ellen, wonderful party."

"Thank you, Margaret. What do you think of my lovely centerpiece in the dining room?"

"It's to die for. Where ever did you get your dress? It's gorgeous."

"I had it sent from Paris," Ellen said. "Margaret, I simply must show you my anniversary present from my husband."

Sasha noticed some friends standing at the entrance to the dining room. "Mother, please excuse me."

"Oh course, dear."

Sasha wove her way through the crowd to join them.

The doorbell rang and a butler opened the door. Taylor Parks and Joseph entered. Joseph, stunned by the size of the home, gazed up at the ceiling. A magnificent chandelier hung from the white plaster ceiling. He peeked down at the attractive gray and white marble floor. The paintings on the walls must have been worth many thousands of dollars.

Lights flashed all around them from two photographers taking pictures. The orchestra was playing. He didn't recognize the music, but it was the most elegant classical music he'd ever heard—though it was a bit overshadowed by the talking and laughing. Overwhelmed, he moved closer to Taylor.

"Your coats," the butler said.

Taylor pulled his coat off and placed it in the butler's hands.

Joseph gave his coat to the butler and said, "Thank you."

A young, distinguished-looking gentleman looked up at Taylor and smiled. Approaching, he said, "Taylor, is that you?"

"Johnson, long time no see." Taylor shook his hand.

Joseph smiled, feeling a bit awkward.

Taylor turned to Joseph and said, "Let me introduce you, this is Joe Abrams; he works for me."

Johnson smiled and reached out and shook Joseph's hand. "Nice to meet you, Joe."

"You too; it's a pleasure."

Joseph studied the fine looking, tall, broad-shouldered man with slicked back black hair. He looked to be in his thirties.

"Johnson here works for General Motors," Taylor told Joseph.

Young and ambitious, Joseph thought.

Turning back to Johnson, Taylor added, "Joe here is a genius; the best thing that ever happened to Parks Company."

Joseph smiled.

He narrowed his eyes to take a better look at Joseph. "Well, you don't say. Maybe I ought to steal him?" He laughed.

"Not a chance, Johnson."

The butler appeared and said, "Champagne."

Taylor grabbed a glass.

Joseph took a glass and said, "Thank you."

The butler nodded.

Just then Robert walked up from behind.

"Taylor."

"Robert, good to see ya, old boy. How long has it been?"

"Too long," Robert responded.

In silence, Joseph pondered on the man standing before him. He was obviously well-educated. There was certain strength to him, yet his demeanor seemed gentle.

"Nice party you got here, and by the way, happy anniversary."

"Thanks, Parks."

Taylor patted Robert on the back. "The wife went all out for this party. Musta cost you a pretty penny."

"I'll say. I might have to get a second job at your shipping company."

Taylor laughed.

Joseph watched the two men talking; they were apparently close friends. He was gazing throughout the room, studying the people. Women moved past him wearing beautiful gowns; their jewelry glimmering in the light. The men looked distinguished—all dressed in either expensive suits or tuxes. He wondered what they did, where they lived, and who they knew.

"I hear business is good," Robert said.

"Couldn't be better. I hired this young man."

Taylor placed his hand on Joseph's back. "Joe, I'd like you to meet Senator Robert Chase."

"Hello, Senator, I'm very glad to meet you."

"Likewise, Joe."

"Joe is one of my managers. This boy has doubled my profits. The kid has some kind of divine favor I tell ya; whatever he touches prospers."

"You don't say," Robert said, smiling.

Joseph smiled.

Just then, another distinguished-looking gentleman with gray hair and a mustache approached them. "Hello, Senator," he said, shaking his hand.

"Hello, Al," Robert said.

"Hello, Governor, so good to see you," Taylor said, shaking his hand.

"Hello, Taylor, it's been a long time."

"Too long. How are things?" Taylor asked.

"They could be better. I'll tell you what, with Warren Harding in office, maybe we'll see a turn around. After Woodrow's stroke, everything seemed to go downhill. Don't get me wrong, Woodrow was a decent president; but after the stroke, we weren't sure if the vice president or his wife was running the country. What about you, Parks? What's new?"

"Hired a new man; he's done great things for the company. I'd like you to meet Joe Abrams. Joe, meet Governor Al Smith."

Joseph was tensed, his face flushing with nervousness, but he met the governor's gaze directly.

"Glad to meet you, Joe."

They shook hands.

"You too, Governor, it's an honor."

This whole night is like a dream, Joseph thought.

In the reception hall, Sasha was chatting and sipping champagne with a couple of friends when she heard her name being called.

"Sasha!" A young, attractive dark-haired woman wearing an off-white sleeveless dress walked towards her. Her hair was styled in a bob.

Happy to see her, Sasha said, "Hi, Sally." She hugged her.

"You look wonderful. Where did you get the dress?" Sally asked.

"Bloomingdale's. You look beautiful too."

"Hi, Marge, Jane," Sally said.

The two responded with, "Hi."

"Where's Alena?" Sally asked.

"She's on her way; she's just running a little late," Sasha said.

"Great party, so many men," Sally said, inspecting the room.

"I'm sure my mother invited every eligible bachelor she could find," Sasha said.

"I'll have to be sure and thank her," Sally said. "Oh look, there's Reginald."

A tall, strikingly handsome, brown-haired, green-eyed man stood on the other side of the living room.

"He's so handsome and so rich." Sally straightened her dress. "Excuse me, ladies, I think I'll get a little better acquainted." She walked toward him.

Out of the corner of her eye, Sasha saw movement outside the patio door. A woman with her short blond hair styled in waves was standing near the rose garden.

"Oh, there's Alena. Let's go outside and get away from the noise."

Joseph stood close to Taylor. Almost everyone that passed them stopped to speak to Taylor. Taylor turned to Joseph and said, "Make yourself at home, my boy," as he walked away.

Joseph moved into the dining room, mesmerized by the assortment of food lying on the large ebony table, covered with a white silk table cloth. Some of the finest dishes were displayed: salmon, lobster, steak, crab, shrimp, salads, French bread. Each dish was decorated like art. An assortment of desserts, cheesecake, chocolate éclairs, and chocolate mousse was perfectly arranged on the smaller table right next to the larger table.

Joseph picked up an elegant china plate, white with gold trim, and a gold knife and fork, and filled his plate. He carried it to the reception hall.

His plate in one hand, he took another glass of champagne from one of the butlers and made his way outside into the gardens.

His eyes lit up when he gazed out at the magnificent view. The Brooklyn Bridge was so bright it glittered. He made his way to a table by the rose garden and sat under a full moon and a blanket of stars.

He took a bite of salmon and gazed up at the balcony, noticing four young women talking there. The two whose faces he could see were very attractive, both with blond hair. The others had their backs to him. He took another bite of his food, and watched as they went into the house.

Later, looking for Taylor, he noticed the same group of girls, this time standing near the entrance talking and laughing. This time there were only three of them—the one with medium length, dark hair was missing.

Should I approach them? What should I say? he thought to himself. His hands began to perspire; his face felt warm.

Suddenly, Joseph heard a ringing sound. Turning, he saw a woman dressed in a brown silk dress was clinking a spoon up against her champagne glass.

"Everyone, everyone, may I have your attention? I'd like the newlyweds—my sister and her husband, Senator Chase, to come forward."

Robert moved over and stood next to the women and reached out his hand, motioning his wife to come to him.

"I would like to propose a toast to two of the most generous and lovely people I know. Though I'm sure you've gone through many hard times, you managed to come out stronger and better people. Congratulations on thirty-five years of marriage."

The guests raised their glasses and congratulated the couple.

"Speech, speech," a man said.

"Yes, thank you to everyone for coming," Robert said. "It's been thirty-five wonderful years, and I thank God every day for giving me this woman by my side."

Mrs. Chase smiled.

"We've been through some tough times, but through it all, we persevered. I couldn't have made it without my lovely wife, Ellen."

Senator Chase kissed his wife gently on the lips. Everyone applauded. Ellen glanced around the room.

"Has anyone seen my daughter?"

Several guests looked around the room.

"Oh well, I'm sure she will turn up somewhere. I do want to thank my lovely daughter. She has stood by her father and me for many years, and we want her to know how much we appreciate and love her."

Again, the guests applauded. They began talking and laughing.

Thirsty, Joseph wove his way in and out of people to get to the punch bowl. "Excuse me, ma'am," he said as he pushed himself past a large woman.

She smiled and nodded.

He strode into the dining room and poured himself a glass of punch before returning to the reception hall.

It was then he saw her. She was dressed in a black velvet dress with a strand of elegant pearls hanging from her neck—thick red lips, small chin, high cheek bones, and beautiful brown eyes. Stunned, his heart began to beat rapidly. He remembered their one brief meeting so long ago.

The museum, the beautiful young girl.

He had never forgotten that face. Joy, excitement, and anxiety flooded his body.

I have to talk to her.

"Joe, Joe."

"Joe!" Taylor yelled.

Joseph flinched and turned toward Taylor.

"What's gotten into you boy?"

"I'm sorry; I thought I saw someone I knew."

"Was it a ghost?"

Joseph, shaken up said, "Uh, what, sir?"

"Never mind, it's getting late. I need to get back and check on my wife."

I can't leave without talking to this woman, Joseph thought. "Can you give me ten minutes?"

Taylor looked down at his watch and let out a small sigh. "All right, just ten minutes."

Joseph turned back around. In a panic, he froze. His eyes canvassed the room back and forth, and up and down the stairs; she was gone.

Frantic, he began to search for her. He made his way through the guests, searching in the dining room and the living room. *Maybe she went outdoors?* He moved in and around people to get outside to the patio, searching every inch of the yard.

IIIIIIIIIIIIIIIIIIIIIIIIIIIIIIIIIIIIIIIIIIIIIIIIIIIIIIIIIIIIIIIIIIIIIIIIIIIIIIIIIIIIIIIII

Sasha ran up the stairs to grab her purse. She'd stashed it in her parents' bedroom. She kissed a couple of her girlfriends goodbye, and walked over to her mother and father, who were now standing by the entrance of the door.

"Mother, Father, I really must go. I have to be at the hospital tomorrow."

Her mother frowned. "Sasha, can't you stay a while longer?"

"I'm sorry, Mother. I really had a lovely time, but I have to work a long day tomorrow."

"All right, darling; if you must, go."

"Thank you for coming, dear," Robert said.

He kissed her on the forehead.

"Thank you, Daddy."

She kissed her mother on the cheek. "Bye, Mother."

"Bye, darling. Do come by more often. You get your own place and we never see you."

"Yes, Mother," Sasha slightly sighed. "Goodnight."

She exited the house and waited for the valet to bring her car.

IIIIIIIIIIIIIIIIIIIIIIIIIIIIIIIIIIIIIIIIIIIIIIIIIIIIIIIIIIIIIIIIIIIIIIIIIIIIIIIIIIIIIIIII

Joseph searched every inch of the garden and found nothing, so he went back into the house, still searching desperately. He paced and fidgeted as he tried to comprehend what was happening. *Where can she be?*

He was walking back into the living room when he heard his name being called.

"Joe, it's getting late, I gotta go."

Joseph lowered his head, took a deep breath, and said, "I'll get our coats."

Joseph remained silent the whole drive home. What began as a wonderful night, ended in heartache. Joseph wondered if he'd ever see her again. He thought to himself, *If I have to search all of New York, I'll find her.*

A Divine Appointment

Joseph rested his forehead on his fingertips and stared down at his desk, paging through the papers as an emotional outlet. It was Monday morning, and work was piled up on his desk. He had two meetings to prepare for and a new advertising campaign to launch, but his mind was far away from his work.

Glaring down at his watch, it was fifteen minutes after nine. Only five minutes had passed from the last time he checked.

He sat for an hour, mesmerized by thoughts of Sasha.

H*ow could I let her get away a second time?*

Gil knocked and stepped into his office. "How was the party?"

Joseph sat stiffly, silently staring into his coffee cup watching the steam rise.

"Are you there?" Gil asked.

"It was fine," he said, reserved.

"Just fine?" Gil looked surprised. "Are you okay?"

"Gil, do you believe in fate?"

"In your case, yes." He sat down in the chair across from Joseph.

Joseph leaned forward in his chair. "Do you remember the girl I told you about? The one that I met over fourteen years ago?"

"Sasha was her name, right?"

"Yes."

"I remember, what about her?"

"You're not going to believe this, but I saw her at the party Friday night."

"Sasha? At the senator's party?"

"Yes."

"What did you do? Did you talk to her? Did she recognize you?"

"She stood there so elegant and graceful. She was the most beautiful woman at the party." Joseph frowned and shook his head. "I turned my head for one minute and she was gone. I searched every inch of the house, but couldn't find her."

"Do you know her last name?"

"No."

"Maybe Taylor might know her, it's worth asking," Gil said.

"I thought about that early this morning, but I learned he went out of the state on business. He won't return for two weeks."

"Two weeks isn't a long time," Gil said.

Joseph looked at Gil solemnly.

"Two weeks seems like eternity. I know it's strange, but I fell in love all over again. I can't rest until I find her."

Gil stood. "If there's anything I can do, tell me."

Joseph nodded.

After Gil slipped out of Joseph's office, he pulled himself together and completed his work.

He left the office early that day and drove around the city with hopes that a miracle would occur and he'd see Sasha. After three hours he went home.

The week was difficult. Joseph thought of Sasha every day.

It was Friday; he left work early to run a few errands.

He drove through midtown. Gil and his girlfriend, Georgia, invited him to join them for dinner later that night.

His car had stopped by a line of unmoving traffic ahead of him. *Must have been an accident,* he thought. With his elbow on the wheel and his head in his hands, he sat still for a moment.

With a sudden urge of impatience, Joseph pulled out of the jam and turned left onto Bellington Avenue and then right onto Main Street, but was stopped again by a red light. Glancing down the street to the side, he noticed a black pickup truck swerving in and out of lanes. Two boys stood in the back acting foolishly—jumping up and down laughing. It was hard to see the driver, though he appeared disoriented. It brought back memories of his own brothers back on his father's farm.

A young boy was standing at the curb staring across the street at a candy shop. He turned toward a woman who was rummaging through some purses. He tugged at her arm, but she kept looking at the handbags.

Suddenly, the little boy dashed into the street. The weaving truck was speeding toward him. Joseph jumped out of his car and ran as fast as he could, pushing the little boy out of the way. The truck hit Joseph and sent him flying back. Joseph heard tires squealing, a crash, and then a scream. Looking to the side, Joseph saw the truck overturned with one man lying next to it and another a few feet away—both appeared to be unconscious.

He looked over at the crying boy lying two feet from the sidewalk. Attempting to move, Joseph moaned in pain.

"Andrew, Andrew. My baby!"

The woman picked up her crying son.

"Is he okay?" Joseph asked, clutching his own bleeding arm.

"He's fine," the woman said, her voice shaking and scared. "I'm so sorry. Thank you so much, you saved my child's life."

Joseph nodded.

"Are you okay?" she asked him.

"I'll be all right."

Joseph began to perspire. His arm stiffened, swelling like a balloon. Moving it caused even greater pain.

As he lay there dazed, he heard a mix of people talking anxiously. "Someone get an ambulance…there's been an accident…Are they okay…I don't know."

More voices: "Did someone call for help…Yeah, help is on the way."

The sun glared down. Joseph lay helpless. His breathing became heavier in the sweltering heat.

Suddenly, a police officer arrived and knelt next to Joseph. "Don't worry, help is on the way," he said.

"That man saved my little boy's life."

Two ambulances arrived—one carried away the two injured men, while the other carried Joseph and the driver of the truck.

Dizzy with pain, Joseph lay still while the medical personnel placed his arm in a splint. The truck's driver lay beside him sobbing, his leg bloody.

The young man looked at Joseph and lowered his head. "I'm sorry," he said quietly.

"It's okay," Joseph said hoarsely. "I'm sure your friends will be okay."

The young man nodded, still crying from the pain.

Fifteen minutes later, the ambulance arrived at the Valley Memorial Hospital. The two medics carried Joseph into a room in the emergency department. A doctor administered medication to help relieve the pain and conducted several tests, including an X-ray. Joseph lay resting in a room.

After two hours, the doctor finally appeared. "You have a broken arm and a slight concussion. You were fortunate; it could have been worse."

"When will I be able to go home?" Joseph asked.

"I'd like to keep you overnight to monitor your concussion. You should be able to go home tomorrow."

Joseph sighed. "All right."

"I'm going to give you a prescription for the pain."

"By the way, doctor, how are the boys in the truck?"

"The driver will be okay, broken leg and a few bruises, but the other two young men were hurt badly. One has three cracked ribs and is still unconscious, the other, severe head trauma, and multiple lacerations to the face. He also has some internal bleeding, but they'll both pull through. The boys had a lot to drink, so I'm afraid they have some explaining to do to the police."

"Thanks for letting me know."

Turning around, the doctor said, "I heard how you risked you life to save that young boy. You're quite the hero."

Joseph smiled slightly.

"I'll send the nurse in with your medication, and you make sure you get plenty of rest."

Joseph nodded.

After being moved to a different ward in the hospital, he asked one of the nurses to call Gil.

Within an hour, Gil rushed into the hospital room. "Are you all right?"

"Fine, just a broken arm and slight concussion. The bad news is I have to stay overnight and probably won't be able to return to work for a week. Let Peterson know. Also, tell him to get the news to Taylor."

"Will do," Gil said. "You just get better."

Joseph nodded.

The next day, as Joseph lay in bed half asleep, he heard someone enter his room.

"Sir," said a pale, brown-haired nurse.

His arm in a cast, he gripped it tightly as he lifted himself from the bed.

"I have some medication for you to take home; the directions are on the back. Here are your things." She handed him a wallet and some keys. "You're free to go."

She turned to leave the room.

Joseph studied the items in his hand and said, "Wait."

She turned around.

"Yes."

"My watch is missing."

The nurse looked at Joseph, baffled.

"That's everything, sir."

"Do you mind if I go back to the emergency department where I first came in to check? The watch has a great deal of value for me; I'd hate to lose it."

"Fine, shall I get you a wheel chair?"

"No, that won't be necessary; I can walk."

Joseph slid off the bed and slowly made his way to the emergency department, stopping at the nursing station.

Glancing down at a red-headed, heavyset nurse, he said, "Excuse me, nurse, I was brought in here last night. I'm missing my gold watch. Did anyone turn one in?"

She looked up at him through her thick eyeglasses. "Let me check."

She looked through the cabinets and checked all of the drawers. "I can't seem to find it. Wait, let me check here."

She pulled a small lead box from under a drawer. "Sometimes we keep lost items in here."

She opened the box and picked up a gold pocket watch with the inscription *JS.*

"Is this it?" she asked.

Joseph gave a sigh of relief.

"Yes, that's it. My father gave it to me when I was only a boy. Thank you, miss."

"You're welcome."

Joseph turned, took two steps, and froze as he stared at the nurse standing in front of him. His heart pounded.

The girl from the party; it's her.

She tilted her head and asked, "Sir, are you all right?"

"Uh, yes, I'm fine." Joseph scrambled to find the words. His heart nearly choking him, it was hard to catch his breath. She turned to walk away.

"Wait!" Joseph lurched toward her, jerking his arm painfully. "Please wait."

"Yes?"

"It's you."

"Excuse me?"

"From the party…Senator Chase's party on Friday."

"Yes, I was there."

As she attempted to leave again, he yelled, "Wait! What is your name?"

She narrowed her eyes, frowning. "Excuse me?"

"I'm sorry; I don't mean to alarm you. I just feel as though we've met."

"Sasha," she said. "My name is Sasha."

It's her. I can't believe I found her. Excitement, shock, and anxiety flooded his body.

"I'm Joe Abrams."

"Nice to meet you, Joe. How do you know the Senator?" she asked.

"I came with a friend, Taylor Parks."

She smiled, "Oh yes, Taylor is a friend of my family's. How do you know him?"

"I work for him."

"Did you enjoy the party?"

"Yes, very much."

"And your husband…did he enjoy it?" Joseph asked.

"Oh, I'm not married; I came alone."

Relief striking through his body, he smiled.

"Look, it is very nice talking with you, but I'm very busy."

"I understand," Joseph said. "Perhaps we will see each other again."

"I hope in a better situation," she said, looking at his cast.

"Oh yes, the doctor said I will be as good as new in a few weeks."

"Well, it was nice meeting you, Joe."

"You too."

He stood still as he watched her walk away. *I should have told her that we've met before,* he thought. He took a deep breath. *No, I'll tell her when the time is right.*

All he could think about as he rushed back to his room was pursuing her. Joseph knew in his heart that he had just seen the woman he would someday marry.

That night, as Sasha sat at her vanity brushing her hair, she thought of the unusual encounter she'd had with the gentleman in the emergency room. She couldn't quite understand it, but she found herself drawn to him. Although it was the first time they'd met, she felt as though she knew him. He appeared odd, yet sweet. He also appeared interested in her, which she found unusual; he didn't even know her. She had to admit he was quite handsome, and he couldn't be too strange if he worked for Taylor Parks.

After brushing her hair, she brushed her teeth and washed her face, kissed her cat goodnight, and went to bed. As she lay in bed, thoughts of the strange man returned. She wondered if their paths would ever cross again. Within minutes, she fell asleep.

Second Chance at Love

While Joseph was confined to his house, he thought of Sasha day and night. Monday of the following week, he returned to work. He stepped into his office; stacks of papers were piled on his desk. It was only nine a.m. and it was all ready hot and humid outside. He wiped the sweat off his forehead with his good hand, and pulled off his jacket and threw it across a chair.

Fanning through the stacks, he smiled, thinking of Sasha. He'd planned to go by the hospital that night in hopes of seeing her again.

After a day of meetings, reports, and phone calls, he left the office at six thirty.

He parked next to the emergency department and walked nervously through the doors directly to the nurses' station. The same large, red-headed nurse was sitting there, head down, studying some notes.

"Excuse me, nurse."

She didn't look up. "Yes."

"I'm looking for a nurse; I ran into her a week ago. I believe her name was Sasha."

Taking off her glasses, the nurse looked up. Joseph could tell she was evaluating him. "You look familiar...Weren't you just in here?"

"Yes, I'm the one with the missing watch."

"Oh, yes. Well, Sasha's off today. She won't be back until Thursday evening."

"Thank you."

His doctor's office was in another wing of the hospital. Disappointed, but not defeated, he went there and strategically changed his doctor's appointment from Friday to Thursday at four p.m.

Thursday couldn't arrive soon enough. Dressed in a brown, Saks Fifth Avenue suit and a beige tie, Joseph walked into the hospital, walking through the emergency room. His eyes peered into every hallway he passed. His heart raced the entire time. He didn't see her, but he decided to come back after his appointment. Joseph was in a daze. He was consumed with thoughts of Sasha. He stopped at the nurses' station for his appointment.

"Sir, sir!" yelled a young, blond nurse who was looking up at him.

"Yes, I'm sorry...Um...I have an appointment."

"Your name?"

"Joe Abrams."

She looked at a schedule on the desk and said, "Yes, here you are. Have a seat in the waiting room. The doctor will be right with you."

"Thank you."

He slowly moved to a chair, glancing down the hall the whole time. *I know she works in a different part of the hospital, but I don't want to take the chance and miss her,* he thought.

After the examination, Joseph made his way to the cafeteria to get a drink. As he entered, he turned, and directly in front of him, stood Sasha. His body shaking, his throat tight; it was hard for him to breathe. At first he had a loss for words. He gazed at her. Even in her white nursing uniform, with little makeup and her hair pinned back, she was beautiful. There was a natural beauty about her that radiated throughout the room. At that moment, no one else existed.

"Oh, hello," she said, smiling.

"Hello," he said.

"Are you here for an appointment?"

"Yes, I just saw the doctor."

Looking at his left arm, she said, "I see the cast is still on."

"Yes, the doctor said a couple more weeks."

His heart was racing. *I can't let her get away again. I need some time with her.*

"Would you like to join me for a soda?" he asked.

"I'd love to, but I have to get back to work. I just finished my break."

It's now or never, he thought.

"I was wondering—if it's not too forward and you're not too busy, if you wouldn't mind joining me for dinner sometime."

"I'd like that."

Intense relief flooded his soul. Smiling broadly, he said, "How about Saturday night?"

"Saturday won't work."

"How about lunch on Sunday?" he asked.

"My family and I attend church on Sunday; perhaps after service? We usually get out around noon."

"Good," Joseph said. "Where should I pick you up?"

She pulled out her pen and a small note pad from her pocket. Holding the paper against the wall, she wrote down her address. "Here you go; you can pick me up there."

"Okay, I'll see you Sunday. Shall we say one?"

"That would be perfect. I should get back to work."

"I'll see you then."

Happy and excited, he had a date with the girl of his dreams. Sunday was only two days away, but it felt like forever.

That night he lay in bed for hours, staring up at the ceiling. Questions filled his mind.

I wonder why she isn't married. Where shall I take her? Perhaps dinner then a show, or maybe for a long drive. Perhaps I'll take her to the park.

Finally, it came to him. *I'll take her to the place we first met: the museum.*

Finally, he drifted off to sleep.

Joseph awoke early Sunday morning. Dressed in white slacks, a dark blue blazer, and a navy tie, he stared at himself one more time in the mirror. He paused to catch his breath.

He straightened his tie, zipped up his blazer, and looked for his car keys. *Where can they be?* After checking the living room, he stormed into the bedroom, and the kitchen. He was beginning to panic. He checked in the bathroom but still nothing.

What if I can't find the keys? What if I'm late?

It dawned on him to check his pant pocket. He pulled out the keys and laughed. He'd put them there so he wouldn't misplace them.

Half an hour later, he arrived at her home. Located in a nice residential area in midtown Manhattan, it was small with a gated fence—simple, but lovely. The lawn was nicely cut; an assortment of flowers lined the pathway of the sidewalk leading to the house. There was a large apple tree to the right of the house and a wooden bench and table to the left.

Joseph felt a sinking feeling in his stomach. He rang the doorbell and she opened the door. He took a deep breath and smiled. She was wearing a long, silk-flowing white dress and a small pearl necklace around her neck. Her soft, deep brown eyes sparkled while her silky, dark black hair fell perfectly at her shoulder.

"Hello," she said.

"Hello. You look…beautiful."

"Thank you."

"Shall we go?" he said.

After graciously opening the car door for Sasha, he fumbled his way around to the driver's seat.

"So, where are we going?" she asked.

He smiled. "I thought we would have lunch first. Do you like Italian?"

"I love Italian," she said, smiling.

"Good, I know a great place."

On the drive to the restaurant, Sasha held her head out the window and smiled. Her black hair flew against the wind. It was hot and humid in the car. Joseph tried to focus on the road, but his eyes were drawn to her. He could smell her sweet perfume. His heart vibrated. This was the most important day of his life.

They dined at the popular Italian restaurant, Antonio's, located in midtown Manhattan.

The restaurant was bustling with people of many races, laughing and speaking several different languages. Three heavyset Italian men stood in the front of the restaurant singing Italian songs. There was an excellent view of the city.

Joseph requested a table near the back of the restaurant—quiet and private.

Once the two were seated, the waitress took their order: grilled shrimp over linguini for Sasha, and spaghetti and Antonio's famous meatballs for Joseph.

"Tell me, Joe, where are you originally from? You speak with a slight accent."

"Italy, although we are Jewish. Our family is originally from Persia. My grandfather settled in Italy when my father was young."

"What brought you to America?"

"It's a long story, but I came with my brothers to visit American colleges; and, due to certain circumstances, I ended up staying."

"So what did you do before you began working for Taylor Parks?"

"Just odds and end jobs," he said, cautiously.

"You never went to college?" she asked.

"Unfortunately, no. You don't mind if I ask you a personal question, Sasha?"

"No, go right ahead."

"How is it that someone so beautiful and as kind as you isn't married?"

She smiled. "I was married many years ago to a wonderful man named Winton. We met at a charity event. He died a few years back."

"I'm sorry," Joseph said.

"He was a warm and generous man. I've not married since."

"Wine?" asked a tall, black haired, mustachioed waiter carrying two bottles of red and white wine in chilled ice.

"Yes, please," Joseph said.

"Red or white?"

Looking at Sasha. "Is red all right?"

"That's fine."

The waiter poured the wine first into Sasha's glass and then Joseph's.

Joseph lifted his glass and said, "A toast."

Sasha smiled and lifted hers.

"To new beginnings."

"To new beginnings," she said, clinking her glass against his.

After lunch, Joseph said, "I thought we could visit a favorite spot of mine: the National Academy Museum."

"Oh, I'd like that; it's one of my favorite spots."

Shooting glances at Sasha, Joseph's heart pounded with anticipation. Being with her felt like the most natural thing in the world. He was hoping that going to the museum would bring back memories of their first encounter.

After a twenty-minute drive, they arrived. Joseph parked the car and dashed around the car to open the door for Sasha.

They strolled through the rooms looking at the beautiful paintings. To the right was *The Heart of the Andes (*1859*)*, the great painting of Mount Chimborazo in Ecuador. To the left, a painting titled *Dance Foyer at the Opera*, by Edgar Degas.

Joseph watched Sasha's eyes light up as she marveled at the beautiful works of art. "I can see you have a real love for art," he said.

"Yes, I wanted to attend art school."

"Why didn't you?"

"My parents, especially my mother, didn't feel it was a realistic field to pursue. I'm afraid they convinced me to give it up. I don't mind though, I love being a nurse."

Joseph's affections grew deeper and deeper for Sasha every moment he was with her. He could feel she was comfortable with him.

They climbed the stairs to the second floor and before they could walk into the next room, Sasha unexpectedly stopped and fastened her eyes on Joseph. Se had an an odd expression. He could tell she was studying him.

"This is going to seem odd, but I feel as though we have met before."

Joseph smiled.

"Probably because we have; I was only seventeen years old when we met in this museum. I had just finished a tour at the university. I bumped into you and you dropped your books."

Her eyes widened, "Yes, I remember. Why didn't you tell me?"

"I wanted to, but wasn't sure if you'd remember."

"What a small world," she said, slightly laughing. "Your appearance is different. I didn't recognize you."

"I had an operation a while back and it somewhat altered my looks. I thought of you every day, Sasha."

"What happened? Where did you go?" she asked.

"It's a long story."

"I have a confession to make to you too, Joe. I came back into the museum every day for two weeks hoping to run into you again."

"Really!" He looked directly into her big, beautiful brown eyes. His voice changed, a little deeper now. "Do you believe in fate, Sasha?"

She turned her head away shyly. "I guess so."

He gently touched her face with his right hand. She glanced up at him.

"I think this is the beginning of a wonderful relationship," Joseph said.

She smiled.

After another half hour at the museum, Joseph drove her home.

He slowly pulled into Sasha's driveway, disappointed that the day was ending. He walked her to the door, his heart trembling the entire time.

"I had a wonderful time,"

"So did I." Joseph didn't want the night to end. "Can I see you again?"

"Of course. I'd like that. Goodnight, Joe."

"Goodnight."

It wasn't long until Joseph and Sasha fell in love. In the weeks to come, they were inseparable apart from work. They went to the theater, long walks on the pier, and picnicked in the park. Joseph learned to play tennis. It was a match made in heaven.

They laughed like a couple of kids. Joseph's heart ached for Sasha, and Sasha had never loved another man the way she loved him.

The Two Shall Become One

It was a beautiful, mid-October night. Gil and Joseph sat at a table in an elegant restaurant on the dock with a view of the ocean, sipping red wine. Sasha and Gil's fiancée, Georgia, were in the bathroom freshening up. Joseph lifted the wine bottle and topped off Gil's glass.

"So have you met the folks?" Gil asked before taking another sip of his wine.

"Tomorrow night," Joseph said. "I'm not looking forward to it. I'm still stunned that her father is Senator Chase. She lives in such a simple, small house in a middle class residential area; I would have never guessed," he said, shaking his head.

Gil laughed.

Joseph gazed outside for a brief moment. The water glistened from the brilliant glare of the moon reflecting down upon it. He sipped more wine, noticing that Gil's mood had dampened.

Gil leaned forward near the candles in the center of the table. "Does Sasha know of your past?"

Joseph shook his head then glanced back out at the bay. "I've been afraid to tell her. I can't chance losing her, Gil. She's the best thing that's ever happened to me."

"She'll understand."

"But I'm so removed from my past; I don't want to ever think of it again."

"You should tell her before she learns another way."

Just then the two women appeared.

"What are you two talking so seriously about?" Sasha asked, kissing Joseph on the cheek.

"How beautiful the two of you are."

"Sure you were. What were you really talking about, Gil?" she asked.

"Taylor wants to open a Chevrolet dealership in New York City and has decided to put Joe in charge."

Sasha, surprised, said, "Why, Joe, that's wonderful. Why didn't you tell me?"

"Congratulations, Joe," Georgia said.

"Well, no congratulations yet; it's still in the works. It could take years before it's a reality."

The waiter arrived with their food and they ordered more wine. The salmon simmered in garlic butter, producing a delicious aroma. The French bread melted in their mouths.

They ate and laughed over dinner for two more hours. After Gil and Georgia said goodnight, Joseph and Sasha drove back to Sasha's place.

Sasha went into the kitchen while Joseph stood in her living room looking out at the sky. The window was slightly open; her green wool curtains blew in the cool breeze.

The room was small with cream carpet, white walls, a light green couch and chair, and two end tables with vases filled with beautiful yellow tulips that Joseph had bought for Sasha. A large, green fern plant stood tall in one corner of the room not far from the fireplace.

Sasha joined Joseph in the living room, carrying a tray with two cups of hot, steaming tea, a bowl of sugar, and a teaspoon.

"Do you want some help?" he asked.

"Please, I seem to be spilling water everywhere."

Grabbing the tray, he set it down on the end table next to the couch. She added a teaspoon of sugar to her tea, stirred the water, and then sat down on the chair next to the fireplace. Joseph grabbed a cup and stood next to her and blew into the cup to cool the tea.

"It's a beautiful night, isn't it?" Joseph said.

"Very."

Looking into her eyes, he knew something was on her mind. "What is it?"

She leaned back in her chair. "Why is it you never talk of your family?"

"Bad memories I guess."

She tilted her head. "What do you mean?"

He took a deep breath. "It's not important."

"I wish you felt comfortable sharing your life with me."

"It's not that, Sasha, it's just…"

"Just what?"

He hesitated. "My past is something I'm trying to forget."

"I've shared my life with you; why can't you share yours with me?"

Joseph knew the day would come when he'd have to tell her. He began to fidget. His hands grew sweaty while his heart pounded loudly. He felt chilled. He closed the window and sat down on the couch.

He held out his right arm, motioning for Sasha to come to him.

She grabbed her tea and sat next to Joseph on the couch.

She turned and looked in his face. He kept a firm grasp on her arm as he spoke to her.

Joseph told Sasha about his life on the farm in Italy. He spoke of his sister, mother, and father, and how close they were. He spoke of both fond memories and tragic ones.

He shared how his father had always favored him and that his brothers were jealous and hated him. He told her about traveling to America, how he'd met her in the museum, and how strangely his brothers acted when he returned to his hotel room. She hung onto every word he spoke. The rest of the terrible story spilled out.

When he said, "The police found thousands of dollars' worth of stolen jewelry in my bag," she gasped, clutching his hand. When he told her that two people had died in the robbery, tears spilled from her eyes. A bitter feeling of grief overtook Joseph. Choking off his words, Sasha gripped his hand tightly.

"I was sentenced to twenty-five years for a crime I didn't commit. I watched my entire life disappear before my eyes. I spent twelve years of my life in prison and almost didn't make it out alive. In the midst of it, God was with me. I saved the life of the warden's daughter and was given a full pardon."

By this time, tears were streaming down his face.

"And your father? Did you try to reach him?"

"I tried, but the letters I sent were returned. I had thought about going back to Italy when I was released, but had no money, and I didn't even know if my father was still alive. I met Taylor Parks on the ship over to America and again while in New York. I looked him up once I got out of prison. He gave me a job."

She pulled a handkerchief from her purse and handed it to him. He wiped the tears from his eyes.

"I don't know what to say. I'm so sorry. I can't imagine what life was like for you."

"No one but you and Gil know of my past."

"I won't say a word. I'm just so sorry."

"God has granted me a second chance. My past is gone and I have a new life. I changed my name from Joseph to Joe. I pray for my family and wish the best for them, but I've moved on. I never want to see my brothers again."

She hugged him.

He laughed nervously while wiping the tears from the corner of his eyes. "I wonder what your parents would say if they knew you were dating a Jewish boy who has spent twelve years in prison."

Looking directly into his eyes, she said, "God will restore all that was lost. I know he will."

She laid her head on Joseph's chest and they held each other.

The next day, Joseph paced back and forth in his apartment, thoughts racing through his mind. *What if her parents learn of my past? How will they feel about Sasha dating a working-class man?*

He looked at himself in the mirror one more time. *Well, God, if I ever needed you before, I need you tonight.*

Later, Joseph picked Sasha up and they made their way to her parents' home. Joseph slowly pulled into Senator Chase's driveway. Sasha got out of the car. Joseph gradually eased himself out.

His hands shaky and his nerves racing, he turned to Sasha apprehensively. Sasha grabbed Joseph by the hand and said, "Relax, he's only my dad."

Sasha rang the doorbell. Joseph took a deep breath and the door opened.

Dressed in an elegant brown, silk flapper dress and smelling of expensive perfume, Ellen said, "Darling, it's so good to see you."

Sasha hugged her and said, "Mother, this is Joe."

"Hello, Joe."

"Mrs. Chase," he said, nodding.

"Oh please, call me Ellen. Do come in."

"Good to see you again, son," Robert said, approaching the door.

"Hello, sir." He reached out and shook the senator's hand.

"Sasha speaks so highly of you," Ellen said. "Come in, come in. Dinner will be served in a few minutes."

A butler walked into the room. "Care for a drink?"

"Wine would be nice," Sasha said.

They moved into a large living room.

"Please have a seat," Ellen said.

Joseph sat on the beige couch next to Sasha. Ellen sat down on one of the chairs. Robert sat on the chair directly across from her.

The butler walked in carrying four glasses of Chardonnay on a silver platter.

Joseph lifted two glasses of wine off the tray. "Thank you."

He handed a glass to Sasha.

The butler handed a glass to Ellen, then Robert.

At first, the conversation focused on Ellen's charity work, the latest events at the country club, and her newest home decorating projects. Joseph listened and smiled. Ellen appeared strong and opinionated. She was the most sophisticated woman Joseph had ever known. He wondered if she'd ever worked a day in her life. She seemed polite and refined, but, from the occasional glances she gave, Joseph could tell she was evaluating him.

Ellen cleared her throat and took a sip of wine then set the glass down on the table next to her. "So tell me, Joe, what college did you attend?"

"I didn't go to college."

"Oh." She glanced at Robert.

"Unfortunately finances didn't allow it."

"I see," she said, frowning slightly, her chin raised high.

"How'd you work your way up in Taylor's business, son?" Robert asked.

"Lots of hard work and diligence, sir."

Sasha, pretending not to notice her mother's behavior said, "Mr. Parks wants to open a Chevrolet dealership in New York and has asked Joe to be in charge."

"You don't say," Robert said. "Well, congratulations."

"Thank you, sir."

Ellen peered at Joseph and asked, "So, tell us about your family."

"I'm from Italy. My father owned a farm. He was quite successful; we owned thirty acres of land."

"I see. So you're Italian." She sipped her wine.

"No, I'm actually Jewish."

She gasped. "Jewish!"

"Yes, ma'am."

She set the glass down, her eyes narrowed and her posture upright. She frowned, looking over at Robert. Just then the butler appeared. "Dinner is served."

During dinner, Joseph and Robert spoke of politics and the work at the shipping company while Sasha interjected at times. Ellen remained silent. After dinner, they sat in the living room and enjoyed chocolate mousse for dessert. Joseph noticed Ellen barely touched hers. From the occasional glares she gave, he could tell she didn't fully approve of him. Mr. Chase on the other hand, seemed quite the opposite—which brought tremendous relief.

Joseph set his dessert plate down on the glass table. "Sir, may I have a word with you?"

"Of course, will you ladies excuse us?"

The men stepped outside onto the veranda balcony. Joseph kept his hands in his pockets so Robert wouldn't see them shaking.

"What it is, Joe?"

"Sir, I know this is soon." He apprehensively glanced up at Senator Chase as tears gathered in his eyes. "I'm in love with your daughter. I would like to know if I can have her hand in marriage."

Mr. Chase smiled and said, "Son, I have to say, I've never seen my daughter so happy. You brought joy into her life for the first time in a very long time. Permission granted."

After breathing a sigh of relief, he shook hands with Robert. "Thank you, sir."

"I know you'll make my daughter very happy."

Joseph nodded. "I will."

Inside, Ellen had been hovering restlessly around the room.

"Honestly, Sasha, it's bad enough he has no breeding, no formal education; but a Jew? What will people think?"

Sasha answered shortly, "Mother, I don't care what people think. I love him and I would marry him tomorrow if he asked."

"Marriage!" she yelled. "Sasha, I simply won't have it. Why, you barely know the man."

"Mother, please calm down and watch your tone. You don't want the whole neighborhood to hear! Joe is a kind, wonderful man. You'll grow to love him once you get to know him."

"He's not of our caliber. I'll not have my daughter marry a Jew and that's all there is to it!"

Just then, Joseph and Robert entered the living room. Ellen quickly turned her head away.

"Well, Sasha, I guess we should be going."

"Yes, I have an early day at work tomorrow," she said.

Joseph watched as Sasha looked at her mother incredulously. Pretending not to notice Ellen's coldness he said, "Thank you again for a wonderful evening, Mrs. Chase."

She nodded and said, reserved, "Yes, you'll have to come back soon."

"Senator, have a good night."

"Likewise, Joe, you have a good night."

Sasha kissed her mother on the cheek, "Goodnight, Mother."

She kissed her father goodnight.

Driving back to Sasha's place, Joseph said, "I don't think your mother likes me."

"Don't worry; she'll learn to love you as I do." She ran her fingers through his hair.

Joseph walked her to her door. He took two deep breaths, gazing intently into her eyes. "Sasha, I have something to ask you."

"What is it?"

"I know we haven't known each other for very long, but I'm so in love with you. I want to spend the rest of my life with you."

He knelt down on one knee. Her eyes widened as she stood staring down at him with a big smile on her face.

"I asked your father's permission and now I'm asking yours."

He pulled a box from his pocket and opened it to reveal a stunning, round, five-carat diamond ring.

Her eyes widen and her jaw dropped before she screeched.

"Sasha, will you marry me?"

"Yes, of course I'll marry you."

He stood and took the ring out of the box and placed it on her finger. As she admired it, he picked her up and swung her around.

"You've made me the happiest man in the world."

The date was Saturday, May 12, 1923; after weeks of planning, the day of the wedding had arrived. Seventy guests were invited, among them... Taylor Parks.

Sasha stood in front of the mirror in a small room in the back of the church she and her parents attended, fixing her wedding veil. She wore a beautiful white wedding gown made of French taffeta and adorned with clear cut crystals and blush beads. It was embellished with diamond-shaped pearl accents. Her hair was tucked perfectly in a bun, and she wore a pearl necklace and pearl earrings.

Alena, her maid of honor, straightened the train on Sasha's dress and looked at her in the mirror. "You look like a princess," she said.

"Thank you."

"Sasha, I know you'll be very happy."

Sasha spoke to her friend's reflection in the mirror. "I know."

They embraced and Alena wiped the tears from her eyes with a small handkerchief she pulled from her purse.

Sasha, too excited to be nervous, sat smiling with her three bridesmaids who were dressed in long, deep red beautiful designer dresses, awaiting the time to march down the aisle.

Dressed in a black satin tuxedo with a small, white rose in the breast buttonhole, Joseph paced the oak floor in another small room toward the back of the church.

"Calm down, you're making me nervous," Gil said.

Gil was dressed in a black tux with a red rose in his coat button hole.

"I can't help it. I feel like any minute my heart is going to jump out of my chest."

He wiped a white handkerchief across his sweaty forehead. "This is the happiest day of my life; why am I so terrified?"

"Don't worry. It's normal. It'll be over soon enough," Gil said, laughing.

Glancing in the mirror, Joseph straightened his tie for the fourth time. Excited, he thought, *I'm marrying the girl of my dreams.* But all of the sudden, a feeling of sorrow ripped through his heart. Thoughts of his father and mother entered his mind.

I can't believe I'm getting married without them. I wish they could be here.

He stood staring in the mirror for several seconds.

"It's time," Gil said.

Joseph inhaled deeply and exhaled.

Joseph, Gil, and two other men who worked with Joseph—they'd been assisting with seating the guests—slowly strolling down the middle aisle of the church. Red roses hung on the end of each church pew. From the corner of his eyes, he watched the eyes of the people upon him. Joseph took his place next to the minister under a canopy of red roses, white tulips, and Gerbera white daisies.

Joseph peered over at Sasha's mother, who was sitting stiffly in her cream silk dress on the front pew. She appeared emotionless. She had kept her distance from him since the night he'd proposed.

Taylor and his wife were sitting in the fourth row.

The Lohengrin *Wedding March* began to play. There stood Sasha with her right arm wrapped around her father's arm. Joseph smiled broadly as he watched her move gracefully down the aisle.

Once she stood next to him, he whispered in her ear, "You look beautiful."

She said, "Thank you."

The ceremony lasted twenty minutes. At the reception, they danced and ate fabulous food—steak, shrimp, and pasta.

Joseph and Sasha decided to honeymoon in France. They stayed at an elegant hotel right on the beach for two weeks.

Joseph had hired two workers to move Sasha's things into his New York apartment. They enjoyed spending days decorating the apartment, nights eating by candlelight, and holding one another while they lay by the fireplace.

Joseph understood now what it meant for "the two to become one." Marrying Sasha made the past that he'd endured worth it.

The Thief

It was a warm, Wednesday morning in 1923. Jacob had just returned from his usual early morning, three-mile walk. The attention he'd paid to his physical health kept him in good shape.

He climbed the stairs and stepped onto the wooden balcony of his four-bedroom, two-story home. The house was made of oak, designed by Matthew, and built by Judah, Luke, and Matthew. It sat on twenty acres of land in the town of Jackson, right outside Kansas City, Missouri.

The winters were bitterly cold and the summers were hot with disastrous weather. They'd been hit with a tornado two years ago. The home was sturdy, so only the large red barn had been destroyed. Everyone had survived.

Rebecca and Dan lived in a small house two miles away. Samuel and Judah also had family homes, less than five miles away, while Luke, Matthew, and Benjamin lived with Jacob.

Jacob watched Judah, Luke, and Dan in the fields, picking corn and tomatoes. They grew an assortment of vegetables. Because the land was flat and the soil was rich, it brought a good crop. Though they were Jewish, they managed to find store owners who purchased their crops.

Matthew and Benjamin sauntered out of the barn covered in hay; they'd been feeding the horses and cattle.

Jacob walked through the front door and removed his dusty, brown old boots, shoving them to the side of the door. He passed the living room, where Samuel was going over financial reports, and entered the kitchen. It was smaller than the one in Italy, but it had running water.

Jacob reached up and grabbed a glass from the cabinet, filled it with water, drank, and refilled the glass.

"Father," Samuel said, standing in the doorway.

"What is it, Samuel?"

"I need your help."

Jacob took another large drink of water then followed Samuel into the living room.

Sitting on a chair next to the window, he said, "What is it?"

"There is a problem that requires your wisdom. I believe one of the men we have hired to assist with the harvest, Nathan, is stealing from us."

Jacob pushed back his chair, and rose. "How do you know this, Samuel?"

"Several weeks ago, I noticed money missing from the safe. I didn't pay much attention because I thought perhaps I miscounted the amount. Then it happened again. One day I walked into the far bedroom, where we keep the safe, and saw Nathan standing right next to it. When I asked him what he was doing, he said he was looking for Judah. Later, I learned that Judah's key to the safe was missing. I also learned that Marian, the housekeeper, and Nathan are involved. Marian carries his child."

Jacob moved to the window. Rubbing his right hand through his white beard, he said "We must know for sure if this is true."

"But how, Father?"

"Have you had the locks changed on the safe?"

"Yes."

"Good. If this is true, they must be brought to justice. How far along is the girl?"

"I believe no more than four months."

"I will not tolerate a thief on my land. Inform your brothers. We will discuss this tonight."

"Yes, Father."

After dinner, the men gathered in the living room. Judah, Matthew, and Luke sat on the green couch, and Jacob sat in a brown rocking chair. Dan, Benjamin, and Samuel stood eat to him.

"I say we confront them straight on," Samuel said.

"And what good will that do?" Judah said. "They will simply deny it."

"Judah is right," Jacob said. "We must catch them in the act."

"But how?" Samuel asked.

"I have an idea," Matthew said. "I had the basement built underneath the barn in case of an emergency. We can set a trap. We can stash money in the barn and catch Nathan in action."

"Yes, it's perfect, Father," Judah said. "We can use Benjamin as bait. Nathan will never expect it."

Luke jumped up from his chair. "I say the whole thing is idiotic! We must get the truth out of him, even if it means using force."

"Luke, why must everything lead to violence with you? Did I not raise you to use more wisdom in your decisions? Sit down, Luke, sit down." Jacob paused and then said, "We will set this trap."

The next day, Samuel and Nathan were out in the fields picking corn. Samuel lifted a basket filled with corn, and placed it near the barn. Nathan, only three feet away, also carried a full basket of corn.

Benjamin ran over to Samuel carrying a small wooden box with a lock. Trying to catch his breath he said, "Samuel, here, Father says to take this to the bank."

"What is it?"

"It's a large sum of money."

Samuel looked inside. The box held hundreds of dollars. Nathan stood next to Samuel and spilled a load of corn into a wheelbarrow. Samuel watched from the corner of his eye as Nathan eyed the money.

"I can't take it today. I have too much to do. Hide it in the barn in the usual place, and I'll take it to the bank in the morning."

"All right," Benjamin said, dashing off into the barn.

Around nine o'clock that night, Jacob and Samuel watched Nathan enter the barn through the back door, carrying a lantern. They carefully glanced through a window and watched him sweep past the cows and two horses. The windows were thin enough so they could hear everything. There were several wooden shelves on the back wall. He started looking for the box of money there. His eyes canvassed every shelf, but he found nothing.

"Nathan."

He gasped, fearful, then turned around. "You frightened me, Marian. Don't ever do that again!"

"I'm sorry. Did you find it?"

"Not yet."

Nathan climbed up an old ladder to the loft to search, while Marian continued to search below.

Jacob and Samuel continued to watch. Some twenty minutes later, Nathan found the small wooden box buried under a few stacks of wood with a small lock attached to it. He carried it back down the ladder.

He showed the box to Marian. She smiled. He spotted a metal bar next to the stable. Sliding the pole through the hasp, he levered it, groaning with effort until the lock finally broke.

He grabbed the money and fanned through it. "At last, our ship has come in."

Marian smiled.

"Let's go," he said.

Holding the money in his left hand, he grabbed Marian's hand with his right.

Suddenly, a hatch on the floor flew open and out climbed Benjamin, followed by Judah, Luke, and Matthew.

Nathan's jaw dropped.

"Your ship has come and gone," Judah said.

Jacob and Samuel entered through the front door of the barn, both carrying lanterns.

"I am ashamed of you, Nathan," Jacob said. "I trusted you"

"Well, what do you have to say for yourself, thief?" Luke said.

Nathan, unable to form words, stood silent. Marian's grip on him tightened.

Jacob turned to Samuel and said, "Go and call the police."

Before Samuel could leave, Nathan pulled a gun out of his pocket and pointed it at Jacob. Samuel gripped his father's arm.

"Nathan, don't do anything foolish," Jacob said.

"Move back, everyone," he said, firmly.

"Nathan, you will never get away with this," Samuel said.

"I've come too far now; I won't let anyone stop me."

"Why, Nathan, why?" Jacob asked. "We gave you everything."

"You gave me nothing!" he yelled. "Now get out of the way before I kill you, old man!"

Jacob and Samuel backed slowly out of the barn, followed by Judah, Matthew, Luke, and Benjamin.

"Marian, grab two of the horses."

"Nathan, let's forget it."

"Do as I say!" he yelled.

She unhitched two horses, saddled them, then led them outside.

Jacob watched from the corner of his eye, as Luke slowly moved toward Nathan. He prayed silently that Luke wouldn't do anything foolish. Nathan's focus was on Jacob and Marian. Luke slowly knelt down to the ground, picked up a small rock, and curled his fist around it.

Luke threw the rock, hitting Nathan between the eyes. Judah, who was closest to Nathan, kicked the gun out of his hand. Luke jumped onto Nathan. Nathan punched Luke in the face; he fell flat on his back. Judah and Matthew began to fight Nathan, wrestling him to the ground.

"Marian, grab the gun!" Nathan yelled.

Benjamin darted after the gun, but Marian reached it first. She picked it up and pointed it at Benjamin.

Breathing heavily, her hands shaking, she said, "Let him go, or I will kill Benjamin."

"Marian, please, think carefully about what you are doing," Jacob pleaded.

"Do as I say!" she yelled.

Judah and Matthew slowly moved over near Jacob and Samuel. Luke followed.

"Marian, put the gun down," Jacob said.

"No," yelled Nathan. "Give the gun to me, now!"

With her outstretched hand, she reached over to hand Nathan the gun. Suddenly, Benjamin kicked it from her hand and ran after it. He was reaching for it when he felt Nathan's strong arm gripped the gun. They wrestled for two seconds, but the gun went off before the others could help.

Jacob froze, terrified.

Both men remained still for several seconds, and then Benjamin slowly picked himself off the ground.

Jacob was breathing heavily. "My son, are you okay?"

"Yes, Father, I'm fine."

Jacob breathed a sigh of relief.

"Nathan, Nathan!" Marian screamed. She ran and knelt beside him.

Jacob peered down at Nathan; he had been shot in the heart.

"It just went off," Benjamin said.

"Samuel, call the police," Jacob said.

Samuel hurried into the house to call the police.

Twenty minutes later, the police arrived and then an ambulance appeared. Jacob watched as two drivers pulled a gurney from the truck and carried Nathan's body away.

The police questioned each of them concerning Marian and the death of Nathan. Jacob tried to appear calm and under control, but the tension and terror took its toll on him. He gasped to catch his breath. Samuel had to do most of the talking.

Marian was hustled away, weeping, into a car.

"They both got what they deserved, Father," Judah said.

"I know this, but it doesn't make it any easier. Well done, my sons, well done."

"Especially Benjamin," Judah said. "That was very brave."

"Yes, but you could have been hurt," Jacob said, sternly. "I couldn't bear to lose another son."

"God protected me, Father."

"Yes, young Benjamin did a courageous thing," Samuel said, grabbing Benjamin by the neck.

Jacob sighed. "Next time you will take the safe route, understood?"

"Yes, Father," he replied.

"Come; let's go back into the house."

The family went into town the next day to eat, celebrate, and give thanks to the Lord for his protection and justice.

The Promotion

After one year of marriage, Sasha, nine months pregnant, sat on the back porch of their home in upper Manhattan, her legs stretched out on a wicker chair. She took a giant bite of a grilled cheese sandwich and set it down on a small wooden table next to a bowl of melted vanilla ice cream. She bit into a dill pickle.

She leaned back and laid a wet towel across her forehead. The scorching heat of the summer months made the pregnancy difficult with frequent headaches, muscle cramps, and nausea. She laid her head back on the chair. Suddenly, the phone rang.

Slowly lifting herself off the chair, she strolled into the kitchen. Supporting her back with one hand, she picked up the phone with the other.

"Hello?"

"Any news? Is the baby coming yet?" Joseph asked.

"No, not yet; the baby will come when it's ready. How's work, darling?"

"Fine. Are you taking care of yourself and following the doctor's orders by staying off of your feet, Sasha?"

"I'm trying, but you know how hard it is. I'm not used to doing nothing."

"I won't have you working."

She smiled. "You mustn't worry, darling, I'll be fine."

"All right, I love you," he said.

"I love you too. What time will nm be home?"

"I've got a meeting at four; I'll try to be home around five thirty."

"Mother's planning to stop by and bring dinner, so try not to be too late. Goodbye."

Ellen and Sasha's relationship had been estranged for several months after Sasha married Joseph, but news of the baby weakened her disapproval of Joseph. She helped Sasha with preparing the nursery and often brought meals to the house.

Ellen was cordial to Joseph when she saw him, but Sasha knew deep down that her mother would never fully approve of him, but she didn't care. After a year of marriage, they were even more in love than they had been at the start.

Joseph worked later than he'd planned to that night. Taylor Parks had come down with pneumonia over the past month, so Joseph was taking on more responsibility. Although the job required long hours, he didn't mind. He loved his job, and business was good. He was strong, ambitious, and thrived on the challenge.

Parks Shipping Company had become one of the most sought after shipping companies in America, extending its services as far as China and Europe. They had recently set up a port in Barcelona, Spain. Sasha had traveled to Spain with Joseph over nine months earlier.

His days in Barcelona were spent meeting with prospective companies while his nights were spent with Sasha.

He smiled, remembering the wonderful time they had drinking Rioja wine, eating fine cheeses, breads, and Gazpacho soup; taking long walks in the Retiro Gardens and viewing countless statues, fountains, and monuments. Thinking about it now, he laughed to himself. *I wonder if our child was conceived on that trip.*

Joseph also worked fervently to get the Chevrolet dealership off the ground. He had numerous meetings with General Motors. He'd spent hours researching the automobile industry and studying their competitor, Ford Motor Company, and their financial structure, advertising, and marketing. He knew every detail involved in the planning and implementation of an automobile company, and vowed that his would be one of the strongest, most successful dealerships in America. The plan was for the dealership to be in place by January 1925, although Joseph knew realistically it would probably take longer.

Checking his watch, it was all ready seven thirty. Sasha would be angry. He'd been working a lot of late nights.

He drove through uptown Manhattan, pulled into their quiet, tree-lined, shady street, and arrived home at eight o'clock. He waved at the next-door neighbor, Willy, who was walking his large German shepherd. Willy enthusiastically waved back. He was a gentle old man, dressed in white pants and a black oversized shirt, with his belly bulging out and a baseball cap covering his white hair.

Joseph pulled up in the driveway of his two-story white home. The lawn was thick, green, the hedges perfectly trimmed. A large Eastern Red Oak tree was in the backyard.

He moved up the stairs onto the wrap-around porch, and entered the front door. He removed his shoes, sliding them behind the door on the vintage chestnut ebony hardwood floor. Sasha wasn't in the living room. He passed the staircase and found her in the dining room.

"Hello," he said.

She gave no response.

He stepped into the room. An expensive orange rug covered the floor. The table was perfectly arranged: a white linen table cloth, perfectly folded napkins, two of her mother's white china with gold trim, and two crystal wine glasses. Candles were lit and centered on the table.

"It looks nice," he said.

She nodded coldly.

"What's the occasion?" he asked.

She frowned. "I wanted to do something special tonight. You said you were coming home at five thirty. Mother came all this way with dinner."

"I'm sorry, Sasha. It's been busy, and I have a lot of work to do."

"You could have at least called, Joe."

"I know, and I'm sorry. It's just…"

"Your dinner is on the stove."

She stood up and threw her napkin on the table, not looking at him once, and stomped up the stairs.

Joseph shook his head and let out a large sigh. *I'll have to make it up to her*, he thought.

He moved to the rear of the house into the kitchen. On the stove was a plate with sliced ham, mashed potatoes, and green beans.

After eating, Joseph crept upstairs; everything was dark. Fumbling his way through the room, he changed his clothes and joined Sasha in bed. After an exhausting day, he fell fast asleep.

That night, while Joseph lay in bed, he had a dream.

A violently rotating column of air swept across America at an extreme speed; destroying homes, buildings, farms, and entire cities. Joseph was standing on a podium in a large coliseum, dressed in a robe of many colors, holding a gold scepter in his right hand.

Before him stood thousands of thin, frail, people seeking refuge from the storm. Many of them held their hands open, and Joseph began handing each one bundles of corn. Then, his brothers appeared before him and knelt down with their hands held out.

Suddenly, awakened by the sound of glass shattering, he leaped up. He glanced over at Sasha's empty side of the bed and yelled, "Is everything okay?"

"Just fine, I dropped a glass," she shouted from downstairs.

It was eight o'clock; the sun was shining bright through the light blue curtains. Joseph slipped into the bathroom. Troubled by the dream, he looked at himself in the mirror. The visions of the people and cities were disturbing, but why were his brothers in the dream? *What did it mean?* he wondered.

After a hot bath, he shaved and combed his hair. He entered the bright kitchen. The brilliant morning sun shone brightly through the yellow and green curtains that hung on the window.

"Good morning," he said.

"Good morning," she said, reserved.

She was sitting down at the white kitchen table next to the open window, her long hair blowing in the cool breeze. She was glancing at the paper; though he could tell her focus was elsewhere. She gently blew into a white china tea cup to cool the steaming herbal tea. Taking a sip, she set the cup down.

He bent and put his arms around her and kissed her. "I'm sorry, please forgive me. I'll make an effort to get home earlier, I promise."

She slightly smiled and nodded.

He went past the gas stove, opened the new refrigerator, and grabbed a jar of milk. He poured himself a glass and then sat down across from her. "How are you feeling?"

"Just fine."

Joseph paused. "I had a dream last night."

"You have many," she said.

"This one was different. It was similar to one I had many years ago when I was a boy, but worse. It was about the nation, and my brothers were in it."

She tilted her head. "Your brothers? What was the dream?"

"A great tornado came to America and destroyed homes and cities. So many people had been affected. I was in a coliseum, standing in the center of a stage. Thin and fragile people began to approach me. I began handing each of them food. Then, all of the sudden, my brothers appeared."

"All of them?" she asked.

"Yes."

"Even Benjamin?"

"Yes. They knelt before me with their hands held out. It was strange."

"What does it mean?"

"I believe God is giving us a warning. A crisis of enormous magnitude is coming to our nation and many families, homes, and businesses will be affected—possibly destroyed."

"What about your brothers?" she asked.

"I'm not sure why my brothers were in the dream. Perhaps a crisis is coming to them as well."

"Perhaps one day you will see them again."

"I wish to never see them again. To me, they no longer exist."

"Surely you haven't forgotten your family completely. What about Benjamin?"

"I hope my younger brother has become a man that I can be proud of. But that was a life of the past. You are my future." He placed his hand on her stomach. "And my child."

She smiled.

He stood up. "I should finish getting ready for work."

Joseph arrived at the office a little past eight wearing a tailored, plaid three-button sports jacket with vest, a deep brown tie, and plaid pants that were cuffed at the bottom. He made several phone calls, had meetings with suppliers, and finished two reports; he worked five hours straight.

At a little past one, he sat in his office eating a chicken salad sandwich. Mrs. Madison knocked on the door. "I'm sorry to bother you, but Mr. Parks' secretary's been trying to reach you. She says it's urgent."

"Thank you, I'll call her."

"Hello, this is Joe Abrams; you were trying to reach me?"

"Hello, Mr. Abrams. Mr. Parks would like to see you immediately."

"All right, I'll be right there."

Leaving his office he said, "Mrs. Madison, tell Gil to meet me at Parks' office."

"Yes, sir."

Joseph's assistant, Nelson Peterson, had gotten a new job as an office manager at Parks Baltimore Shipping Company, and Gil had replaced Peterson as Joseph's assistant manager.

Joseph felt vaguely uneasy about the nature of the summons. Did Taylor's health take a turn for the worse? Was there some problem with General Motors?

It took him twenty minutes to drive across town to the new luxury four-story building that Taylor had purchased two miles from Wall Street. He stepped out of the car. The sun was scorching. Joseph wiped his forehead with his sleeve and breathed deeply then entered the building. Taylor's secretary, a pretty brunette in her early thirties, was sitting behind a polished brown mahogany desk. She smiled once she saw Joseph. "You may go in, they're expecting you," she said in a gentle and polite voice. She pointed straight to the conference room next to Taylor's office.

He stepped in and twelve members of the board, including Taylor, were sitting around a large ebony conference table.

"Glad you could make it, Joe," Taylor said hoarsely. "Come in; please, have a seat."

Joseph sat at one of the chairs surrounding the large table.

"How are you feeling?" Joseph asked.

"Much better. Doc said I'm over the worst."

The room was stuffy, the air still, even though a window was open. The men were all dressed in suits and ties. Joseph studied them as they sat fixed and comfortable around the heavy table. There was some small talk; laughter came from Ralph Moore, the stout, blond board member in his late forties. Larry Jackson, who had thick gray sideburns, smiled, listening to Ralph.

Joseph looked toward John Beans, a large bald-headed man in his sixties. His piercing, deep green eyes were watching Joseph. John always wore a frown on his face. Joseph smiled; John turned his head.

Minutes later, Gil stepped into the office.

"I hope you don't mind, I've Gil asked to come."

"No, no, come; the more the better," Parks said.

Gil sat down right next to Joseph.

Parks began to cough. He rose up and motioned for his secretary to bring some water.

Setting it down in front of Parks, she said, "Mr. Parks, your wife called earlier."

"What'd she want?"

"I told her you were in a meeting, sir. She wanted to make sure you are taking your medication."

"Next time she calls, tell her to stop making such a fuss!" he shouted.

"Yes, sir." She slipped out, gently closing the door.

"I've asked you all here for a reason. Getting sick this past month has got me thinkin'. I'm not getting any younger and the wife has been buggin' me to do some more travelin'. I'm not plannin' on retirin' yet," he said, strongly. "However, I'm feeling like I need to retreat from much of the hands-on stuff. The business has grown, as you all know." He paused and took another drink of water.

"I've decided to appoint a vice president, someone who will be in charge of the whole operation—the shipping company and the Chevrolet dealership. He will be my appointed Chief of Operations, and the only person above him will be me. I need someone with integrity and confidence; someone that I can trust.

It takes a great deal of wisdom to run a business like this, and there's only one man I can think of who can do it."

Taylor stood and moved over to Joseph and smiled. He turned to the rest of the board and said, "That person is Joe."

Joseph's jaw dropped, his eyes widened. He looked at Gil and smiled. Gil shook his head.

Did he just say, vice president? Joseph thought to himself.

"Joe has proven his ability to lead and he is the only person I would trust with my business. I am giving Joe complete reign over this company."

Is this a dream or is this real? I can't believe what I'm hearing. I can't believe this is happening, thought Joseph.

"I don't know what to say," Joseph said, stunned.

"Say you'll take the job!" Taylor shouted.

Joseph laughed. "I'll take it."

"Good, Joe. This seventh day of July, 1924, you are officially the Vice President of Taylor Parks Shipping Company and the up and coming Chevrolet Automotive Dealership."

Taylor coughed several times.

"Are you all right ?" Joseph asked.

"I'm fine. The Board will brief you. I need to get home and get some rest.

We'll talk, son."

"Thank you."

Bill Edwards, a gray-haired man with an oval-shaped face, was the first to stand and shake Joseph's hand. "Congratulations, son, you deserve it."

The other board members gathered around him and shook hands.

Joseph and Gil left the conference room. Gil placed his hand gently across Joseph's shoulders. "Once again, God has shone down on you, Joe. I admire you."

Joseph was still shaking his head in disbelief. He chuckled. "I can't believe what just happened. I can't wait to tell my wife. Can I have a minute, Gil. I need to use the bathroom."

"All right." Gil sat down.

Joseph walked into the bathroom. He moved over to the mirror. Tears fell from his face. He glanced at himself for a few minutes. Then he slid down and sat in the corner of the bathroom. He looked up and said, "God. Thank you. You have been my rock. In the midst of my suffering, you never let me down. You got me out of prison. You gave me a job. You gave me an incredible woman, and soon, I'll be blessed with a wonderful child. And if that's not enough, now you've given me the promotion of a life time. Vice President? How...Why? I'm at a loss for words. I don't deserve all this."

Just than a scripture came to Joseph. One he had heard while attending church with Sasha. '*Blessed are the meek, for they shall inherit the earth. Blessed are those who hunger and thirst for righteousness for they shall be filled. Blessed are the merciful, for they shall be shown mercy, blessed are the pure in heart, for they shall see God.'*

He remembered the words of the Pastor. *'When you live a life pleasing to the Lord, he will bless you. Even in the midst of your test and your trails, when you remain steadfast, you will be blessed.*

He stood, grabbed a towel, ran some water from the sink, and washed his face. He said, God, I will continue to serve you all the days of my life. I won't let you down,"

When he entered the reception office, Taylor's secretary said, "Oh, Mr. Abrams. I have a message from your secretary. Your wife has gone into labor."

Frantic, Joseph began patting down his pant pockets. "Where are my keys? Where'd I park my car?"

"Calm down." Gil said. "I'll drive you to the hospital."

Gil drove as fast as he could. The whole way, Joseph's heart beat rapidly. He got nervous at every car pulling in front of them. "Isn't there a faster way?"

"I'll get you there as fast as I can, calm down; I know she's fine."

Joseph was breathing heavily, thinking the whole time. *I should have been there when she went into labor. I hope she's all right.*

Gil finally pulled up at Valley Memorial Hospital. Joseph jumped out of the car and rushed into the emergency department while Gil parked. He was directed to the Maternity Ward.

Running up to a nurse sitting behind the desk. he said, "I need to find my wife, Sasha Abrams."

Studying the chart, she said, "She's in room 244."

He darted down the hallway, praying she was okay. Looking at the room numbers on each door, he passed room 241, room 242, room 243, and finally arrived at room 244.

His heart was pounding as he stepped in. There Sasha lay smiling, holding a tiny, black-haired, brown-eyed, pink-faced baby in her arms. He knelt beside her, staring at the tiny infant in astonishment. He kissed Sasha on the forehead. "Are you all right?" his voice was soft.

"I've never been better," she said, smiling. "What shall we call our son?"

He paused. Rubbing the child's tiny forehead with the tip of his fingers, he said, "Justice shall be his name."

She smiled, "Hmm... Justice. It fits. Justice Robert Abrams."

He smiled, placing one of his fingers into the small hand of his son. "I pray my son will be wise and bring justice where injustices have been done." He smiled. "This is the happiest day of my life."

He stayed with her all night, leaving the room only to eat and use the bathroom.

She was released from the hospital a few days later.

The Stocks

Joseph stepped into the luxury four-story office building in uptown Manhattan with a view of Wall Street. He removed his long, black wool scarf and coat, and hung them on a shining bronze coat rack. It had been a bitterly cold winter. His face was chilled from the icy wind that had brushed up against it. He swiftly rubbed his frozen hands together to try and bring back the circulation. Despite the winter, things were good. Joseph earned a six figure income, and he and Sasha were blessed with another son, Caleb.

He straightened his button-down gray designer jacket and light blue tie. He glanced at the clock on the wall. The time was two twenty five. Christmas was only two days away and the work was piled on his desk.

The Chevrolet dealership was established as planned. By the end of 1927, Chevrolet as a whole was outselling Ford. The company stood tall as the manufacturer of some of the best American cars.

But Joseph knew the dreams God gave him about the coming crisis to America were true. A recession had begun. He'd saved thousands of dollars. He and Sasha purchased two abandoned warehouses, one located in midtown Manhattan, and the other near Brooklyn in a poor neighborhood. They'd planned to establish soup kitchens for the poor.

As he entered his office, his secretary motioned to him. "Sir, Mr. McDermott called and asked to move the meeting to Monday."

"All right."

"And your wife called. She wanted to remind you that you're dining with Senator Basin and his wife tonight, and that the time has been changed from eight to seven o'clock."

"Oh, and one more thing, there is a gentleman here to see you." She gestured towards the waiting room where a plump, gray-haired man looking to be in his late fifties who was slightly bald on top was sitting.

"Did he say what he wanted?"

"No, sir."

"All right, send him in and hold my calls please."

"Yes, sir."

Joseph stepped into his new office. "The polished mahogany desk glistened, as did the black leather chair sitting behind it. It was filled the most expensive furniture money could buy.

The gentleman stepped into Joseph's office.

"Thank you for agreeing to see me, Mr. Abrams." He shook Joseph's hand.

"You're welcome Mr…"

"Grant, Grant Bishop."

"Well, you're welcome, Mr. Bishop."

"Please, just call me Grant."

"Please, have a seat," Joseph said.

He sized up the large office. "Nice office you have here."

"Thank you. So what can I do for you, Grant?"

"It's actually what I can do for you. Since the end of World War I, there's been a growth of industry which has been unmatched by anything that came before. It's brought new comforts into people's lives," he said, glancing around Joseph's office. "What's even better is the impact it's had on the stock market. Under Coolidge, the stock market began its spectacular five-year rise. Now it's 1928, and the market is stronger than ever."

Grant talked for almost five minutes. Joseph, staring at his watch, said, "Mr…I mean Grant, I don't mean to interrupt you, but I've only got a few minutes."

"No, no, not at all. Let me get to the point. I've worked as a broker for the New York Stock Exchange for two years now; and, well, this American International Group has made a lot of money for a lot of people. We'd like for you to consider investing with us."

Joseph leaned back in his chair. "I've never been one to invest in the stock market. I'm not much of a gambler."

"Joe, I'm not asking you to gamble. This is an investment for you, your wife, and your kids. Why, for some of our clients, in just over two years, we've doubled, and in some cases, tripled their dollar value. The wealthiest of men in the nation invest in the stock market, even Parks. Someone like you could easily discern which investments would be a sure thing. Why, we'd all make more money with your wisdom."

Joseph smiled.

"Thank you, Grant. I'll give it some thought. I'm sorry I don't have more time to discuss this, but my wife and I are meeting some friends for dinner tonight; I need to get home."

"I understand." He stood up. "You've been very generous with your time." He shook Joseph's hand. "Give it some thought. You won't be sorry, Joe."

Joseph nodded.

After Grant left, Joseph pondered on the conversation. Joseph couldn't explain it, but a feeling mounted deep within him, causing him to think that the root of the disaster he felt coming soon come to America would be from the stock market.

He made two more calls and then headed home in his black Chevrolet series M Copper- Cooled model.

He pulled up to the mansion that he and Sasha moved into one year ago, ten miles north of Manhattan. The home sat on ten acres of land. It was built of beautiful golden-gray bricks and displayed the finest craftsmanship, including French doors and stained-glass windows.

The perfectly trimmed lawn was covered with snow. The back yard had tall oak trees and a playhouse for the kids.

He climbed five stairs and walked onto the icy brown stone. The patio was edged with plant bowls that were bear in the winter months. He shivered from the cold as he entered the house. He rubbed his hands together and blew on them to relieve the stiffness.

"Sasha!" He heard his voice echo from the high gable roof. He glanced up the white staircase covered with an expensive white rug.

The upper part of the house was given over to eight rooms: five bedrooms, including a master room, study, and a playroom for the children. The downstairs had a family room, dining room, kitchen, living room with a fireplace, and a large reception room for entertaining guests.

He'd taken only two steps when his oldest son, now four, flew into his arms. "Papa! Papa!"

Joseph picked him up and rubbed his fingers through his brown, wavy hair. Though Justice resembled Joseph as a boy, he'd inherited his deep brown eyes from Sasha.

"Were you a good boy today?"

"Yes!" he shouted, gripping Joseph by the neck.

Sasha entered the room carrying five month old Caleb.

Joseph smiled. Caleb looked just like Benjamin had as a baby—sandy hair, small face, and dashing smile.

"Hello, darling," she said. She gently kissed Joseph. "Senior Basin called and had to cancel dinner. His wife is feeling a little under the weather."

I'm sorry to hear that, but to be honest, I was looking forward to a nice evening at home."

"I put a roast in the oven. Dinner will be ready soon." Sasha went upstairs.

Joseph swung Justice around several times. "Let's go and get something to drink."

He whisked him into the kitchen onto the marble tile floors and rich-looking ebony cabinets. There were brand-new kitchen appliances: stove, refrigerator, and a sparkling white, and stainless porcelain sink.

Joseph poured them both a glass of water. He watched Justice slurp the water down, spilling half of it on the floor. He smiled. "Why don't you go upstairs and join your mother, and I'll be right up."

"Okay, Papa."

He dashed up the stairs.

Joseph took a towel and dried the floor.

Several hours later, after dinner, Joseph Justice a bedtime story. Caleb was fast asleep.

Sasha strolled down the stairs dressed in her nightgown. His eyes looked directly into hers. Even after five years of marriage, he was still awestruck by her.

Joseph joined her in the living room. They sat on the sofa, snuggled by the fire.

Joseph snuggled close to Sasha on the sofa, by the fireplace.

After several minutes, he asked, "Sasha, does your father own stock?"

"Of course," she said. "Why?"

"The dreams I've had. You know of the storm coming to the nation. I can't explain it, but I've sensed for some time now that the stock market will be the root."

"Well, Daddy's always invested; he's made a lot of money that way."

"I know it sounds odd, Sasha, but I'm concerned over this. It's a gamble."

"Daddy says, the stock market's a gamble only if you don't know how to use it to your advantage, He's invested his whole life."

"I think it's time he reconsider, Sasha. I feel strongly about this."

"I'll talk to him."

"Thank you. Did I tell you I loved you today."

"Yes, but I can never hear it enough. I love you too."

They sat for another hour before retiring for the evening.

The next morning Sasha rose early. It was Christmas Eve. Thy planned to attend church tht evening and then spend the remainder of the night at Sasha's parents' home. She strolled out of the bathroom. Joseph was buttoning his shirt.

"I can't believe you have to go into the office today," she said.

"It's only for a couple of hours."

"Remember, it's Christmas Eve. the children have prepared something special at the church."

"I won't forget."

"I don't want you staying late at the office."

Joseph frowned. He grabbed his tie and threw it around his neck. "Sasha, I said I'd be there on time. I need to finish up a few things."

"Okay, it's just that this night is important to the boys."

"I'll be there, I promise."

Joseph barely made it on time for the children's play. Sasha was a little annoyed but they had a wonderful evening. She was thankful to be with her family.

Christmas morning, Justice ripped opened the package of one of his Christmas presents. His face lit up when he saw the train station and toy railroad. Caleb sat in his high chair, apple sauce covering his mouth, giggling and banging the toy pony he'd received against the high chair.

Joseph bought Sasha a fifteen-carat diamond necklace from Tiffany's. Sasha bought Joseph a tailored black suit, a new tie, and gave him a quilt she'd spent a year making. He was more thrilled about his quilt than any other gift.

Robert and Ellen and a few close friends arrived at noon. They ate dinner at two o'clock. Sasha made grilled chicken, mashed potatoes, spinach salad, homemade bread, and lemon tart for dessert.

Robert wasn't feeling well, so he and Ellen left early. Sasha was concerned, but Joseph assured her he was fine.

As they sat in the living room eating lemon tart, the sound of beautiful voices came from outside. Sasha opened the door and nine Christmas carolers graced them with songs. They stood and listened. It was the perfect ending to a perfect night.

It was one of the best Christmases Joseph ever had.

The Great Depression

The date was Sunday, October 27, 1929. That evening, Joseph stood by the window in the living room, drinking a cup of hot tea. A pale moon shone, reflecting on the white snow covering the yard. Thousands of stars filled the sky. His eyes followed a shooting star soaring through the sky. He wondered where or if it would land. He sat down on a chair next to the fireplace, where the fire was burning bright and hot.

"Joe." Once again Sasha called out, "Joe."

"I'm in the living room," he said.

Sasha stepped into the living room and sat in the chair next to his.

"Are the children in bed?"

"Yes, I put them down fifteen minutes ago. Mother called. She and Daddy were listening to the radio earlier. The stocks have taken a significant turn for the worse."

Joseph took a deep breath. "I know; I read it in the newspaper. The market hasn't looked good for some time now, especially over the past three days."

She leaned forward. "Do you suppose it's happening, Joe? The dreams that God has given you…are they coming true?"

"I don't know, but we should prepare for the worst."

The next day, Monday morning, a ceiling of gray clouds covered the sky. Joseph had an early meeting at the shipping company. He entered the building and noticed several men huddled around the radio. He walked over to join them. "What is it?"

"Stock markets taken a horrible turn," Nelson Peterson said.

Joseph listened intently.

The radio announcer said, "Wall Street is feeling pretty restless, and that anxiety has extended to the rest of the country. Today, the losses have worsened. This is a crisis of historical magnitude. Thirteen million shares have changed hands. What a horrific day for the markets."

Joseph hung his coat up on the rack and slipped into a spare office near the rear of the building. Gil and Nelson followed.

"What do you make of it, Joe?" Gil asked.

Joseph set his briefcase down on the floor next to the desk, and then sat down. He took a deep breath and frowned. "It feels like a nightmare coming to life."

"These seven months of Hoover's administration have been the worst we've seen in years. More than half of all Americans are living in poverty," Gil said.

"I don't know that one man is to blame for what's happening," Joseph said.

"Construction's in a slump" Peterson said. "Not to mention the suffering this recession's put on businesses. I hear Chevrolet's the only automobile company that's making a profit. Everyone else's sales have declined."

Joseph stood. "We are heading into what appears to be one of the worst crises this nation has seen, and now is the time to use our resources. I have a feeling it's only going to get worse. One thing I do know for sure, gentlemen, is that this company has never been more prepared. We will do everything we can to help."

The company had begun an aggressive advertising strategy that helped Chevrolet to outsell their competitors almost three to one. The shipping company continued to expand under Joseph's leadership. Joseph had also saved hundreds of thousands of dollars and purchased double the supplies needed for the company for over three years and stored them in a large warehouse he'd bought.

He looked at Gil. "Call the board and set a meeting for four p.m. today."

"I'll get on it," Gil said.

"Nelson, get me last month's financial reports."

"Will do."

The next day was the most devastating day for the financial markets. Sixteen million shares changed hands and many could not find buyers. People were calling it "Black Tuesday."

A month had passed since the beginning of the financial crisis, and Joseph sat in his kitchen listening to the radio. "Henry Ford declared, on November, 4 1929, that things are better today than they were yesterday. A week later, Hoover said that any lack of confidence in the economic future of American enterprises is foolish. But here it is, mid-November and thirty billion dollars have disappeared; the same amount of money spent during World War I."

Sasha walked into the room and sat next to Joseph as he listened incredulously about the crisis upon the nation.

The radio announcer went on to say, "The collapse in stock prices has caused the president and all the business leaders to accept that the economy is in a profound depression of unimaginable consequences."

"Joe, what's going to happen?"

"I don't know, Sasha, but I fear we haven't seen the worst."

"The crash of the stock market has worsened. Daddy says the economy has all ready suffered severely."

"He's right; but if I'm interpreting the dreams God has given me correctly, the worst is yet to come, due to the poor policies created by the US government. Calvin Coolidge's administration favored business and the wealthy who invested in these businesses. When Coolidge signed that Revenue Act in 1926, it reduced federal income and inheritance taxes. In other words, the rich got richer and the poor got poorer. The economy's unstable and most people don't have enough money to satisfy their needs."

"Father has a meeting with the president next week."

"Good," Joseph responded. "I don't believe our political leaders have truly grasped the magnitude of this crisis."

He leaned forward with his elbows on his knees, held his head down, and ran both hands through his hair.

"What's going to happen?" Sasha asked.

He looked directly into Sasha's eyes. "The worst economic nightmare of American history is going to happen."

Six months later, many people had lost their jobs, businesses closed, salespeople had been fired, and factories cut their production. Joseph was determined to do everything he could to help.

He and Sasha turned one of the warehouses they'd purchased into a soup kitchen as they'd planned. The empty building was cold and damp, but Joseph hired a construction team who built a kitchen with running water and bathrooms, painted the building white, and put in concrete floors. Round tables and chairs, enough to seat two hundred people, were purchased.

It was Christmas Eve. Justice and Caleb were spending the night with their grandparents while Sasha assisted in the soup kitchen, serving food to the hungry.

Sasha's heart hurt as she looked from face to face. The people looked destitute, lifeless, fragile, and weak; for many, the meal they received at the soup kitchen once a day was their only meal.

Sasha glanced at a small girl who looked to be eight years old with a dirty face and curly hair, wearing wrinkled pants. Sasha walked over and sat down in the chair beside her. The young girl's face was reddened by the cold air coming into the building. Sasha removed the red scarf from her neck and wrapped it around the girl.

"Hello," Sasha said.

She quickly glanced at Sasha then turned her head. After several seconds of silence she shyly said, "Hi."

"What's your name?"

Another pause. "Clara."

"That's a lovely name. Where are your parents?"

The girl held her head low. After several seconds of silence, she said quietly, "My father died."

"I'm so sorry," Sasha said.

"My mother said she was going to look for work and she would be back for me soon. I was staying with my grandmother. She never came back."

Sasha shook her head as tears gathered in her eyes. Her stunned mind and emotions scrambled for something to say. "Are you here alone?"

She pointed with her slender, bony finger toward the feeding line. "No, my grandmother is over there in line for more food."

Sasha glanced over and saw a thin, white-haired woman hunched over—her wrinkled, frail hand gripping a scuffed up wooden cane. Sasha wondered how she could care for the girl. The woman looked as though she could barely support herself.

After a moment of silence, "I won the third-grade spelling bee. I got twenty-five cents," she said, smiling.

Sasha smiled. "That's wonderful."

Clara frowned. "But my grandmother took my twenty-five cents to buy food."

Sasha rubbed the little girl's back.

She looked across the table and there sat a frail man in his late sixties. His head was hanging down, his clothes were filthy. With his shaky hand, he lifted the fork filled with mashed potatoes to his mouth and slowly chewed his food. His eyes were bloodshot. Sasha knew he had nowhere to go. Her heart ached for these people. If only she could do more.

That night, she and Joseph decided to make the other building they'd purchased into a shelter to house the homeless. It would be big enough for two hundred beds. Joseph planned to begin work on the building once he returned to the office.

The next day, Sasha and Joseph spent Christmas Day serving meals at the soup kitchen: turkey, dressing, mashed potatoes, cranberry sauce, and pumpkin pie.

A few days later, Joseph was on his way out of the office when the phone rang.

Joseph received the news from his wife that Taylor Parks had passed away. Joseph fell silent at the tragic words. He sat staring, eyes wide and unable to form words.

After a moment of silence, his voice hoarse, he asked, "But how…when?"

"I just found out. The double pneumonia caused his heart to enlarge. He was hospitalized several hours ago and he just stopped breathing."

He took the news hard. In many ways, Taylor had been like a father to him.

The funeral was held three days later. There were over three hundred people in attendance: several politicians, businessmen, and well-respected leaders. Taylor was loved by many people. Tribute was paid to the successful businessman with a great sense of humor who had helped so many people.

Joseph spoke about Taylor. Tears streamed down his face as he remembered old times, like the day he first met Taylor on the ship as a boy, or the time he saw him in New York. He spoke about how Taylor gave him his first job. He owed him so much. After the funeral, everyone gathered at the Parks' mansion and told stories of their friend.

State of Relief

It was a warm day in April. Joseph joined two senators and the governor for lunch at a restaurant in uptown Manhattan to discuss the devastating effects of the past three years. The hardship brought on by the Depression had affected Americans deeply. President Herbert Hoover had underestimated the seriousness of the crisis, called it "a passing incident." Hoover did not think the federal government should offer relief to the poverty-stricken population, so many business executives had laid off workers.

Senator Sam Wilson took a drink of milk. The milk dripped into his thick, black beard. He wiped his mouth with his white linen napkin. "The president is considering making a major expansion of the national money supply. Let's hope it works. Unemployment's so high, poverty has actually become common," he said. "Can it get any worse?"

Joseph nodded.

Senator John Basin bit into a slice of French bread. "Hoover rejected a proposal to implement unemployment insurance. Instead, he offered the jobless 1.5 billion dollars in loans, and we know that plan failed. "

"It's a tragedy," the governor said. "Doctors have to treat patients for free, teachers work for charity—and what's Hoover doing about it? Absolutely nothing."

Joseph fixed his eyes carefully on the Governor. He had an oval-shaped head with thin, white hair, and eye glasses.

"I'll tell you one thing's for sure: Hoover won't be re-elected." He took a sip of cold tea. "That's why, gentleman…I plan to run for president," said the governor sternly.

Joseph leaned forward toward the center of the table, fascinated and attentive. "Excellent," said Basin,

"Yes, were glad to hear it," Wilson said.

"We need sound leadership and good ideas. And I'll tell you another thing; I need people beside me with integrity and who are committed to the needs of people." The governor turned toward Joseph. "That's why, Joe, I need your help to get into office."

Joseph, stunned, sat silent for a moment, his heart pounding with anticipation. "I'd be honored, Governor Roosevelt."

"Good, good."

Joseph felt Franklin D. Roosevelt was one of the strongest, most ambitious men he knew. Though he was confined to a wheel chair due to a crippling illness, it had proved to be no political problem. In his eyes, the governor personified greatness. Joseph felt the energetic governor was a leading progressive reformer and thought he would make an excellent president.

"First things first, I'll need someone to show the sympathetic side of me." Looking at Joseph, the governor said, "Got any suggestions?"

God give me the wisdom and the words to say, Joseph prayed. "Well, sir, I believe we can start by helping to provide aid to railroads, financial institutions, and businesses right here in New York City."

"I couldn't agree with you more, Joe."

"My wife and I have turned two of our abandoned warehouses into shelters for the poor. They also serve as soup kitchens,"

Joseph said. "I'd like to purchase more land to build several others. We've got more than 750 thousand New Yorkers reported to be dependent upon city relief. We can't help everyone, but we can make a difference in some of their lives."

"Good, Joe, good. I'll make sure you have the funds to do it. As of today, you are in charge of the State Relief Administration."

Joseph was elated. *I can't wait to tell Sasha.*

Back at the house, Sasha was in the kitchen preparing dinner. Her face was flushed from the hot stove. She turned on the facet, grabbed the lower portion of the white apron she was wearing, and slightly dipped it in the cold water. She then whipped it across her face to cool off.

Justice and Caleb sat close by, playing with toy cars.

She added a half a cup of milk to the mashed potatoes, stirred the peas, and added a little salt. As she was taking the pot roast out of the oven, the phone rang. "Hello," she said. "Mother…I'm having a hard time understanding you. Slow down, what is it?"

"It's your father…he's in the emergency department. They had to hospitalize him. I think it's his heart. I'm so scared, Sasha."

Sasha dropped the phone, grabbed Justice and Caleb, and ran out the door. She drove through midtown, past the Brooklyn Bridge, and arrived at Memorial Valley Hospital thirty minutes later.

She parked the car. Holding Caleb in one arm, and Justice's hand with the other, she flew through the doors of the emergency department.

By the time she got to the nurses' station, she was breathing heavily. "I'm looking for a patient, Robert Chase," she said, her voice quivering.

The nurse glanced down her chart. Sasha heard her name being called. She turned around and saw MaryAnn, the nurse she worked with years ago. MaryAnn gently placed her hands on Sasha's arms. "Your father had a heart attack."

Sasha felt a sinking feeling in her stomach. She covered her mouth with her hand as tears began to form in her eyes. "How… bad is it?"

"We don't know yet. I'll let you know as soon as I find out. Come with me, I'll take you to your mother."

Sasha followed MaryAnn down a long hallway into the small waiting room. Her mother sat with two balled-up tissues on her lap and holding a third in her slender fingers.

"Mother."

She ran to her and wrapped her arms around her. She held her tight for some time. They cried.

Her eyes were bloodshot. "He complained of shortness of breath and tightness around his chest. I'm so scared," said Ellen.

"Mother, everything will be okay. Mary Ann, is there a phone I can use?"

"Of course, come with me."

Sasha called Joseph's office twice, but his secretary was unable to locate him. Twenty minutes later she dialed the phone number for a third time with trembling hands, this time reaching him in his office. Her voice hoarse and quivering, she said, "Come quick…My father's had a heart attack."

Joseph arrived at the hospital twenty minutes later and was directed to the waiting room. Sasha flew into his arms.

"How is he?" he asked.

She lowered her chin to her chest. Tears gathered and fell down her face as she spoke. "We don't know."

Several hours had passed and still no word from the doctors.

"How about we take the kids to the cafeteria to get something to eat?" Joseph said.

She nodded.

"Can I bring you something, Mother?"

"No, I haven't an appetite. You go on, the kids must be famished."

"All right, we'll be right back."

Joseph grabbed sandwiches and milk. Sasha found it difficult to eat. She sat motionless, never flinching.

"Please, take a few bites," Joseph pleaded. "You'll need your strength."

Glancing at the plate in front of her, she lifted the turkey sandwich and took a small bite. She managed to take two more bites before moving the plate to the side.

Once the children finished eating, they went back to the waiting room.

Four long hours passed. Justice was asleep on a chair and Caleb slept in his father's arms. Sasha rested her head on Joseph's shoulder.

Finally the doctor walked in. Sasha and her mother leaped out of their seats. Joseph picked Caleb up and stood beside Sasha. He grabbed her hand.

"Will he be okay?" Sasha asked. She gripped Joseph's hand so tight his fingers turned white.

"Your father's heart attack was quite severe. However, he pulled through the operation."

"What does that mean?" Ellen asked, nervously.

"Well, he has a ways to go, but I see no reason why he won't fully recover."

Sasha breathed a sigh of relief. "Oh thank goodness." She hugged her mother.

"May we see him?" Ellen asked.

"Yes."

"Thank you, doctor."

"Joe, why don't you take the children home? I want to stay a bit longer with mother. I'll be along in a while."

"Okay."

Joseph carried Caleb in one arm and Justice in the other. He arrived home thirty minutes later and put the boys to bed. He made himself a cup of tea and sat in the living room waiting for Sasha to come home with more news.

Two hours later, Joseph heard Sasha pull into the driveway. He greeted her at the door. She'd spent an hour with her father, and then drove her mother home. Her father remained unconscious, but his condition was stable.

Joseph wanted to tell her about his meeting with Governor Roosevelt, but the time and mood didn't warrant such celebratory news. It had been a long and emotionally exhausting day, mentally and physically. They went straight to bed.

Regardless of how tired he was, Joseph lay awake for almost an hour, pondering on his new responsibilities. Joseph knew God had prepared him his whole life for this.

He remembered the words his father spoke to him before he boarded the ship to travel to America.

"The Lord has special plans for you, Joseph. You were chosen to do something great. You are a fruitful vine near a spring whose branches climb over a walls. Someday, Joseph, you will understand what those words mean."

Joseph smiled. *I understand, Father. I understand.*

Thirty minutes later, he drifted off to sleep.

Journey to Familiar Land

Jacob, Judah, and Samuel sat in the dining room of Jacob's home in Jackson, Missouri, discussing the family's financial situation. It was a cloudy, grim day in May of 1932. The past three years had brought tremendous hardship for the family.

Jacob took a sip of tea before studying the financial report in front of him.

"What are we going to do, Father?" Samuel asked.

Shaking his head, Jacob said, "I don't know. The situation worsens every day. We are in the worst drought in history. We've all ready been forced to lower the price of our crop—receiving only a fourth of its worth because merchants are stocking less in their stores. Sales are so low."

Judah's thirteen-year-old son, Jeremiah, ran into house. He flung the door back and dashed into the dining room. "Father, come quick!"

"What is it, Jeremiah?" Judah asked.

His voice shook. "One of the horses…it's not moving."

Judah leaped up from the table and followed his son with Samuel and Jacob not far behind. They walked into the barn where one of the beautiful chestnut ranch horses lay still on its side. Matthew knelt down beside the horse, rubbing its stomach.

"What's wrong with him?" Judah asked.

"It's been sick for two days now," Matthew said. "The horse is nearly dead." He looked up at Jacob. "I'll have to put him down."

Tears gathered in Jeremiah's eyes. He grabbed Judah's arm. "No, Father, please don't let him do it!"

"We have no choice; the animal is too sick."

Jeremiah knelt beside the horse and wept. Jacob's heart hurt when he saw the grief in his grandson's face.

Judah placed his arm on his son's back. "Jeremiah, let's go into the house."

"No, Father, please, I beg you!" He pushed his father's arm away.

Judah grabbed his son, dragging him out of the barn. "We have no choice." He pulled his weeping son into the house with Jacob and Samuel right behind him. They sat in the living room. Benjamin, who had been upstairs reading, joined them.

Five minutes later, a gun shot went off. Jeremiah leaped from his seat and ran upstairs.

Jacob shook his head. "What was wrong with the horse?"

"I believe it was a respiratory disease," Samuel said. "The animal has had a decreased appetite and nasal discharge for weeks. Since we've let go of all the workers, there's been no one to properly care for the animals. With our wives and children, we are forced to devote most of our time harvesting double the crops for less than half payment. We've all ready lost half of everything we own."

Luke came in through the back door. He and Judah's eldest son, Elijah, had just delivered a wagonload of corn, tomatoes, and wheat to the local store owner in town.

"Here you are, Father," Luke said. He handed Jacob forty dollars. Luke shook his head. "The crop was worth almost two hundred dollars and they gave us almost nothing! I wanted to walk away, but knew we needed the money."

Jacob rose to his feet and paced the living room floor. "The farmers' problems have become increasingly severe for everyone. We need to thank God that we haven't lost everything."

"But, Father, it's only a matter of time before we do," Judah said.

Samuel leaned forward on his elbows. "Judah is right. We have spent much of our savings and collected our insurance policies. My wife has had to sell some of her jewelry just to make ends meet."

"And what do you suggest we do?" Jacob asked.

"Many of the farmers have migrated to the cities," Luke said. "There are said to be jobs there."

"I have heard of the tales of the big cities," Jacob said. "Men waiting in dreary lines outside soup kitchen doors... unemployment has swept the country. If they can't make a living in the city, what makes you think we can?"

"But, Father, we must try," Luke said. "If we stay here any longer, we will lose everything. Even Benjamin cannot get a job."

"He's right, Father. A college education has no value here," Benjamin said.

Jacob paused. "I have heard that Congress is trying to pass an Agricultural Act to help support farmers."

"It may be years until it's in place—if ever," Luke said. "Besides, we cannot depend on that."

Jacob took a deep breath. "But how would we all live in the city?"

"We have an idea," Judah said. "Matthew, Samuel, Luke, Benjamin, and I will travel to New York to find work. We will work wherever jobs are available and send money home. Once the drought is over, we will return."

"But what if you cannot find jobs?" Jacob asked.

"Father, you always said God will be with us wherever we go," Benjamin said.

Jacob looked at Benjamin and Judah. "I will not allow Benjamin to travel."

"But, Father, he is the only one with a college education; perhaps he can find work where we can't," Judah said.

"No."

"But, Father, please," Benjamin said.

"I said 'No'! I will not take the chance and lose Benjamin as I lost Joseph. That is my final word. The four of you will go."

That night, Judah, Samuel, Luke, and Matthew packed their things.

The next morning, Jacob handed Judah money he had stored for emergencies. "Use this to survive until you find work," Jacob said. He laid his arm on Judah's shoulder. "Be careful. My prayers are with you."

"We will, Father. Don't worry, we will be fine," Judah said.

Rebecca and Dan drove them to the train by horse and carriage.

They traveled through Illinois, Kentucky, Indiana, Ohio, Pennsylvania, and finally arrived in New York. The train ride took longer than they'd expected. There was trouble with one of the tracks and the conductor had problems with people trying to get on the train for free.

A dreary, dark atmosphere covered the city. They walked in search of transportation to a hotel, along the way passing men sleeping on street corners and people lying on the sidewalk. They took a trolley to a hotel on the east side of lower Manhattan. They passed tarpaper shacks on the streets.

Judah shook his head. "This crisis has truly affected everyone."

The carriage stopped in front of a hotel in the eastern side of Manhattan. It was an old, dingy brick building. When they entered, it spelled of old cigars. A giant man sat behind the desk. He looked rough, but was gentle and kind when he spoke. After checking them in, he pointed to the discolored stairs behind them. They settled on the second floor of the hotel. Filthy curtains hung from the windows and the wooden floors and blankets were stained and dirty. The room smelled of urine, but it was cheap.

They ate dinner at a small restaurant four blocks up the road. Judah peered out onto the streets. Though it was late May, the clouds were gray and the mood was dim. "I feel as though I am in a ghost town."

Matthew nodded.

"I am haunted by thoughts of Joseph," Samuel said.

Silently, Luke drank his milk.

"It is difficult for all of us, but our focus must be elsewhere," Judah said. "What happened to our brother was a long time ago. We cannot change our past, but we must secure our future."

"He's right," Luke said. "There must be no more mention of Joseph."

"We will grab a newspaper on the way back to the room and begin our search tomorrow," Judah said.

Jobs were scarce; there were few options. The Electric Company, Con Edison, and the lumber mill were hiring a few men. Judah and Luke went to apply at the electric company, while Samuel and Matthew went to the lumber mill.

Samuel and Matthew arrived at nine. They stared, stunned. There must have been over five hundred men in line, though only seven jobs were available.

Sweat dripped from Matthew's forehead. His shirt was drenched. "I can't believe my eyes. I knew the situation was bad, but this I can't comprehend."

Discouraged and exhausted, they had walked almost five miles to get there.

Samuel said, "Let's go. We will be wasting our time here."

Judah and Luke encountered the same at the lumber mill. There were two hundred men in line for four jobs.

Judah tried to remain strong, but he knew that this would be a far greater challenge than they'd imagined.

Several miles away, Joseph was in a large seven-story, abandoned hotel, meeting with Gil, Sam Matthews, the manager of a construction company, and his assistant, Greg Stevens.

They were discussing the expansion of the homeless-shelter project. As the crisis grew, the rescue programs Joseph had established multiplied.

Joseph, Gil, Sam, and Greg climbed the steps to the third floor. Staring at the filthy, grim building, Sam said, "It needs quite a bit of work, but it's got potential, Joe. What are the plans?"

"I plan to restore four buildings to be used for shelters. Three others will be located in Brooklyn, Harlem, and New Jersey. One of the buildings, like this one, is an abandoned hotel, and two were old warehouses used to store furniture. They are big enough to hold 150 to 250 beds. I also want kitchens built in each building."

"How many men you think it'd take to complete this?" Gil asked.

Gil had been promoted to one of the managers at the Manhattan Shipping Company and oversaw foreign trade. He also helped Joseph with the relief efforts in the state of New York.

Sam rubbed his fingers through his brown hair. "I haven't seen the other buildings, but if they're anything like this one, I'd say about two hundred men. That's the only way we'd have it done by the end of July. I'd put fifty men on each project."

"I'd like the work to begin in two weeks. I want Gil to oversee the hiring of the men," Joseph said.

Sam nodded.

Joseph finished the meeting at half past three. He had plans to meet Sasha and the boys at her parents' house for dinner.

He slid behind the steering wheel of his car. He started the engine then headed east. The drive to Sasha's parents' house was long and hot. Thoughts filled his mind; there was much to do.

Although foreign trade was down, Parks Shipping Company shipped cargo to more than three hundred ports because the company had increased the types of cargo they delivered: mainly automotive parts.

The Chevrolet dealership was growing. The business continued to act as though there were nothing wrong, and that the public had money to spend. Joseph didn't wait for public demand for their products to rise; he created that demand even during the most difficult of times.

Joseph appointed Peterson, Gil, and two board members, Al and Jim, to run the companies, allowing him to devote more time to the relief efforts. He continued to attend regular weekly meetings and stayed involved in the major decision making.

After dinner, the boys spent the night with their grandparents while Joseph and Sasha went home.

Sasha noticed Joseph had passed the exit to their home. "Where are you going?"

"I thought we'd go for a drive," he said.

It was six thirty and the sun was still shining bright. They put the windows down and let the hot air blow into the car. Joseph turned left on Second Street, and then took a right on Brooklyn Boulevard.

Sasha peered out the window and saw small shacks that looked like torn tents alongside the sidewalk. She saw a family living in their car. One man lay on a ragged blanket on the hot cement. She shook her head. Her heart ached for the people. But she felt some hope thinking of the additional shelters Joseph was building. They would provide many people with a roof over their heads and food.

Sasha had found time to assist in the shelters. She used her nursing skills to provide much needed medical care. She solicited help from two doctors from Valley Memorial who provided first aid, gave immunizations, and distributed medications.

Joseph drove for two more miles down lower east part of Manhattan. Children played in abandoned parks. Two black children, about eight-years-old, were walking past the park, barefoot on the hot sidewalk. African Americans' jobs were often taken away from them and given to Whites, so many of their children suffered the worst.

Sasha planned to meet with Eleanor Roosevelt and a few of the senators' wives to champion for Black rights by creating a bill to stop the prohibited discrimination. During a past meeting, Eleanor shared how she felt the bill had a greater chance of passing once her husband got elected president, but she was determined to begin the process now.

"Joe, so many of the children are malnourished and they have no shoes to walk to school. They look ill and weak. I want to begin a lunch program in the schools. I'd also like to purchase shoes to give away at one of the warehouses."

"I like the idea, Sasha."

"God would be pleased; don't you think, Joe?"

Joseph smiled, "Yes, very."

Joseph Faces His Past

Three weeks flew by; Judah, Samuel, Luke, and Matthew sat in their hot and humid hotel room—jobless. Though the sun was shining bright, it was a grim and dark Tuesday morning.

With enough money to last two more weeks, Judah, desperate and discouraged, picked up the paper, praying for a glimmer of hope. After an uninterested first glance, he threw the paper down. "It's useless. We've read the paper for days now and still nothing."

Matthew, who was standing by the window watching the people stroll by, picked up the paper and sat on the edge of the bed as he fanned through the pages.

Luke lay on the bed resting, while Samuel sat on the other bed reading a letter from their father. "Father asked how things are. He asked if we have found employment. What should we tell him?"

Luke leaned on his elbow. "The truth; that we failed."

"No," Judah said sternly. "We will do no such thing. We will continue to search until we find something."

Samuel frowned. "And when will that be? There are no jobs to be found. We've searched the whole city. What is there left to do?"

"We've come a long way and we cannot fail," Judah said, firmly.

Matthew was staring at the newspaper in his hand. He jumped to his feet. "We may be onto something. It says here that Parks Shipping Company is hiring two hundred men to assist with the construction of four abandoned buildings.

Once completed, the buildings will be used for shelters to house the homeless."

"Yes; and there will be ten thousand men applying!" Luke yelled.

"Then we will simply get there first. We have the skills. Maybe one, if not two of us, will get a job," Matthew said.

"Let me see that." Judah grabbed the paper from Matthew.

"It also says they're opening a shelter downtown and that they provide food twice a day. I say we check out of the hotel and go to the shelter. We can save what little money we have left," Matthew said. "What other choice do we have?"

Samuel rubbed his hand through his beard. "I agree, let's check out of the hotel first thing in the morning."

Judah laid the newspaper down. "We will go now. The paper said the shelter is due to open first thing in the morning. The line for the shelter probably out numbers the lines for jobs."

"He's right," Matthew said. "We should check out tonight."

They packed and took a trolley to the corner of Fourth and Broadway. It was only noon and one hundred people were already in line.

The next day by five a.m., over seven hundred people stood in line. The first two hundred were allowed to enter.

They stepped into the large warehouse-like shelter. Judah peered around the room; white walls, wooden floors, hundreds of beds, and white sheets and a pillow on each seemed inviting considering the circumstances. Toward the rear of the building was a simple but clean kitchen. Judah could see people towards the back preparing the food.

A tall, heavyset man with dark brown, wayward hair directed the men to the far side of the room. They placed their things on the beds. They were told that the first meal was served at eleven and the second at four.

The shipping yard was two miles away and was scheduled to begin recruiting Thursday morning.

The men took turns standing in line at the shipping yard. Judah and Luke stood for four hours, followed by Matthew and Samuel. By five o'clock Thursday morning, all four were in line with only twenty men in front of them.

The next morning, Joseph arranged to meet with Nelson and Gil at the shipping yard to discuss the hiring process. He promised Sasha he'd be finished in time to attend Justice's nine o'clock piano recital.

He stepped into the building. Gil's office was located on the main floor right next to Peterson's office. There was a spare office located near the back of the room that Joseph occupied when he made visits.

They met in Gil's office. Gil laid out the plans and Joseph studied them carefully. He flipped the page which listed the specific needs: painters, builders, and appliance specialists. Fifty men would be assigned to each building.

The meeting lasted one and a half hours. Joseph folded the papers and handed them to Gil, giving Gil the okay to move ahead.

He then stepped into the rear office, grabbed his hat, threw his tailored plaid jacket over his shoulders, and looked down at his watch. At eight thirty, he turned off the light and headed outside.

He squinted from the sizzling sun blaring down on his face. There were hundreds of men lined up outside. Joseph shook his head realizing that, for many, this might be their last hope.

He pulled his car keys out of his pants and shot another quick glance at the line. He hesitated at first, and then moved closer to the line. Staring at four men in line, he thought, *Is my vision playing tricks on me?*

He took five more steps. His heart began to beat rapidly; it was eighty degrees, but his body felt chilled. Joseph turned around and stormed back into the building, passing Gil who was talking to the assistant. He went into the rear office and slammed the door shut.

Joseph tried to comprehend what was happening. He fidgeted, pacing the floor. *Was it really them?* he thought. *How?* He felt sick to his stomach. He leaned up against the door. Tears began to stream down his face. Sorrow, grief, and rage engulfed him.

A knock at the door. Joseph didn't respond.

Another knock. This time Gil said, "Joe, you okay?" He tried to enter, but Joseph's body was blocking the door.

Again, he asked, "Is everything all right?"

Finally, Joseph opened the door. He wiped the tears from his eyes and sat down on the chair next to the desk. His body was shaking.

"What's wrong?" Gil asked.

Joseph, unable to form words at first, sat silent. Finally, his voice shivering, he said, "I…I saw them."

"Saw who?"

"My….brothers."

"Where? When? How?" Gil asked.

"They are standing in line."

"Are you sure it was them?"

"Yes. There was a man—it looked like my brother Matthew, so I decided to get a closer look. It was him and the rest of my brothers. After all of these years…I can't believe this is happening. Is God punishing me?" He began to weep uncontrollably.

Gil placed his arm around Joseph's shoulders.

Once Joseph regained his composure, Gil asked, "What are you going to do?"

"I don't know."

"Did they recognize you?"

Joseph leaned forward on his elbows. "I can't be sure." A moment of silence. "Bring them here. Take the four of them into your office for a private interview."

"You'll need to point them out to me."

Joseph and Gil stepped outside. Joseph pointed to a man with a light blue shirt, wavy blond hair, and sun-darkened skin. Next to him was a man five feet five inches tall with thick, black hair, a black mustache, and a clipped beard. He pointed to the two standing right behind them.

Gil went to where the four were standing. He motioned for them to follow him. He brought them into his office.

Ten minutes later, Joseph prepared himself to enter the room. He listened quietly as Gil questioned the men regarding their background.

I wonder if they'll recognize me. My appearance has changed, especially after the surgery in prison. It altered my looks.

He hesitated at first, and then he opened the door.

"This is Joe Abrams, the head of the company," Gil said.

Judah nodded, while the others stood still.

They don't recognize me, he thought.

Joseph studied each of his brothers. Judah's appearance was that of someone slightly weathered; he looked as though he'd suffered hard times. He was thinner, his hair gray and black, and his face lined. Matthew maintained his handsome features; his shoulders had broadened, and his hands were callused. Samuel was still large and well built; now, though, with streaks of gray lining his brown hair, and his face was aged and worn. Luke looked the same; his hair was longer and he'd grown a mustache.

"Who are you?" Joseph asked.

"We've traveled a long way to seek employment," Judah said. "We heard there are greater opportunities for work in New York."

"Where are you from?" The men spoke with a strong Italian accent. After years in America, Joseph had learned to speak without his accent.

"We are originally from Italy, but traveled to America with our families," Samuel said.

"Are you brothers?"

"Yes," Judah said.

"Is it just the four of you?" Joseph asked.

"Yes," Judah said, "and our younger brother, Benjamin."

"Is your father still living?"

"Yes, we own a farm outside of Kansas City, in a city called Jackson," Samuel said.

So my father is still alive, Joseph thought. "What about your mother?"

"Our mother died when we were young and our stepmother died many years ago in Italy."

Joseph felt as though a knife entered his heart. "Excuse me," he said.

He hurriedly walked out of the office into the bathroom stall and wept. He covered his mouth with his hand to hold back his moans.

Minutes later, he went to the sink, washed his face, pulled a napkin out the cabinet, and wiped his face dry.

He felt the rage within him draining the color of his face. He stormed back into the office. "Why did you really come to New York?" Joseph barked.

"We told you," Judah said. "We came to find temporary work to help save our farm."

"How can I be assured you are who you say you are?"

"Why would we lie?" Samuel said.

"We have heard of spies coming from Europe."

Luke laughed.

Joseph frowned. "I should have you all arrested!"

"On what charge!" Luke yelled, jumping out of his seat. "We've done nothing wrong!"

"Then prove it," Joseph said. "Bring your younger brother here."

"We cannot, our little brother is needed on the farm," Judah said.

Joseph's anger intensified every moment he was with them. With his outstretched arm, Joseph pointed at Luke. "I will have this one arrested until you can prove your story." His anger burned greatest for Luke. He flashbacked to Luke sitting on the witness stand many years ago when he was on trial for robbery and murder; Luke's testimony had been the most damaging.

"Our families are depending on us, we could lose our farm," Judah pleaded. Joseph paused. "Bring your brother back to me, and then I will give you all jobs." Glaring at Luke, he added, "This one will stay."

"We will bring back our brother, with one request. I will ask that Matthew also remain," Judah said. "We are short on funds and cannot afford for all us to make the trip home."

Joseph peered at Matthew. "All right."

Joseph had Luke taken into the police station for questioning. He hated Luke. But after several hours, he was released. There wasn't significant cause to detain him. Joseph's decency allowed him to make sure Luke and Matthew were provided with food and a roof over their heads at one of the shelters.

That night, Joseph sat at the dining table. He rubbed his temples with both hands and stared at the floor.

Why, God why? he thought. *Why would you torment me forcing me to see my brothers once again?*

Sasha entered the room and sat beside him.

"What are you going to do?"

"I don't know; I'm torn. I'm afraid my anger got the best of me and I had Luke arrested. I felt so much rage."

"Anyone would feel the same," she said. "We should take the next train to see your father."

"It's not that simple, Sasha." He leaned forward, placing his elbows on the table.

"Your father would be proud of the man you've become—all that you've done."

"I want desperately to see my father, but I can't just show up at his farm twenty-five years later—after he's thought I was dead all of these years. I fear it would destroy him. I can't just pick up where I left off."

"In time, I'm sure he would forgive your brothers," Sasha said.

"I do wonder what kind of man Benjamin has become."

"That's right, he was only a small child when you left home."

"I pray he has turned out to be the good man."

"I'm sure young Benjamin has become a kind and sensitive man, just like his older brother," Sasha said. She rubbed her hand through Joseph's hair.

He let out a sigh. "Only time will tell."

"What do you mean?"

"I demanded my older brothers bring Benjamin to me. I had to see him."

"I can't wait to see him," she said. "Actually, I can't wait to meet all of your brothers. I want to thank them."

Joseph laughed. "For what?"

"I married the most wonderful man on earth, and it's all due to your brothers. God took your misfortune and turned it into my fortune."

He smiled and wrapped his arm around her. "You are a peculiar one."

"No, just very blessed."

They went to bed at nine. Sasha fell asleep. Joseph tossed and turned all night. Thoughts flooded his mind. *What brought them to America? Is my father well?* His heart urged him to take a train the next day, but his head said to wait.

After two hours, he fell asleep.

Benjamin's Journey

It was Thursday morning. Judah and Samuel had been on the stuffy and humid train for over a day, which seemed like one week.

Judah looked out the window and watched cows grazing in miles of fields. He was dreading the conversation he would soon have with his father and the look he expected to see on his face. He'd rehearsed the words over and over. It would be a difficult task to convince his father to allow Benjamin to travel to New York.

After what seemed like an eternity, they finally arrived in Jackson, Missouri. They had arranged to have Rebecca's husband, Dan, pick them up. Jacob didn't know they were coming home.

They drove to Jacob's house in Dan's horse and carriage. Jacob was sitting on the balcony, drinking iced tea. He peered up and saw the men approaching.

Jacob stood when Judah and Samuel stepped out of the carriage. He strode down the stairs, his cane in one hand, holding the wooden rail with the other.

Jacob hugged Judah and Samuel. "Where are the others?" He asked.

Judah hung his head. He hesitated, and then told his father that they were still in New York.

Jacob frowned. "Why would you leave your brothers? What happened?"

Samuel suggested that they step into the house and out of the hot sun in order to explain what happened.

They told Jacob of the man they'd met in New York City and how he'd accused them of being spies from Europe. The man demanded they bring their younger brother back with them to prove their story. Then, he would grant each of them jobs.

Jacob rose to his feet. He insisted they return at once and bring back their brothers. Judah reminded his father of the hardship they'd seen, and told him that things would only get worse. All of them had been assured employment, which would help to save the farm.

Jacob yelled, "How could you do such a thing? To leave your brothers behind in a foreign city and travel without them! That city has brought me nothing but grief! I demand you return and bring back Matthew and Luke!"

"Father, we must return with Benjamin, otherwise we are doomed," Judah pleaded.

"How can I be assured that Benjamin will be returned safely?"

"We will guard him with our lives, Father," Judah said. "I promise; no harm will come to him. We are only there to earn enough money to save the farm. Then we will return."

"Father, I beg you to reconsider," Samuel said.

Jacob stood still for several seconds. He glanced out the window and saw his grandchildren playing in the fields. He knew in his heart that times would only get worse. The farm might have to be sold. *What other choice do I have?* he thought.

With apprehension, he agreed to allow Benjamin to go.

That night, they ate dinner together. At eight a.m. the next day, Judah, Samuel, and Benjamin caught the next train to New York.

They arrived on Thursday at nine a.m. They rode a trolley to the shipping company where Luke and Matthew were waiting for them. Peterson escorted Judah, Samuel, and Benjamin to the office where they waited. The men embraced each other.

Gil called Joseph. Joseph left his downtown office and drove to the shipping yard.

Joseph went in the front door, and started down the long hallway to the office where his brothers waited. He stepped in and his eyes went straight to Benjamin.

"This is our youngest brother, Benjamin," Judah said.

Benjamin's shirt was tucked loosely into faded black pants. The young man had broad shoulders and sandy brown hair.

He's so big and so handsome. He'd be twenty-six now, Joseph thought.

Joseph's mind wandered back to the little boy he'd held in his arms before leaving for America. He smiled and shook Benjamin's hand. "It's nice to meet you."

"You too," Benjamin said. He seemed surprised by the welcome.

Joseph's brothers were standing. He gestured toward five chairs, side by side, near the window.

"Please, sit down," Joseph said.

Joseph felt tightness in his throat. He gasped for air. He needed water. Excusing himself, he left the office and hurried to a small kitchen at the end of the hall. He grabbed a glass from the cupboard and filled it, drinking intensely.

Joseph was deeply moved by the sight of his younger brother. Tears began to fill his eyes. He wanted to take Ben's hand and tell him he missed him, and hold him in his arms. He wiped his face on his shirt sleeve and gulped the rest of the water down. He then returned to his brothers.

Sweeping past the others, he went straight to Benjamin. "Would you like something to drink? Coffee, tea, water?"

"Yes please. Water would be nice," Benjamin said.

Joseph motioned to Peterson, "Have an assistant bring water for everyone."

Peterson left the office.

Looking at Benjamin, he asked, "How is your father?"

"He's well."

"And your farm?"

"We are still struggling, but we are survivors," Benjamin said. "Thank you for asking."

Joseph felt a strong connection to Benjamin.

Minutes later, a petite, brown-haired woman entered the office carrying a tray with five glasses and of water. She laid the try on a small side table. As she turned to leave, Joseph asked her to send in Gil.

Gil came to the door.

"See that they're provided with food and a place to stay," Joseph said.

Gil nodded.

Joseph shot a glance at each of the men before speaking directly to Judah. "Be here tomorrow at eight a.m."

"We will, and thank you," Judah said.

Joseph nodded.

Joseph left work early. He sat on the back porch in the rear of the house, gazing out into the yard.

Sasha arrived home after picking the children up from her mother's house. She called, "Joe, are you here?"

"I'm out back," he said.

She peeked out the door. "I'm going to get the kids some milk and cookies. Would you like anything?"

"No, thank you," he said quietly.

Fifteen minutes later, she strode over to him and sat on a wicker chair beside his.

"Joe, what are you doing home so early?"

"I felt like taking the rest of the day off."

"I'm dying to know, did you see Benjamin?"

"Yes, Judah and Samuel returned with him, just as I asked."

"How did it go?"

"He's grown into a fine young man. He's bright and appears to be well mannered—everything I had hoped he would be."

"That's wonderful," she said, smiling.

She reached for his hand and squeezed it. "Joe, when are you going to tell them? Especially Benjamin. The sooner they know the truth, the sooner you can be reunited with your father."

He didn't answer. He stood and walked to edge of the porch and leaned against the post. After a long silence, he said, "I'm going for a walk…I'll be back."

"Don't be long," she said.

He walked through towers of trees and headed into a field, strolling through thousands of wildflowers. He'd thought the fresh air would help clear his mind, but after half an hour, it hadn't helped.

Joseph passed a lake. Two fishermen dressed in overalls were sitting on a rock, fishing. He flashed back to a time when he and his father had gone fishing in the Nera River in Italy, surrounded by the woodland hills; he'd remembered catching his first fish that day.

He continued to walk, passing houses on hilly green grass. His feet began to ache; the hot sun beamed down on him. He was thirsty, but four words consumed his mind: *What should I do?*

After spending time with Benjamin, he didn't want to lose him again.

Still undecided, he made his way home.

Joseph skipped dinner that night. He spent the whole night tossing and turning. He thought long and hard. Finally, it came to him.

A New Day

The next day, Joseph left for the office at six a.m.

He flipped through the pages of a financial report from the Chevrolet dealership and made three calls, two to domestic companies in South Carolina and Florida, and one to a company in France. A cargo of Chevrolet car parts had been shipped to three companies, and he called to check on the shipments.

Joseph had telephoned Gil earlier to have a driver pick up his brothers up and bring them to his office. He also told Gil to meet him in his office at eight thirty with Peterson.

He paced his office floor, thoughts racing through his mind the entire time. *This isn't going to be easy. My emotions have to be intact.*

His brothers were brought to the luxurious office two blocks from Wall Street. Joseph realized the importance of the moment; he needed to stay calm, straight faced. "I hope your stay at the hotel was decent."

"Yes, thank you again," Samuel said.

"You have a very nice office," Matthew said.

"Thank you. Have a seat, gentlemen."

There were five chairs next to his desk. Luke pulled off his brown cap before sitting down.

"May I get you all something to drink?"

"No, thank you," Samuel said.

Joseph shot a quick glance at each of them. "I'm sure you're all wondering why I called you here so early."

Judah nodded.

"I'd like to invite you to join my wife and me for dinner tomorrow night at our home."

Samuel looked at Judah. Matthew and Luke looked stunned.

"That would be nice," Samuel said.

Judah nodded, slightly smiling.

"Shall we say seven p.m.?"

"Yes, seven would be fine," Judah said.

"Do any of you drive?" Joseph asked.

"Yes," Judah said.

"Good, I'll see that you're provided with a car while you're here."

"Thank you," Judah said.

"Also, as I promised, I'll see to it that you all get jobs. You'll start next week."

"We don't know how much to thank you," Judah said.

Joseph nodded.

"That's all," Joseph said.

Luke rose first and placed his cap back on his head. The others stood.

"Thank you again. We look forward to it," Judah said.

Joseph nodded.

As the men turned to leave, Joseph called out, "Benjamin."

They stopped.

"You may go; I wish to speak to your younger brother… alone."

They left the room. Benjamin remained.

"I know that times are hard, and, considering the distance you've come, I want to assist you any way I can."

He handed Benjamin a thick white envelope. "There's a significant amount of money in there. It's for your father and the five of you while you're here."

Benjamin smiled. "I don't know what to say. Thank you."

"You're welcome." Joseph smiled. His affections for Benjamin grew stronger every time he saw him. Ben was gentle and kind; he reminded him of their mother.

Joseph walked with Benjamin out of his office. "I'll see you tomorrow."

Benjamin nodded and smiled. "I look forward to it."

Joseph stopped by Mrs. Madison's desk and asked her to send Gil and Peterson into his office. He met with Gil and Peterson for thirty minutes. He had constructed a plan that involved them both. Everything needed to be perfect.

Saturday afternoon, Joseph walked into the kitchen after dropping the boys off at their grandparents' home. Sasha was preparing dinner. Joseph suggested they allow the chef to prepare the meal, but Sasha loved to cook and insisted on doing it herself. She'd also given the housekeeper the night off.

Her hair was tucked tightly into a bun with her wayward bangs hanging across her forehead and her face flushed from the hot oven. She was making the dough for the homemade rolls. Earlier, she'd pulled a chicken out of the refrigerator; after cutting it into pieces and seasoning it with salt and pepper, she placed the chicken in a roasting pan and put it in the oven. There were five raw potatoes in a large white bowl next to the kitchen sink.

Joseph poured himself a glass of water. "What can I do to help?"

"You can peel the potatoes for the potato salad," she said.

He reached up in the top cabinet and grabbed a large brown bowl. He pulled a paring knife from the drawer next to the sink and began to peel the skin off of one of the potatoes.

"I was surprised that you asked your brothers to dinner, considering everything that's happened," Sasha said.

Joseph was silent.

"Is must be difficult being around them–except for Benjamin, of course."

"Fortunately, I'm not around them much. I only offered them jobs because I knew my father was in need."

"What are your plans?"

"Only time will tell."

She looked intently at Joseph, her head tilted and her eyebrows raised. "What do you mean?"

"Let's just say, I'm expecting an intriguing evening."

At seven, Sasha placed a beautiful crystal vase holding gardenias on the dining room table. The light green linen tablecloth was set with Ellen's china, crystal glasses, and perfectly folded white napkins.

Joseph appeared calm, but his mind was racing. *I have to maintain a straight face. Remember why they're here.*

Five minutes later, the doorbell rang.

"Hello, come in," Joseph said.

Samuel stepped in first, followed by Judah, Matthew, Benjamin, and Luke. Joseph watched Matthew studying the architecture of the home, his eyes peering up at the beautiful white staircase and the handcrafted banister.

Sasha appeared, dressed in a lovely blue dress with a long strand of pearls hanging from her neck. Her black hair, now medium in length, was styled in waves.

"This is my wife, Sasha Abrams."

"Hello, Mrs. Abrams. It is so nice to meet you. Thank you for inviting us to dinner," Judah said.

"You're very welcome; and please, call me Sasha."

“These are my brothers, Samuel, Luke, Matthew, and Benjamin.”

“It’s nice to meet all of you.”

“I’ll take your jackets,” Joseph said.

Summer days were hot in New York, but evenings often got cool. The men pulled off their suit jackets and handed them to Joseph. He moved over to the closet near the front door and hung the jackets up.

Sasha motioned them toward the living room.

“Please, make yourselves at home.”

Joseph was two steps behind them when Sasha grabbed his arm. “Joe, will you help me carry out the refreshments?” She slid her arm through his, nestling close to him.

“So those are your brothers,” she whispered. “I must say, Benjamin is quite handsome. Matthew is handsome as well.”

Joseph was silent. He lifted a tray with five glasses of cold tea from the kitchen counter, while Sasha carried the appetizers: bread, cheese, and fresh crab. They strode into the living room. Joseph offered each of them tea.

Sasha placed the tray of snacks beside a stack of small plates on the glass table in front of the couch. “Dinner will be ready in a bit. Please, help yourselves.”

“Thank you,” Benjamin said. He reached for a slice of cheese.

She noticed Luke peering at the stunning artwork on the walls.

“You have a beautiful home,” Luke said.

“Thank you. Please, have a look around the house,” she said.

“I’ll give you a tour,” Joseph said.

Joseph took them into the parlor, which was next to the kitchen. The fireplace was marble, handmade oriental carpet covered the ebony hardwood floors, and two exquisite paintings hung on the wall—one of Madrid, Spain, that Joseph had bought for Sasha on a trip years ago, the other of New York City.

They swept through the reception room; it was large enough to hold one hundred people, with high ceilings and stained-glass windows. Joseph watched as Matthew studied the walls, floors, and windows. He remembered his brother's love and talent for building.

After showing them the downstairs, he led them upstairs, stopping first in the master bedroom.

"This is our room."

One by one they walked into the 450-square-foot bedroom.

"This is the most beautiful bedroom I've ever seen. It's larger than our Father's entire downstairs," Matthew said. The walls were as white as the carpet. There was a thick white comforter that covered the bed. Matthew touched the polished ebony dresser with his right hand as he examined its carpentry. Photos of Joseph, Sasha, and her parents covered one wall. Earlier, he had removed the photos of the boys—their appearance greatly favored him as a child. He didn't want to risk them finding out who he was—at least, not yet.

"Do you mind waiting in here for a minute? I want to check to make sure the other rooms are presentable." Joseph asked.

"No, not at all," Luke said.

Matthew walked into a small side room. "Take a look at this. There's a bathroom in here. It's unbelievable."

Luke strolled in. "So this is how the rich live," he said, shaking his head.

"Look at the closet," Judah said. "I've never seen so many clothes."

Samuel and Benjamin stared at the enormous walk-in closet.

"I still can't understand why he would invite us to his home. One minute he's threatening to throw us in jail, and now he's treating us like kings. It's unusual," Judah said.

"Perhaps he's showing kindness because we traveled back to Missouri as he asked. It was a long, miserable, and unnecessary trip," Samuel said.

"What does it matter, brothers?" Luke said. "Let's just enjoy the night."

Minutes later, Joseph returned. "All right, please follow me."

Once they finished seeing the inside of the house, Joseph escorted them out back. The lawn was perfectly cut; there was a small garden to the right with an assortment of flowers from tulips, roses, to gardenias. White and yellow daisies surrounded two large oak trees in the center while to the left there was a swing set and slide. They walked farther down the hillside, which was covered with a strong mix of bushes, shrubs, and flowers. Straight ahead was a brilliant view of downtown Manhattan. The city glistened. Joseph pointed east. The Statue of Liberty stood tall. His mind flashed back to the first time he saw it with his brothers on the ship from Italy.

After a few minutes he said, "Shall we go back in?"

They strolled back into the house, and Sasha came out to greet them. "Dinner is ready."

They sat in the dining room and ate and talked. Joseph's attention was fixed on Benjamin most of the time. Joseph gave a detailed overview of the automotive and shipping company. When the men talked of life in Italy and their families, Joseph changed the subject. Hearing about a life that he'd been robbed of brought too much grief.

Joseph looked at Luke. He acted polite, but from his facial expressions and body language, Joseph sensed an inner anger that still consumed his brother.

Matthew seemed to have matured. He spoke more articulately and appeared well-mannered, a change from the immature, selfish boy he once knew.

Samuel sat quiet for most of the night. Judah spoke sternly, but Joseph discerned the years had been hard on him. Judah told them he'd lost his son to the fever. Joseph thought of what his own father's reaction must have been when he learned of his death.

Sasha asked, "Shall we have dessert outside on the patio?"

Joseph nodded.

They sat outside and ate strawberry shortcake. Thirty minutes later, the doorbell rang.

"I wonder who that could be?" Sasha asked.

"I'll get it," Joseph said.

Joseph opened the door. Gil and Peterson stepped in.

He brought them out back. Sasha slipped back into the kitchen and prepared two more desserts and coffee.

They talked for twenty more minutes. Joseph pulled his gold pocket watch from his pant pocket, glancing at it briefly.

Judah glanced at the watch. He tilted his head. "Your watch… where did you get it?"

I didn't mean to show them that, thought Joseph. He quickly stuffed the watch in his pocket. "A small store in Manhattan."

"My father owned one like it," Judah said. "He gave it to my brother who passed away many years ago."

Joseph's heart sank. A bitter feeling swept through him. He leaped up out of his seat. "It's late. I have a busy day tomorrow."

"We don't want to outstay our welcome," Samuel said. He rose out of his chair. "Thank you for a wonderful night," he said, glancing at Sasha.

"Yes, thank you," Matthew said.

She nodded. "You're welcome."

The men went back to the hotel.

One hour later, there was a knock at the men's hotel room door. Matthew opened the door. Joseph stormed into the room, Gil and Peterson following.

"There's been a theft at my house."

A moment of silence. "Surely you don't think we were involved," Judah said.

"I assure you, my brothers and I would never steal from you," Samuel said.

Joseph gave them a stony look. "I hope for your sake this is true. I would hate to think that I could open my home to all of you, feed you dinner, and be treated this way."

"We don't understand," Luke said. "We haven't done anything."

Joseph glared at Luke, fury in his eyes. "Then you wouldn't mind if we checked your jackets, would you?"

Luke glared straight back at Joseph, eyes narrowed. He turned around, picked up his jacket from off the desk, and handed it to Joseph.

Joseph searched the pockets, finding nothing. He pointed to Samuel and said, "Gil, check his."

"We don't know what this is about, but I can assure you we've taken nothing," Judah said.

Gil checked Samuel's pockets. "He's clean."

Peterson stuck his hand in Judah's jacket and pulled out the key to the hotel.

"Check his," he pointed to Matthew.

Peterson checked Matthew's jacket and came up empty.

With his piercing brown eyes, Joseph looked straight at Benjamin. Joseph held his hand out motioning for Benjamin to bring him his jacket. Joseph reached his hand in the side pocket and pulled out a fifteen-carat diamond necklace. Eyes wide and jaw dropped, Benjamin froze.

Joseph held the necklace up. "This necklace belongs to my wife."

Judah grabbed Benjamin with both arms. "What have you done, you ignorant boy?"

"I swear I don't know where that came from. I don't know how it got in my pocket." Looking at Joseph, Benjamin said, "I swear by Almighty God, I would never steal from you."

"I left you alone in my bedroom, there was plenty of time to have taken the necklace," Joseph said.

"I swear, my brother is not a thief," Matthew said.

"Then how did it get in his coat pocket!" Joseph shouted.

Matthew bent his head.

"Our brother is not a thief; your must believe us," Luke said.

"Perhaps we should call the police to straighten this out," Joseph said.

"No please, do not involve the police. We will do whatever you ask," Judah pleaded.

Joseph looked Benjamin straight in the face before turning to Judah. "I will forget this dreadful act on one condition. You must leave at once and go back home, and I won't press charges."

"Except for Benjamin; I demand he stay and work for me. He will work off the price of the necklace."

"We cannot go back without our younger brother," Samuel said.

"You have no other choice. I will press charges against your brother, and he will spend a very long time in prison. The necklace is worth over five thousand dollars."

"Please, Mr. Abrams, you don't understand," Judah said. "My father has lost one son whom he loved more than anything; he cannot bear to lose another. Take me instead. I will stay and do whatever you say. I will work for you for the rest of my life if I have to," he pleaded.

Joseph, surprised, thought, *Now you're willing to give your life for your brother, while before you watched him be imprisoned for a crime he didn't commit.*

"I will say this only one more time. Benjamin will work for me, and the rest of you will leave."

Suddenly, Joseph felt an arm tight around his waist, and a hand holding a knife against his throat.

Gil leaped forward.

"One more move, and I will kill him!" Luke said. "I mean it, one move, and he's dead!"

Joseph stood still, breathing lightly. He felt the sharp knife penetrate his skin. Peterson and Gil froze.

"We'll pack up our things tonight, and we will leave—but not without our little brother," Luke said.

Joseph spoke to Gil and Peterson. "Leave the room."

"We're not leaving you here!" Gil said, adamantly.

"I want you both to leave. I mean it…I'll be okay."

Gil paused. "Are you sure?"

"Yes."

Once they left, Luke released Joseph.

Joseph stood still. After a long pause, he finally spoke. His voice coarse, he turned to Judah. His eyes began to tear.

"How is it you could defend your brother now, but allow the other to be punished for a crime that you know he didn't commit?"

Judah was taken back by his words.

"I don't understand."

"You watched your younger brother being taken off to prison, yet you did nothing!" Tears began to stream down Joseph's face.

"How do you know these things?" Samuel asked.

It was difficult to talk. He began to breathe heavily. "I'm Joseph…your brother."

Luke dropped the knife to the floor. The men stood, stunned. Though it was silent, the room seemed to tremble.

Joseph wiped the tears from his eyes. "I am Joseph Abraham Solomon. My father is Jacob and my mother was Rachel."

Judah's mouth hung open. Benjamin slowly moved toward Joseph. He looked directly into Joseph's eyes. "Joseph, my brother." He threw his arms around him.

Joseph began to cry. His grip tightened on his younger brother. "I lost you once…I couldn't bear to lose you again."

Judah stepped up to Joseph, staring him straight in the face. His eyes were red as tears streamed down his cheek. "How can you ever forgive us?" He began to cry harder.

Joseph held out his hand and hugged him. "I endured twelve years of hardship in prison. But God has used my life to help to save the lives of thousands of people. What was intended for evil, God used for good."

Samuel embraced Joseph. They wept in one another's arms. Tears began to fall from Matthew's eyes. Joseph reached out his hand, and motioned for Matthew to come to him. He embraced his brother.

Gasping for air, Luke said, "I'm so…ashamed. I…I don't deserve to live for what I've done. I am most to blame." He began to weep uncontrollably, and then fell to the floor.

Joseph knelt beside him and looked him in the face. "I forgive you."

The men cried and embraced one another.

Joseph shared his life story with them: life in prison, Parks Shipping Company, his rise to power and wealth, his life with Sasha, and his work with Governor Roosevelt. The men spoke of their lives in Italy: the hardships they encountered, the move to America to flee the war, and life in Missouri.

Joseph said, "You must tell Father I am alive. Tell him all is well. God brought me here for a purpose. Tell our father to pack your things; I will make a home for all of you here."

The Journey Home

Jacob was sitting in his home reading the paper, when he suddenly heard a horse and carriage. He went outside and down the stairs, moving slowly toward the carriage. He hugged his sons.

They went into the living room. Rebecca came out of the kitchen where she was making cookies to greet them. Benjamin handed Jacob the envelope filled with money.

Jacob opened it and smiled, but asked, "How could you earn such a large amount in a short period of time?"

Judah bent his head, and then slowly looked up at his father. He began to weep. Jacob's eyes narrowed as he leaned forward in his chair.

"Father, Joseph…Joseph is alive," Judah said.

Jacob frowned. "Why would you say such a horrible thing?"

"It is true, Father. Joseph is alive. He has become a wealthy and powerful man. Here are photos of him and his wife," Samuel said.

Jacob stared at the photos. It was difficult to recognize Joseph; his appearance had changed.

Rebecca brought a tray holding a pitcher of cold water and glasses and sat down to join them.

For half an hour, the men spoke of their trip to New York and how they had found Joseph. They told their father the horrible story of their betrayal many years ago. Matthew remained quiet, but Luke cried, taking all of the blame.

When Jacob heard the whole story, he froze. He felt as though a ton of bricks hit his chest. Anger, rage, and grief engulfed him. Rebecca ran out of the house crying. Jacob left the room and went into his bedroom, where he wept bitterly.

How could they lead me to believe my son was dead, all these years? How can I ever forgive them? he thought.

"My son! My son!" he screamed, burying his head in his pillow.

Jacob remained in his room for hours. The pain that gripped him was unbearable. Finally coming out, he found that all his children had left the house. Glancing out the window, Jacob saw the sun forcing the gray clouds out of the sky. It depicted his mood. The overwhelming joy of knowing his beloved son was alive was lessening the disheartening news of his sons' betrayal.

He found Benjamin on the porch and asked him questions about Joseph.

Benjamin shared in detail the successful, wealthy, and powerful man Joseph had become. He told him that Joseph had established homeless shelters and soup kitchens, and he had helped hundreds, if not thousands, of people. He told of Joseph's work with Governor Roosevelt. Jacob felt warmth and life flow through his body. He smiled as he thought to himself; *My Joseph has become a great man.*

Benjamin told Jacob of Joseph's wishes for the family to move to New York City.

Joseph had agreed to purchase the farm to save time and expedite the move to New York.

Joseph sat in his office, heavy in thought. Visions of his father's face consumed his mind. The thought of calling terrified him, but he couldn't wait any longer. His brothers were sure to have told Jacob by now.

How will my father take the news of my brothers' betrayal? he thought. *It is, for most, an unforgivable crime.*

After minutes of staring at the telephone, he lifted the receiver and dialed the number.

"Hello," Benjamin said.

"Benjamin, it's Joseph."

"Joseph, it's wonderful to talk to you."

"Is our father there?"

"Yes, he's out on the porch. I will go and get him."

Benjamin slipped out on the porch to get his father.

"Hello."

Joseph's heart sank when he heard his father's hoarse voice. It was difficult to talk. "Father…it's Joseph…your son." He began to cry.

"Joseph…I can't believe it's you. My precious son. It is true. You really are alive," Jacob said, crying.

Gasping for air, Joseph said, "Father…I've missed you."

"I just can't believe I'm hearing your voice. This is truly the happiest day of my life. I have my precious son back. Benjamin was just telling me of the great man you have become. I am proud of you, Joseph. I cannot bear to think of the hardships you have encountered. My heart aches to think you were in prison."

"I am fine now, Father. God has blessed me with great wealth and I have helped thousands of people."

"Why did you not come home when you were released from prison, Joseph?"

"At first, I didn't have the money to travel to Italy. I wrote letters but they were returned. It was after the war."

"I see. Well soon, my son, we will be reunited and no one will ever separate me from you again."

"Yes, Father, I'm making arrangements now."

Joseph planned to hire an architect to design houses for his family on the land in upper Manhattan he and Sasha were purchasing.

"I can't wait to see you, Father. When will you come?"

"We will begin packing tonight. My son, until we see one another, remember how much I love you," Jacob said, crying.

"I love you too, Father…goodbye."

"Goodbye, Joseph."

Joseph hung up the phone, placed his head in the palms of his hands, and wept.

Jacob moved into the dining room, sat at the table, and wept. Benjamin sat beside him.

A part of Jacob wanted to take Benjamin, and Rebecca and her family to catch the next train to New York, and forget his other sons existed. But they'd been through too much, and his grandchildren meant everything to him. Jacob prayed to God to grant him grace to forgive their horrible act. He asked Benjamin to get his brothers.

Samuel and Luke were in the barn feeding the animals, while Judah and Matthew were mending a broken fence on the side of the barn.

They joined Jacob in the dining room. The men remained silent.

At first, it was hard for Jacob to look at them. He spoke to them coldly, telling them that there was much to do. The animals and the remaining crop would need to be sold. They needed to pack only those items necessary for the trip.

They began that night.

When Jacob thought of Joseph, his heart was happy and his spirit uplifted.

They boarded the train a week later. Joseph had insisted they travel first class.

The train ride seemed endless. One minute felt like an hour. Jacob stared at the pictures of Joseph, his wife, and his children for hours.

My beloved son is alive.

He had a new song in his heart that filled his spirit with peace and joy.

It was nine a.m. on Sunday morning. Joseph, Sasha, and their two sons stood outside the train station awaiting Jacob's arrival. Joseph's heart felt as though it would leap out of his body. The wait was agonizing.

Finally, the train approached. Joseph moved closer. His mind was racing and his breathing labored.

Joseph's eyes canvassed the passengers detraining. His eyes began to tear; his heart beat faster every minute. He was so excited; he found it hard to contain himself.

Finally, Benjamin climbed down the steps, followed by Matthew, Samuel, Luke, and Judah. Judah turned and held out his hand, assisting a wrinkled, white-haired man dressed in blue pants and a plaid shirt off the train.

Joseph cried when he saw his father. Though his father walked with a slight limp, he was still strong and robust.

Joseph ran to him and fell on his knees and wept. He wrapped his arms around Jacob.

Jacob knelt, tears streaming down his cheeks. He held Joseph's face in his hands. "My son, God has returned you to me. I wake up with joy in my heart now."

Joseph looked into his father's eyes. "I've…missed you…I love you."

Jacob held his son in his arms, and they both wept for a long time.

Joseph stood and helped his father up. Rebecca was crying bitterly. She ran to Joseph and hugged him. They cried in each other's arms.

He wiped his tears, and then motioned for Sasha to come to him. "This is my wife, Sasha."

She wiped the tears from her face and hugged Jacob.

"And these are my two sons, Justice, eight, and Caleb, five."

Jacob smiled, knelt down, and kissed both of Joseph's sons.

"You remember my husband, Dan. These are my two sons, Josiah and Joel, and my daughter, Hadassah," Rebecca said.

Joseph and Sasha hugged Dan and the children. Judah introduced his family, as did Samuel.

"God has restored my family. I have my son, my precious Joseph," Jacob said. "I have surely seen his grace and wonders."

Joseph wrapped his arms around his father. "I have lived in a foreign land for over twenty-five years. It's been a long journey, but finally I'm home. God has restored my hope and my identity."

Joseph had homes built for Judah, Samuel, Rebecca, and their families, as well as Luke and Matthew, on the land he'd purchased in upper Manhattan. Jacob and Benjamin lived with Joseph and Sasha.

Luke and Matthew worked at the shipping yards, assisting with repairs and ship maintenance. Benjamin was hired as an assistant manager in the Chevrolet dealership in downtown Manhattan. Samuel helped manage the finances of the dealership, and Judah and Dan were trained as automobile mechanics.

Although the country was still suffering great devastation, Chevrolet continued to expand its advertising budget, and took the lead in its field.

After Roosevelt was elected president, Joseph had even more power to implement relief efforts on a national level. Many homeless people took refuge in his shelters. Sasha and Rebecca often volunteered in the shelters in Manhattan.

Joseph helped President Roosevelt to implement a program called the Civilian Conservation Corps. It provided jobs for 250 thousand unemployed men to work on rural local projects. The program was highly successful and operated in every state.

It was a sunny day in April, and nearly one year had passed since Joseph's reunion with his family.

Sasha and Joseph strolled hand in hand down the long, narrow path alongside a small, crystal-clear stream; the sun shone bright, and the cool crisp air blew against their skin. Jacob was at the house resting.

"I don't think I've ever told you this, but you were right," Joseph said.

"What do you mean?" Sasha asked.

"Many years ago, when I first told you of my past, you said God would restore all that was lost. You were right."

She smiled and gripped his hand tight.

Jacob lived another fifteen years and passed away at the age of ninety-seven.

Joseph requested that, when the day came, that he too would pass away, the name on his tombstone must read: Joseph Abraham Solomon.

THE PRODIGAL
(first chapter)

Chapter 1

Clint woke up in a small, filthy, smelly room that had only one dusty window. He groaned from the agonizing pain in his neck where they'd struck him. The thick rope binding his hands and feet was so tight, his skin was peeling off. He was huddled near the door; his legs were stiff and sore.

W*here am I*, he thought. Clint didn't know how long he'd been there. He rolled over on his right side and moaned as he tried to sit up. He tilted his head against the wall; he could vaguely remember. A vision of Abby being shot pierced his mind. "Oh God, let her be okay," he said in a

whisper. *I've got to get out of here. She's got to be all right. God please, let her be okay.* Clint studied the room and noticed a wooden door. The glass window looked easy to break. *If I can just pry myself loose, I could get out of here.* He leaned forward to try and free himself from the coarse rope, but it was useless. His heart was beating violently in his chest. Hours passed and fear gnawed at his mind and he was heavy from torment as sweat poured profusely from his forehead down his body.

October was scorching hot in the Democratic Republic of Congo. Thoughts flooded his mind. *It will take a miracle to get out of here. Is Abby still alive? Will I ever see her again? I never got to say goodbye to my Dad. Tell him I love him. Ask him to forgive me.* "God help me," he said quietly.

Minutes later, the sound of men yelling caused his stomach to jump. Waves of fear ran through his body as one of the voices got louder. He heard the sound of chains clanking. Suddenly, the door flew open. Clint strained in the glare of the bright sun. The large black man who had held Chiamaka stood there, his face engulfed with rage. Clint froze instantly fearing that he would see death.

The man untied Clint's hands and his feet. "Get up!" His voice was deep and it was hard to understand him. Clint rolled onto his knees, his body was stiff. The man yanked him to his feet and shoved him up against the wall before pushing him forward.

At first, it was hard to walk. He felt the roughness of the ground through the hole in his shoe. The man pushed him again, this time more forcefully. Clint fell to his knees. The man grabbed his arm with such force, it felt as though it would rip right out of its socket.

When he regained his footing, the man led him in front of a small hut. The leader of the group was standing there. The leader began barking orders in his native tongue. The others, who seemed to fear him, stood almost at attention. Two of them left and entered

the hut. One of them returned with a wooden chair, which he set before the

leader.

The village looked deserted. There was one car that looked like a jeep. There must have been at least twenty men. They were heavily armed with guns, dressed in trousers. Clint wondered if the village was used as some type of military base. There was a heap of guns stacked up near one of the huts. He was being locked up in one of the wood houses. Three men were standing close to the leader.

"Sit," said the leader. His voice was calm and rational.

The large man who'd brought him outside pushed him down on the chair.

"I will ask you again. Where is the rest of the money?" There was intensity in his face.

Blinded by the sun shining directly into his eyes, Clint paused, straining to see the man's scowling face. His hand fluttered nervously. "I told you. My father gave it to me. I don't have any more money."

The leader nodded to the large black man. The man punched Clint in the stomach. Clint cried out, feeling a deep wrenching pain in his gut.

"Where is the rest of the money?"

Quietly he said, "That's all I have."

The man took two steps closer to him. He smacked Clint across the face with the back of his hand. The force sent him flying out of the chair and onto the hard ground. Clint could taste warm blood as it ran down his lips. The man kicked him in his gut. Excruciating pain shot through him as he let out a groan.

His words slurred this time, "I swear…I don't have any more money."

The man balled his fist and before he could strike again, Clint yelled, "Alright, alright, I'll get you more money! I'll do whatever you say!" He could hardly breathe from the pain. The leader walked over to one of the other men. He looked at Clint. "I knew he would eventually talk. Lock him up."

The large man grabbed Clint's arm, dragged him back to the room, threw him down to the ground, and tied his legs and hands, again. Clint heard him lock the door. He lay down on his side shivering with his legs against his chest.

It was hard to believe he was being held like a common criminal. He hadn't done anything wrong. How could God let this happen? Was he wrong to think he cared? What kind of a God is he? Is he punishing me?

A glimmer of hope. Maybe he could bargain with them and they'd let him go. But the reality of that soon shifted his emotions. His stomach tightened and his body began to shake violently from pain and fear. Tremors swept over him like powerful waves, he cringed to get them to stop.

As the hours passed, depression descended upon him. It was then, that it hit him. He would probably die. At that point, he began to face the consequences of his past actions and the current situation. The loss of freedom and pain of separation from his loved ones, especially Abby; not knowing whether she was dead or alive became torture.

Visions of Abby continued to resonate through his mind. He quietly said, "God help me . . .

please." He leaned back against the cement wall his mind in a daze. Clint wondered how the path he'd taken led him to the devastating presence he now faced. *Are all my mistakes catching up to me?* he thought. Visions of his past spread through his mind, back three years when he was fighting in the war in Germany.

www.janiceparker.tateauthor.com